Lucas Trask of Traskon was not an admirer of the Space Vikings; raiding, pillage and killing were not avocations to his liking. And on this long-awaited day of his marriage to the lovely Lady Elaine, all unpleasant thoughts seemed far away.

But Lucas was to be suddenly awakened to a world of chaotic violence, where murder followed murder, and the only motive to rival avarice was revenge. For Lucas, the old life was dead, and the new life he had chosen led out into the trackless realms of galactic space and the surfaces of pillaged planets with one objective always in mind—the death of Lady Elaine's murderer.

SPACE VIKING

Ace Science Fiction Books by H. Beam Piper

H. BEAM PIPER

SPACE VIKING

ACE SCIENCE FICTION BOOKS
NEW YORK

SPACE VIKING

An Ace Science Fiction Book / published by arrangement with
the author

PRINTING HISTORY
This printing / September 1983

ISBN: 0-441-77784-8

Ace Science Fiction Books are published by The Berkley Publishing Group,
200 Madison Avenue, New York, New York 10016.
PRINTED IN THE UNITED STATES OF AMERICA

SPACE VIKING

GRAM

I

THEY STOOD together at the parapet, their arms about each other's waists, her head against his cheek. Behind, the broad leaved shrubbery gossiped softly with the wind, and from the lower main terrace came music and laughing voices. The city of Wardshaven spread in front of them, white buildings rising from the wide spaces of green treetops, under a shimmer of sun-reflecting aircars above. Far away, the mountains were violet in the afternoon haze, and the huge red sun hung in a sky as yellow as a ripe peach.

His eye caught a twinkle ten miles to the southwest, and for an instant he was puzzled. Then he frowned. The sunlight blazed on the two thousand foot globe of Duke Angus' new ship, the *Enterprise*, back at the Gorram shipyards after her final trial cruise. He didn't want to think about that, now.

Instead, he pressed her closer and whispered her name, "Elaine," and then, caressing every syllable, "Lady Elaine Trask of Traskon."

"Oh, no, Lucas!" Her protest was half joking and half apprehensive. "It's bad luck to be called by your married name before the wedding."

"I've been calling you that in my mind since the night of the Duke's ball, when you were just home from school on Excalibur."

She looked up from the corner of her eye.

"That was when I started calling me that, too," she confessed.

"There's a terrace to the west at Traskon New House," he told her. "Tomorrow, we'll have our dinner there, and watch the sunset together."

"I know. I thought that was to be our sunset-watching place."

"You have been peeking," he accused. "Traskon New House was to be your surprise."

"I always was a present-peeker, New Year's and my birthdays. But I only saw it from the air. I'll be very surprised at everything inside," she promised. "And very delighted."

And when she'd seen everything and Traskon New House wasn't a surprise any more, they'd take a long space-trip. He hadn't mentioned that to her, yet. To some of the other Sword-Worlds—Excalibur, of course, and Morglay and Flamberge and Durendal. No, not Durendal; the war had started there again. But they'd have so much fun. And she would see clear blue skies again, and stars at night. The cloudveil hid the stars from Gram, and Elaine had missed them, since coming home from Excalibur.

The shadow of an aircar fell briefly upon them and they looked up and turned their heads in time to see it sink with graceful dignity toward the landing-stage of Karvall House, and he glimpsed its blazonry—sword and atom-symbol, the badge of the ducal house of Ward. He wondered if it were Duke Angus himself, or just some of his people come ahead of him. They should get back to the guests, he supposed. Then he took her in his arms and kissed her, and she responded ardently. It must have been

2

all of five minutes since they'd done that before.

A slight cough behind them brought them apart and their heads around. It was Sesar Karvall, gray-haired and portly, the breast of his blue coat gleaming with orders and decorations and the sapphire in the pommel of his dress-dagger twinkling.

"I thought I'd find you two here," Elaine's father smiled. "You'll have tomorrow and tomorrow and tomorrow together, but need I remind you that today we have guests, and more coming every minute."

"Who came in the Ward car?" Elaine asked.

"Rovard Grauffis. And Otto Harkaman; you never met him, did you, Lucas?"

"No, not by introduction. I'd like to, before he spaces out." He had nothing against Harkaman personally; only against what he represented. "Is the Duke coming?"

"Oh, surely. Lionel of Newhaven and the Lord of Northport are coming with him. They're at the Palace now." Karvall hesitated. "His nephew's back in town."

Elaine was distressed; she started to say, "Oh, dear! I hope he doesn't—"

"Has Dunnan been bothering Elaine again?"

"Nothing to take notice of. He was here, yesterday, demanding to speak with her. We got him to leave without too much unpleasantness."

"It'll be something for me to take notice of, if he keeps it up after tomorrow."

For his seconds and Andray Dunnan's, that was; he hoped it wouldn't come to that. He didn't want to have to shoot a kinsman to the house of Ward, and a crazy man to boot.

"I'm terribly sorry for him," Elaine was saying.

3

"Father, you should have let me talk to him. I might have made him understand."

Sesar Karvall was shocked. "Child, you couldn't have subjected yourself to that! The man is insane!" Then he saw her bare shoulders, and was even more shocked. "Elaine, your shawl!"

Her hands went up and couldn't find it; she looked about in confused embarrassment. Amused, Lucas picked it from the shrub onto which she had tossed it and draped it over her shoulders, his hands lingering briefly. Then he gestured to the older man to precede them, and they entered the arbored walk. At the other end, in an open circle, a fountain played, white marble girls and boys bathing in the jade-green basin. Another piece of loot from one of the Old Federation planets; that was something he'd tried to avoid in furnishing Traskon New House. There'd be a lot of that coming to Gram after Otto Harkaman took the *Enterprise* to space.

"I'll have to come back, some time, and visit them," Elaine whispered to him. "They'll miss me."

"You'll find a lot of new friends at your new home," he whispered back. "You wait till tomorrow."

"I'm going to put a word in the Duke's ear about that fellow," Sesar Karvall, still thinking of Dunnan, was saying. "If he speaks to him, maybe it'll do some good."

"I doubt it. I don't think Duke Angus has any influence over him at all."

Dunnan's mother had been the Duke's younger sister; from his father he had inherited what had originally been a prosperous barony. Now it was mortgaged to the top of the manor house aerial-mast. The Duke had once assumed Dunnan's debts, and refused to do so a second time.

Dunnan had gone to space a few times, as a junior officer on trade-and-raid voyages into the Old Federation. He was supposed to be a fair astrogator. He had expected his uncle to give him command of the *Enterprise*, which had been ridiculous. Disappointed in that, he had recruited a mercenary company and was seeking military employment. It was suspected that he was in correspondence with his uncle's worst enemy, Duke Omfray of Glaspyth.

And he was obsessively in love with Elaine Karvall, a passion which seemed to nourish itself on its own hopelessness. Maybe it would be a good idea to take that space-trip right away. There ought to be a ship leaving Bigglersport for one of the other Sword-Worlds, before long.

They paused at the head of the escalators; the garden below was thronged with guests, the bright shawls of the ladies and the coats of the men making shifting color-patterns among the flowerbeds and on the lawns and under the trees. Serving robots, flame-yellow and black in the Karvall colors, floated about playing soft music and offering refreshments. There was a continuous spiral of changing costume color around the circular robo-table. Voices babbled happily like a mountain river.

As they stood looking down, another aircar circled low, green and gold, lettered PANPLANET NEWS SERVICE. Sesar Karvall swore in irritation.

"Didn't there use to be something they called privacy?" he asked.

"It's a big story, Sesar."

It was; more than the marriage of two people who happened to be in love with each other. It was the marriage of the farming and ranching barony of Traskon and the

Karvall steel mills. More, it was public announcement that the wealth and fighting men of both baronies were now aligned behind Duke Angus of Wardshaven. So it was a general holiday. Every industry had closed down at noon today, and would be closed until morning-after-next, and there would be dancing in every park and feasting in every tavern. To Sword-Worlders, any excuse for a holiday was better than none.

"They're our people, Sesar; they have a right to have a good time with us. I know everybody at Traskon is watching this by screen."

He raised his hand and waved to the news-car, and when it swung its pickup around, he waved again. Then they went down the long escalator.

Lady Lavina Karvall was the center of a cluster of matrons and dowagers, around whom tomorrow's bridesmaids fluttered like many-colored butterflies. She took possession of her daughter and dragged her into the feminine circle. He saw Rovard Grauffis, small and saturnine, Duke Angus' henchman, and Burt Sandrasan, Lady Lavina's brother. They spoke, and then an upper-servant, his tabard blazoned with the yellow flame and black hammer of Karvallmills, approached his master with some tale of domestic crisis, and the two went away together.

"You haven't met Captain Harkaman, Lucas," Rovard Grauffis said. "I wish you'd come over and say hello and have a drink with him. I know your attitude, but he's a good sort. Personally, I wish we had a few like him around here."

That was his main objection. There were fewer and fewer men of that sort on any of the Sword-Worlds.

6

II

A DOZEN men clustered around the bartending robot—his cousin and family lawyer, Nikkolay Trask; Lothar Ffayle, the banker; Alex Gorram, the shipbuilder, and his son Basil; Baron Rathmore; more of the Wardshaven nobles whom he knew only distantly. And Otto Harkaman.

Harkaman was a Space Viking. That would have set him apart even if he hadn't topped the tallest of them by a head. He wore a short black jacket, heavily gold-braided, and black trousers inside ankle-boots; the dagger on his belt was no mere dress-ornament. His tousled red-brown hair was long enough to furnish extra padding in a combat-helmet, and his beard was cut square at the bottom.

He had been fighting on Durendal, for one of the branches of the Royal house contesting fratricidally for the throne. The wrong one; he had lost his ship, and most of his men and, almost, his own life. He had been a penniless refugee on Flamberge, owning only the clothes he stood in and his personal weapons and the loyalty of half a dozen adventurers as penniless as himself, when Duke Angus had invited him to Gram to command the *Enterprise*.

"A pleasure, Lord Trask. I've met your lovely bride-to-be, and now that I meet you, let me congratulate both." Then, as they were having a drink together, he put his foot in it by asking, "You're not an investor in the Tanith Adventure, are you?"

He said he wasn't, and would have let it go at that. Young Basil Gorram had to get his foot in, too.

"Lord Trask does not approve of the Tanith Adventure," he said scornfully. "He thinks we should stay home and produce wealth, instead of exporting robbery and murder to the Old Federation for it."

The smile remained on Otto Harkaman's face; only the friendliness was gone. He unobtrusively shifted his drink to his left hand.

"Well, our operations are definable as robbery and murder," he agreed. "Space Vikings are professional robbers and murderers. And you object? Perhaps you find me personally objectionable?"

"I wouldn't have shaken your hand or had a drink with you if I did. I don't care how many planets you raid or cities you sack, or how many innocents, if that's what they are, you massacre in the Old Federation. You couldn't possibly do anything worse than those people have been doing to one another for the past ten centuries. What I object to is the way you're raiding the Sword-Worlds."

"You're crazy!" Basil Gorram exploded.

"Young man," Harkaman reproved, "the conversation was between Lord Trask and myself. And when somebody makes a statement you don't understand, don't tell him he's crazy. Ask him what he means. What *do* you mean, Lord Trask?"

"You should know; you've just raided Gram for eight hundred of our best men. You raided me for close to forty vaqueros, farm workers, lumbermen, machine operators, and I doubt I'll be able to replace them with as good." He turned to the elder Gorram. "Alex, how many have you lost to Captain Harkaman?"

Gorram tried to make it a dozen; pressed, he admitted to a score and a half. Roboticians, machine supervisors, programmers, a couple of engineers, a foreman. There was grudging agreement from the others. Burt Sandrasan's engine works had lost almost as many, of the same kind. Even Lothar Ffayle admitted to losing a computerman and a guard-sergeant.

And after they were gone, the farms and ranches and factories would go on, almost but not quite as before. Nothing on Gram, nothing on any of the Sword-Worlds, was done as efficiently as three centuries ago. The whole level of Sword-World life was sinking, like the east coast-line of this continent, so slowly as to be evident only from the records and monuments of the past. He said as much, and added:

"And the genetic loss. The best Sword-World genes are literally escaping to space, like the atmosphere of a low-gravity planet, each generation begotten by fathers slightly inferior to the last. It wasn't so bad when the Space Vikings raided directly from the Sword-Worlds; they got home once in a while. Now they're conquering planets in the Old Federation for bases, and staying there."

Everybody had begun to relax; this wouldn't be a quarrel. Harkaman, who had shifted his drink back to his right hand, chuckled.

"That's right. I've fathered a dozen bastards in the Old Federation, and I know Space Vikings whose fathers were born on Old Federation planets." He turned to Basil Gorram. "You see, the gentleman isn't crazy, at all. That's what happened to the Terran Federation, by the way. The good men all left to colonize, and the stuffed shirts and yes-men and herd-followers and safety-firsters stayed on Terra and tried to govern the Galaxy."

"Well, maybe this is all new to you, Captain," Rovard Grauffis said sourly, "but Lucas Trask's dirge for the

Decline and Fall of the Sword-Worlds is an old song to the rest of us. I have too much to do to stay here and argue with him.''

Lothar Ffayle evidently did intend to stay and argue.

''All you're saying, Lucas, is that we're expanding. You want us to sit here and build up population pressure like Terra in the First Century?''

''With three and a half billion people spread out on twelve planets? They had that many on Terra alone. And it took us eight centuries to reach that.''

That had been since the Ninth Century, Atomic Era, at the end of the Big War. Ten thousand men and women on Abigor, refusing to surrender, had taken the remnant of the System States Alliance navy to space, seeking a world the Federation had never heard of and wouldn't find for a long time. That had been the world they had called Excalibur. From it, their grandchildren had colonized Joyeuse and Durendal and Flamberge; Haulteclere had been colonized in the next generation from Joyeuse, and Gram from Haulteclere.

''We're not expanding, Lothar; we're contracting. We stopped expanding three hundred and fifty years ago, when that ship came back to Morglay from the Old Federation and reported what had been happening out there since the Big War. Before that, we were discovering new planets and colonizing them. Since then, we've been picking the bones of the dead Terran Federation.''

Something was going on by the escalators to the landing-stage. People were moving excitedly in that direction, and the news-cars were circling like vultures over a sick cow. Harkaman wondered, hopefully, if it mightn't be a fight.

''Some drunk being bounced,'' Nikkolay Trask dismissed it. "Sesar's let all Wardshaven in here, today. But, Lucas, this Tanith Adventure; we're not making any hit-and-run raid. We're taking over a whole planet; it'll be another Sword-World in forty or fifty years. A little farther away, of course, but—"

"Inside another century, we'll conquer the whole Federation," Baron Rathmore declared. He was a politician and never let exaggeration worry him.

"What I don't understand," Harkaman said, "is why you support Duke Angus, Lord Trask, if you think the Tanith adventure is doing Gram so much harm."

"If Angus didn't do it, somebody else would. But Angus is going to make himself King of Gram, and I don't think anybody else could do that. This planet needs a single sovereignty. I don't know how much you've seen of it outside this duchy, but don't take Wardshaven as typical. Some of these duchies, like Glaspyth or Didreksburg, are literal snake-pits. All the major barons are at each other's throats, and they can't even keep their own knights and petty-barons in order. Why, there's a miserable little war down in Southmain Continent that's been going on for over two centuries."

"That's probably where Dunnan's going to take that army of his," a robot-manufacturing baron said. "I hope it gets wiped out, and Dunnan with it."

"You don't have to go to Southmain; just go to Glaspyth," someone else said.

"Well, if we don't get a planetary monarchy to keep order, this planet will decivilize like anything in the Old Federation."

"Oh, *come*, Lucas!" Alex Gorram protested. "That's pulling it out too far."

"Yes, for one thing, we don't have the Neobarbarians,'' somebody said. ''And if they ever came out here, we'd blow them to Em-See-Square in nothing flat. Might be a good thing if they did, too; it would stop us squabbling among ourselves.''

Harkaman looked at him in surprise. ''Just who do you think the Neobarbarians are, anyhow?'' he asked. ''Some race of invading nomads, Atilla's Huns in spaceships?''

''Well, isn't that who they are?'' Gorram asked.

''Nifflheim, no! There aren't a dozen and a half planets in the Old Federation that still have hyperdrive, and they're all civilized. That's if 'civilized' is what Gilgamesh is,'' he added. ''These are homemade barbarians. Workers and peasants who revolted to seize and divide the wealth and then found they'd smashed the means of production and killed off all the technical brains. Survivors on planets hit during the Interstellar Wars, from the Eleventh to the Thirteenth Centuries, who lost the machinery of civilization. Followers of political leaders on local-dictatorship planets. Companies of mercenaries thrown out of employment and living by pillage. Religious fanatics following self-anointed prophets.''

''You think we don't have plenty of Neobarbarian material here on Gram?'' Trask demanded. ''If you do, take a look around.''

''Glaspyth,'' somebody said.

''That collection of overripe gallows-fruit Andray Dunnan's recruited,'' Rathmore mentioned.

Alex Gorram was grumbling that his shipyard was full of them; agitators stirring up trouble, trying to organize a strike to get rid of the robots.

''Yes,'' Harkaman pounced on that last. ''I know of at least forty instances, on a dozen and a half planets, in the last eight centuries, of anti-technological movements. They had them on Terra, back as far as the Second Century Pre-Atomic. And after Venus seceded from the First Federation, before the Second Federation was organized.''

''You're interested in history?'' Rathmore asked.

''A hobby. All spacemen have hobbies. There's very little work aboard ship in hyperspace; boredom is the worst enemy. My guns-and-missiles officer, Van Larch, is a painter. Most of his work was lost with the *Corisande* on Durendal, but he kept us from starving a few times on Flamberge by painting pictures and selling them. My hyperspatial astrogator, Guatt Kirbey, composes music; he tries to express the mathematics of hyperspatial theory in musical terms. I don't care much for it, myself,'' he admitted. ''I study history. You know, it's odd; practically everything that's happened on any of the inhabited planets has happened on Terra before the first spaceship.''

The garden immediately around them was quiet, now; everybody was over by the landing-stage escalators. Harkaman would have said more, but at that moment he saw half a dozen of Sesar Karvall's uniformed guardsmen run past. They were helmeted and in bulletproofs; one of them had an auto-rifle, and the rest carried knobbed plastic truncheons. The Space Viking set down his drink.

''Let's go,'' he said. ''Our host is calling up his troops; I think the guests ought to find battle stations, too.''

III

THE GAILY-DRESSED crowd formed a semicircle facing the landing-stage escalators; everybody was staring in embarrassed curiosity, those behind craning over the shoulders of those in front. The ladies had drawn up their shawls in frigid formality; many had even covered their heads. There were four news-service cars hovering above; whatever was going on was getting a planetwide screen showing. The Karvall guardsmen were trying to get through; their sergeant was saying, over and over, "Please, ladies and gentlemen; your pardon, noble sir," and getting nowhere.

Otto Harkaman swore disgustedly and shoved the sergeant aside. "Make way, here!" he bellowed. "Let these guards pass." With that, he almost hurled a gaily-dressed gentleman aside on either hand; they both turned to glare angrily, then got hastily out of his way.

Meditating briefly on the uses of bad manners in an emergency, Trask followed, with the others. The big Space Viking plowed to the front, where Sesar Karvall and Rovard Grauffis and several others were standing.

Facing them, four men in black cloaks stood with their backs to the escalators. Two were commonfolk retainers; hired gunmen, to be precise. They were at pains to keep their hands plainly in sight, and seemed wishing themselves elsewhere. The man in front wore a diamond sunburst jewel on his beret, and his cloak was lined with pale blue silk. His thin, pointed face was deeply lined about the mouth and penciled with a thin black mustache. His eyes showed white all around the irises, and now and then his mouth would twitch in an involuntary grimace. Andray Dunnan; Trask wondered briefly how soon he would have to look at him from twenty-five meters over the sights of a pistol. The face of the slightly taller man who stood at his shoulder was paperwhite, expressionless, with a black beard. His name was Nevil Ormm; nobody was quite sure whence he had come, and he was Dunnan's henchman and constant companion.

"You lie!" Dunnan was shouting. "You lie damnably, in your stinking teeth, all of you! You've intercepted every message she's tried to send me."

"My daughter has sent you no messages, Lord Dunnan," Sesar Karvall said, with forced patience. "None but the one I just gave you, that she wants nothing whatever to do with you."

"You think I believe that? You're holding her a prisoner; Satan only knows how you've been torturing her to force her into this abominable marriage."

There was a stir among the bystanders; that was more than well-mannered restraint could stand. Out of the murmur of incredulous voices, one woman's was quite audible:

"Well, really! He actually *is* crazy!"

Dunnan, like everybody else, heard it. "Crazy, am I?" he blazed. "Because I can see through this hypocritical sham? Here's Lucas Trask—he wants an interest in Karvallmills; and here's Sesar Karvall—he wants access to iron deposits on Traskon land. And my loving uncle—he wants the help of both of them in stealing Omfray of Glaspyth's duchy. And here's this loan shark of a Ffayle, trying to claw my lands away from me, and Rovard Grauffis, the fetchdog of my uncle who won't lift a finger to save his kinsman from ruin, and this foreigner Harkaman who's swindled me out of command of the *Enterprise*. You're all plotting against me.''

''Sir Nevil,'' Grauffis said, ''you can see that Lord Dunnan's not himself. If you're a good friend to him, you'll get him out of here before Duke Angus arrives.''

Ormm leaned forward and spoke urgently in Dunnan's ear. Dunnan pushed him angrily away.

''Great Satan, are you against me, too?'' he demanded.

Ormm caught his arm. ''You fool, do you want to ruin everything, now?'' He lowered his voice; the rest was inaudible.

''No, curse you, I won't go till I've spoken to her, face to face!''

There was another stir among the spectators; the crowd parted, and Elaine was coming through, followed by her mother and Lady Sandrasan and five or six other matrons. They all had their shawls over their heads, right ends over left shoulders; they all stopped except Elaine, who took a few steps forward and confronted Andray Dunnan. He had never seen her look more beautiful, but it was the icy beauty of a honed dagger.

''Lord Dunnan, what do you wish to say to me?'' she asked. ''Say it quickly and then go; you are not welcome here.''

''Elaine!'' Dunnan cried, taking a step forward. ''Why do you cover your head; why do you speak to me as a stranger? I am Andray, who loves you. Why are you letting them force you into this wicked marriage?''

''No one is forcing me; I am marrying Lord Trask

16

willingly and happily, because I love him. Now, please, go and make no more trouble at my wedding."

"That's a lie! They're making you say that! You don't have to marry him; they can't force you. Come with me now. They won't dare stop you. I'll take you away from all these cruel, greedy people. You love me, you've always loved me. You've told me you loved me, again and again."

Yes, in his own private dream world, a world of fantasy that had now become Andray Dunnan's reality, an Elaine Karvall whom his imagination had created existed only to love him. Confronted by the real Elaine, he simply rejected the reality.

"I never loved you, Lord Dunnan, and I never told you so. I never hated you, either, but you are making it very hard for me not to. Now go and never let me see you again."

With that, she turned and started back through the crowd, which parted in front of her. Her mother and her aunt and the other ladies followed.

"You lied to me!" Dunnan shrieked after her. "You lied all the time. You're as bad as the rest of them, all scheming and plotting against me, betraying me. I know what it's about; you all want to cheat me of my rights, and keep my usurping uncle on the ducal throne. And you, you falsehearted harlot, you're the worst of them all!"

Sir Nevil Ormm caught his shoulder and spun him around, propelling him toward the escalators. Dunnan struggled, screaming inarticulately like a wounded wolf. Ormm was cursing furiously.

"You two!" he shouted. "Help me, here. Get hold of him."

Dunnan was still howling as they forced him onto the escalator, the backs of the two retainers' cloaks, badged with the Dunnan crescent, light blue on black, hiding him. After a little, an aircar with the blue crescent blazonry lifted and sped away.

"Lucas, he's crazy," Sesar Karvall was insisting. "Elaine hasn't spoken fifty words to him since he came back from his last voyage."

Lucas laughed and put a hand on Karvall's shoulder. "I know that, Sesar. You don't think, do you, that I need assurance of it?"

"Crazy, I'll say he's crazy," Rovard Grauffis put in. "Did you hear what he said about his rights? Wait till his Grace hears about that."

"Does he lay claim to the ducal throne, Sir Rovard?" Otto Harkaman asked, sharply and seriously.

"Oh, he claims that his mother was born a year and a half before Duke Angus and the true date of her birth falsified to give Angus the succession. Why, his present Grace was three years old when she was born. I was old Duke Fergus' squire; I carried Angus on my shoulder when Andray Dunnan's mother was presented to the lords and barons the day after she was born."

"Of course he's crazy," Alex Gorram agreed. "I don't know why the Duke doesn't have him put under psychiatric treatment."

"I'd put him under treatment," Harkaman said, drawing a finger across under his beard. "Crazy men who pretend to thrones are bombs that ought to be deactivated, before they blow things up."

"We couldn't do that," Grauffis said. "After all, he's Duke Angus' nephew."

18

"I could do it," Harkaman said. "He only has three hundred men in this company of his. Why you people ever let him recruit them Satan only knows," he parenthesized. "I have eight hundred; five hundred ground-fighters. I'd like to see how they shape up in combat, before we space out. I can have them ready for action in two hours, and it'd be all over before midnight."

"No, Captain Harkaman; his Grace would never permit it," Grauffis vetoed. "You have no idea of the political harm that would do among the independent lords on whom we're counting for support. You weren't here on Gram when Duke Ridgerd of Didreksburg had his sister Sancia's second husband poisoned."

IV

THEY HALTED under the colonnade; beyond, the lower main terrace was crowded, and a medley of old love songs was wafting from the sound outlets, for the sixth or eighth time around. Lucas looked at his watch; it was ninety seconds later than the last time he had done so. Give it fifteen more minutes to get started, and another fifteen to get away after the marriage toasts and the felicitations. And no marriage, however pompous, lasted more than half an hour. An hour, then, till he and Elaine would be in the aircar, bulleting toward Traskon.

The love songs stopped abruptly; after a momentary silence, a trumpet, considerably amplified, blared; the *Ducal Salute*. The crowd stopped shifting, the buzz of voices ceased. At the head of the landing-stage escalators there was a glow of color and the ducal party began moving down. A platoon of guards in red and yellow, with gilded helmets and tassled halberds. An esquire bearing the Sword of State. Duke Angus, with his council, Otto Harkaman among them; the Duchess Flavia and her companion-ladies. The household gentlemen, and their ladies. More guardsmen. There was a great burst of cheering; the news-service aircars got into position above the procession. Cousin Nikkolay and a few others stepped out from between the pillars into the sunlight; there was a similar movement at the other side of the terrace. The ducal party reached the end of the central walkway, halted and deployed.

"All right; let's shove off," Cousin Nikkolay said, stepping forward.

Ten minutes since they had come outside; another five to get into position. Fifty minutes, now, till he and Elaine—Lady Elaine Trask of Traskon, for real and for always—would be going home.

"Sure the car's ready?" he asked, for the hundredth time.

His cousin assured him that it was. Figures in Karvall black and flame-yellow appeared across the terrace. The music began again, this time the stately *Nobles' Wedding March,* arrogant and at the same time tender. Sesar Karvall's gentleman-secretary, and the Karvall lawyer, executives of the steel mills, the Karvall guard-captain. Sesar himself, with Elaine on his arm; she was wearing a shawl of black and yellow. Lucas looked around in sudden fright. "For the love of Satan, where's our shawl?" he demanded, and then relaxed when one of his gentlemen exhibited it, green and tawny in Traskon colors. The bridesmaids, led by Lady Lavina Karvall. Finally they halted, ten yards apart, in front of the Duke.

"Who approaches us?" Duke Angus asked of his guard-captain.

He had a thin, pointed face, almost femininely sensitive, and a small pointed beard. He was bareheaded except for the narrow golden circlet which he spent most of his waking time scheming to convert into a royal crown. The guard-captain repeated the question.

"I am Sir Nikkolay Trask; I bring my cousin and liegelord, Lucas, Lord Trask, Baron of Traskon. He comes to receive the Lady-Demoiselle Elaine, daughter of Lord Sesar Karvall, Baron of Karvallmills, and the sanction of your Grace to the marriage between them."

Sir Maxamon Zhorgay, Sesar Karvall's henchman, named himself and his lord; they brought the Lady-Demoiselle Elaine to be wed to Lord Trask of Traskon. The Duke, satisfied that these were persons whom he could address directly, asked if the terms of the marriage-agreement had been reached; both parties affirmed this. Sir Maxamon passed a scroll to the Duke; Duke Angus began to read the stiff and precise legal phraseology. Marriages between noble houses were not matters to be left open to dispute; a great deal of spilled blood and burned powder had resulted from ambiguity on some point of succession or inheritance or dower-rights. Lucas bore it patiently; he didn't want his great-grandchildren and Elaine's shooting it out over a matter of a misplaced comma.

"And these persons here before us do enter into this marriage freely?" the Duke asked, when the reading had ended. He stepped forward as he spoke, and his esquire gave him the two-hand Sword of State, heavy enough to behead a bisonoid. Trask stepped forward; Sesar Karvall brought Elaine up. The lawyers and henchmen obliqued off to the sides. "How say you, Lord Trask?" he asked, almost conversationally.

"With all my heart, your Grace."

"And you, Lady-Demoiselle Elaine?"

"It is my dearest wish, your Grace."

The Duke took the sword by the blade and extended it; they laid their hands on the jewelled pommel.

"And do you, and your houses, avow us, Angus, Duke of Wardshaven, to be your sovereign prince, and pledge fealty to us and to our legitimate and lawful successors?"

"We do." Not only he and Elaine, but all around them, and all the throng in the gardens, answered, the spectators in shouts. Very clearly, above it all, somebody, with more enthusiasm than discretion, was bawling: *"Long live Angus the First of Gram!"*

"And we, Angus, do confer upon you two, and your houses, the right to wear our badge as you see fit, and pledge ourself to maintain your rights against any and all who may presume to invade them. And we declare that this marriage between you two, and this agreement between your respective houses, does please us, and we avow you two, Lucas and Elaine, to be lawfully wed, and who so questions this marriage challenges us, in our teeth and to our despite."

That wasn't exactly the wording used by a ducal lord on Gram. It was the formula employed by a planetary king, like Napolyon of Flamberge or Rodolf of Excalibur. And, now that he thought of it, Angus had consistently used the royal first person plural. Maybe that fellow who had shouted about Angus the First of Gram had only been doing what he'd been paid to do. This was being telecast, and Omfray of Glaspyth and Ridgerd of Didreksburg would both be listening; as of now, they'd start hiring mercenaries. Maybe that would get rid of Dunnan for him.

The Duke gave the two-hand sword back to his esquire. The young knight who was carrying the green and tawny shawl handed it to him, and Elaine dropped the black and yellow one from her shoulders, the only time a respectable woman ever did that in public, and her mother caught and folded it. He stepped forward and draped the Trask colors over her shoulders, and then took her in his arms. The cheering broke out again, and some of Sesar Karvall's guardsmen began firing a pom-pom somewhere.

It took a little longer than he had expected to finish with the toasts and shake hands with those who crowded around. Finally, the exit march started, down the long walkway to the landing-stage, and the Duke and his party moved away to the rear to prepare for the wedding feast at which everybody but the bride and groom would celebrate. One of the bridesmaids gave Elaine a huge sheaf of flowers, which she was to toss back from the escalator; she held it in the crook of one arm and clung to his with the other.

"Darling, we really made it!" she was whispering, as though it were too wonderful to believe.

One of the news-cars—orange and blue, that was Westlands Telecast & Teleprint—had floated just ahead of them and was letting down toward the landing-stage. For a moment, he was angry; that went beyond the outer-orbit limits of journalistic propriety, even for Westlands T & T.

Then he laughed; today he was too happy for anger about anything. At the foot of the escalator, Elaine kicked off her gilded slippers—there was another pair in the car; he'd seen to that personally—and they stepped onto the escalator and turned about. The bridesmaids rushed forward, and began struggling for the slippers, to the damage and disarray of their gowns, and when they were half way up, Elaine heaved the bouquet and it burst apart among them like a bomb of colored fragrance, and the girls below snatched at the flowers, shrieking deliriously. Elaine stood, blowing kisses to everybody, and he was shaking his clasped hands over his head, until they were at the top.

When they turned and stepped off, the orange and blue aircar had let down directly in front of them, blocking their way. Now he was really furious, and started forward with a curse. Then he saw who was in the car.

Andray Dunnan, his thin face contorted and the narrow mustache writhing on his upper lip; he had a slit beside the window open, and was tilting the barrel of a submachine gun up and out of it.

He shouted, and at the same time tripped Elaine and flung her down. He was throwing himself forward to cover her when there was a blasting multiple report. Something sledged him in the chest; his right leg crumpled under him. He fell.

He fell and fell and fell, endlessly, through darkness, out of consciousness.

V

HE WAS CRUCIFIED, and crowned with a crown of thorns.
Who had they done that to? Somebody long ago, on Terra.
His arms were drawn out stiffly, and hurt; his feet and legs
hurt, too, and he couldn't move them, and there was this
prickling at his brow. And he was blind.

No; his eyes were just closed. He opened them, and
there was a white wall in front of him, patterned with a
blue snow-crystal design, and he realized that it was a
ceiling and that he was lying on his back. He couldn't
move his head, but by shifting his eyes he saw that he was
completely naked and surrounded by a tangle of tubes and
wires, which puzzled him briefly. Then he knew that he
was not on a bed, but on a robomedic, and the tubes would
be for medication and wound drainage and intravenous
feeding, and the wires would be to electrodes imbedded in
his body for diagnosis, and the crown-of-thorns thing
would be more electrodes for an encephalograph. He'd
been on one of those things before, when he had been
gored by a bisonoid on the cattle range.

That was what it was; he was still under treatment. But
that seemed so long ago; so many things—he must have
dreamed them—seemed to have happened.

Then he remembered, and struggled futilely to rise.

"Elaine!" he called. "Elaine, where are you?"

There was a stir and somebody came into his limited
view; his cousin, Nikkolay Trask.

"Nikkolay," he said. "What happened to Elaine?"

Nikkolay winced, as though something he had expected to hurt had hurt worse than he had expected.

"Lucas." He swallowed. "Elaine . . . Elaine is dead."

Elaine is dead. That didn't make sense.

"She was killed instantly, Lucas. Hit six times; I don't think she even felt the first one. She didn't suffer at all."

Somebody moaned, and then he realized that it had been himself.

"You were hit twice," Nikkolay was telling him. "One in the leg; smashed the femur. And one in the chest. That one missed your heart by an inch."

"Pity it did." He was beginning to remember clearly, now. "I threw her down, and tried to cover her. I must have thrown her straight into the burst and only caught the last of it myself." There was something else; oh, yes. "Dunnan. Did they get him?"

Nikkolay shook his head. "He got away. Stole the *Enterprise* and took her off-planet."

"I want to get him myself."

He started to rise again; Nikkolay nodded to someone out of sight. A cool hand touched his chin, and he smelled a woman's perfume, nothing at all like Elaine's. Something like a small insect bit him on the neck. The room grew dark.

Elaine was dead. There was no more Elaine, nowhere at all. Why, that must mean there was no more world. So that was why it had gotten so dark.

He woke again, fitfully, and it would be daylight and he could see the yellow sky through an open window, or it would be night and the wall-lights would be on. There would always be somebody with him. Nikkolay's wife, Dame Cecelia; Rovard Grauffis; Lady Lavina Karvall —he must have slept a long time, for she was so much older than he remembered—and her brother, Burt Sandrasan. And a woman with dark hair, in a white smock with a gold caduceus on her breast. Once, Duchess Flavia, and once Duke Angus himself.

He asked where he was, not much caring. They told him, at the Ducal Palace. He wished they'd all go away, and let him go wherever Elaine was.

Then it would be dark, and he would be trying to find her, because there was something he wanted desperately to show her. Stars in the sky at night, that was it. But there were no stars, there was no Elaine, there was no anything, and he wished that there were no Lucas Trask, either.

But there was an Andray Dunnan. He could see him standing black-cloaked on the terrace, the diamonds in his beret-jewel glittering evilly; he could see the mad face peering at him over the rising barrel of the submachine gun. And then he would hunt for him without finding him, through the cold darkness of space.

The waking periods grew longer, and during them his mind was clear. They relieved him of his crown of electronic thorns. The feeding tubes came out, and they gave him cups of broth and fruit juice. He wanted to know why he had been brought to the Palace.

"About the only thing we could do," Rovard Grauffis told him. "They had too much trouble at Karvall House as it was. You know, Sesar got shot, too."

"No." So that was why Sesar hadn't come to see him. "Was he killed?"

"Wounded; he's in worse shape than you are. When the

shooting started, he went charging up the escalator. Didn't have anything but his dress-dagger. Dunnan gave him a quick burst; I think that was why he didn't have time to finish you off. By that time, the guards who'd been shooting blanks from the rapid-fire gun got in a clip of live rounds and fired at him. He got out of there as fast as he could. They have Sesar on a robomedic like yours. He isn't in any danger.''

The drainage tubes and medication tubes came out; the tangle of wires around him was removed, and the electrodes with them. They bandaged his wounds and dressed him in a loose robe and lifted him from the robomedic to a couch, where he could sit up when he wished; they began giving him solid food, and wine to drink, and allowed him to smoke. The woman doctor told him he'd had a bad time, as though he didn't know that. He wondered if she expected him to thank her for keeping him alive.

"You'll be up and around in a few weeks," his cousin added. "I've seen to it that everything at Traskon New House will be ready for you by then."

"I'll never enter that house as long as I live, and I wish that wouldn't be more than the next minute. That was to be Elaine's house. I won't go to it alone."

The dreams troubled his sleep less and less as he grew stronger. Visitors came often, bringing amusing little gifts, and he found that he enjoyed their company. He wanted to know what had really happened, and how Dunnan had gotten away.

"He pirated the *Enterprise*," Rovard Grauffis told him. "He had that company of mercenaries of his, and he'd bribed some of the people at the Gorram shipyards. I thought Alex would kill his chief of security when he found out what had happened. We can't prove anything—we're trying hard enough to—but we're sure Omfray of Glaspyth furnished the money. He's been denying it just a shade too emphatically.''

"Then the whole thing was planned in advance?''

"Taking the ship was; he must have been planning that for months, before he started recruiting that company. I think he meant to do it the night before the wedding. Then he tried to persuade the Lady-Demoiselle Elaine to elope with him—he seems to have actually thought that was possible—and when she humiliated him, he decided to kill both of you first.'' He turned to Otto Harkaman, who had accompanied him. "As long as I live, I'll regret not taking you at your word and accepting your offer, then.''

"How did he get hold of that Westlands Telecast and Teleprint car?''

"Oh. The morning of the wedding, he screened Westlands editorial office and told them he had the inside story on the marriage and why the Duke was sponsoring it. Made it sound as though there was some scandal; insisted that a reporter come to Dunnan House for a face-to-face interview. They sent a man, and that was the last they saw him alive; our people found his body at Dunnan House when we were searching the place afterward. We found the car at the shipyard; it had taken a couple of hits from the guns at Karvall House, but you know what these press-cars are built to stand. He went directly to the shipyard, where his men already had the *Enterprise;* as soon as he arrived, she lifted out.''

He stared at the cigarette between his fingers. It was almost short enough to burn him. With an effort, he leaned forward to crush it out.

"Rovard, how soon will that second ship be finished?''

Grauffis laughed bitterly. "Building the *Enterprise* took everything we had. The duchy's on the edge of bankruptcy now. We stopped work on the second ship six months ago because we didn't have enough money to keep on with her and still get the *Enterprise* finished. We were expecting the *Enterprise* to make enough in the Old Federation to finish the second one. Then, with two ships and a base on Tanith, the money would begin coming in instead of going out. But now—"

"It leaves me where I was on Flamberge," Harkaman added. "Worse. King Napolyon was going to help the Elmersans, and I'd have gotten a command in that. It's too late for that now."

Lucas picked up his cane and used it to push himself to his feet. The broken leg had mended, but he was still weak. He took a few tottering steps, paused to lean on the cane, and then forced himself on to the open window and stood for a moment staring out. Then he turned.

"Captain Harkaman, it might be that you could still get a command, here on Gram. That's if you don't mind commanding under me as owner-aboard. I am going hunting for Andray Dunnan."

They both looked at him. After a moment, Harkaman said, "I'd count it an honor, Lord Trask. But where will you get a ship?"

"She's half finished now. You already have a crew for her. Duke Angus can finish her for me, and pay for it by pledging his new barony of Traskon."

He had known Rovard Grauffis all his life; until this moment, he had never seen Duke Angus' henchman show surprise.

"You mean, you'll trade Traskon for that ship?" he demanded.

30

"Finished, equipped and ready for space, yes."

"The Duke will agree to that," Grauffis said promptly. "But, Lucas, Traskon is all you own. Your title, your revenues—"

"If I have a ship, I won't need them. I am turning Space Viking."

That brought Harkaman to his feet with a roar of approval. Grauffis looked at him, his mouth slightly open.

"Lucas Trask—Space Viking," he said. "Now I've heard everything."

Well, why not? He had deplored the effects of Viking raiding on the Sword-Worlds, because Gram was a Sword-World, and Traskon was on Gram, and Traskon was to have been the home where he and Elaine would live and where their children and children's children would be born and live. Now the little point on which all of it had rested was gone.

"That was another Lucas Trask, Rovard. He's dead, now."

VI

GRAUFFIS excused himself to make a screen-call and then returned to excuse himself again. Evidently Duke Angus had dropped whatever he was doing as soon as he heard what his henchman had to tell him. Harkaman was silent until after he was out of the room, then said,

"Lord Trask, this is a wonderful thing for me. It's not been pleasant to be a shipless captain living on strangers' bounty. I'd hate, though, to have you think, some time, that I'd advanced my own fortunes at the expense of yours."

"Don't worry about that. If anybody's being taken advantage of, you are. I need a space captain, and your misfortune is my own good luck."

Harkaman started to place tobacco into his pipe. "Have you ever been off Gram, at all?" he asked.

"A few years at the University of Camelot, on Excalibur. Otherwise, no."

"Well, have you any conception of the sort of thing you're setting yourself to?" The Space Viking snapped his lighter and puffed. "You know, of course, how big the Old Federation is. You know the figures, that is, but do they mean anything to you? I know they don't to a good many spacemen, even. We talk glibly about ten to the hundredth power, but emotionally we still count, 'One, Two, Three, Many.' A ship in hyperspace logs about a lightyear an hour. You can go from here to Excalibur in thirty hours. But you could send a radio message announcing the birth of a son, and he'd be a father before it was received. The Old Federation, where you're going to hunt Dunnan, occupies a space-volume of two hundred billion cubic lightyears. And you're hunting for one ship and one man in that. How are you going to do it, Lord Trask?"

"I haven't started thinking about how; all I know is that I have to do it. There are planets in the Old Federation where Space Vikings come and go; raid-and-trade bases, like the one Duke Angus planned to establish on Tanith. At one or another of them, I'll pick up word of Dunnan, sooner or later."

"We'll hear where he was a year ago, and by the time we get there, he'll be gone for a year and a half to two

32

years. We've been raiding the Old Federation for over three hundred years, Lord Trask. At present, I'd say there are at least two hundred Space Viking ships in operation. Why haven't we raided it bare long ago? Well, that's the answer: distance and voyage time. You know, Dunnan could die of old age—which is not a usual cause of death among Space Vikings—before you caught up with him. And your youngest ship's-boy could die of old age before he found out about it.''

"Well, I can go on hunting for him till I die, then. There's nothing else that means anything to me.''

"I thought it was something like that. I won't be with you, all your life. I want a ship of my own, like the *Corisande*, that I lost on Durendal. Some day, I'll have one. But till you can command your own ship, I'll command her for you. That's a promise.''

Some note of ceremony seemed indicated. Summoning a robot, he had it pour wine for them, and they pledged each other.

Rovard Grauffis had recovered his aplomb by the time he returned accompanied by the Duke. If Angus had ever lost his, he gave no indication of it. The effect on everybody else was literally seismic. The generally accepted view was that Lord Trask's reason had been unhinged by his tragic loss; there might, he conceded, be more than a crumb of truth in that. At first, his cousin Nikkolay raged at him for alienating the barony from the family, and then he learned that Duke Angus was appointing him vicar-baron and giving him Traskon New House for his residence. Immediately he began acting like one at the death-bed of a rich grandmother. The Wardshaven financial and industrial barons, whom he had known only distantly, on the other hand, came flocking around him, offering assistance and hailing him as the savior of the duchy. Duke Angus' credit, almost obliterated by the loss of the *Enterprise*, was firmly reestablished, and theirs with it.

There were conferences at which lawyers and bankers argued interminably; he attended a few at first, found himself completely uninterested, and told everybody so. All he wanted was a ship; the best ship possible, as soon as possible. Alex Gorram had been the first to be notified; he had commenced work on the unfinished sister-ship of the *Enterprise* immediately. Until he was strong enough to go to the shipyard himself, he watched the work on the two thousand foot globular skeleton by screen, and conferred either in person or by screen with engineers and shipyard executives. His rooms at the ducal palace were converted, almost overnight, from sickrooms to offices. The doctors, who had recently been urging him to find new interests and activities, were now warning of the dangers of over-exertion. Harkaman finally added his voice to theirs.

"You take it easy, Lucas." They had dropped formality and were on a first-name basis now. "You got hulled pretty badly; you let damage-control work on you, and don't strain the machinery till it's fixed. We have plenty of time. We're not going to get anywhere chasing Dunnan. The only way we can catch him is by interception. The longer he moves around in the Old Federation before he hears we're after him, the more of a trail he'll leave. Once we can establish a predictable pattern, we'll have a chance. Then, some time, he'll come out of hyperspace somewhere and find us waiting for him."

"Do you think he went to Tanith?"

Harkaman heaved himself out of his chair and prowled about the room for a few minutes, then came back and sat down again.

"No. That was Duke Angus' idea, not his. He couldn't put in a base on Tanith, anyhow. You know the kind of crew he has."

There had been an extensive inquiry into Dunnan's associates and accomplices; Duke Angus was still hoping for positive proof to implicate Omfray of Glaspyth in the piracy. Dunnan had with him a dozen and a half employees of the Gorram shipyards whom he had corrupted. There was some technical ability among them, but for the most part they were agitators and trouble-makers and incompetent workmen. Even under the circumstances, Alex Gorram was glad to see the last of them. As for Dunnan's own mercenary company, there were about a score of former spacemen among them; the rest graded down from bandits through thugs and sneak-thieves to barroom bums. Dunnan himself was an astrogator, not an engineer.

"That gang aren't even good enough for routine raiding," Harkaman said. "They'd never under any circumstances be able to put in a base on Tanith. Unless Dunnan's completely crazy, which I doubt, he's gone to some regular Viking base planet, like Hoth or Nergal or Dagon or Xochitl, to recruit officers and engineers and able spacemen."

"All that machinery and robotic equipment and so on that was going to Tanith; was that aboard when he took the ship?"

"Yes, and that's another reason why he'd go to some planet like Hoth or Nergal or Xochitl. On a Viking-occupied planet in the Old Federation, that stuff's almost worth its weight in gold."

"What's Tanith like?"

"Almost completely Terra-type, third of a Class-G sun. Very much like Haulteclere or Flamberge. It was one of the last planets the Federation colonized before the Big War. Nobody knows what happened, exactly. There wasn't any interstellar war; at least, you don't find any big slagpuddles where cities used to be. They probably did a lot of fighting among themselves, after they got out of the Federation. There's still some traces of combat damage around. Then they started to decivilize, down to the pre-mechanical level—wind and water power and animal power. They have draft-animals that look like introduced Terran carabaos, and a few small sailboats and big canoes and bateaux on the rivers. They have gunpowder, which seems to be the last thing any people lose.

"I was there, five years ago. I liked Tanith for a base. There's one moon, almost solid nickle iron, and fissionable ore deposits. Then, like a fool, I hired out to the Elmersans on Durendal and lost my ship. When I came here, your Duke was thinking about Xipototec. I convinced him that Tanith was a better planet for his purpose."

"Dunnan might go there, at that. He might think he was scoring one on Duke Angus. After all, he has all that equipment."

"And nobody to use it. If I were Dunnan, I'd go to Nergal, or Xochitl. There are always a couple of thousand Space Vikings on either, spending their loot and taking it easy between raids. He could sign on a full crew on either. I suggest we go to Xochitl, first. We might pick up news of him, if nothing else."

All right, they'd try Xochitl first. Harkaman knew the planet, and was friendly with the Haulteclere noble who ruled it. The work went on at the Gorram shipyard; it had taken a year to build the *Enterprise*, but the steel-mills and engine-works were over the preparatory work of tooling up, and material and equipment was flowing in a steady stream. He let them persuade him to take more rest, and day by day grew stronger. Soon he was spending most of his time at the shipyard, watching the engines go in —Abbot lift-and-drive for normal space, Dillingham hyperdrive, power converters, pseudograv, all at the center of the globular ship. Living quarters and workshops went in next, all armored in collapsium-plated steel. Then the ship lifted out to an orbit a thousand miles off-planet, followed by swarms of armored work-craft and cargo-lighters; the rest of the work was more easily done in space. At the same time, the four two-hundred-foot pinnaces that would be carried aboard were being finished. Each of them had its own hyperdrive engines, and could travel as far and as fast as the ship herself.

Otto Harkaman was beginning to be distressed because the ship still lacked a name. He didn't like having to speak of her as 'her,' or 'the ship,' and there were many things soon to go on that should be name-marked. *Elaine*, Trask thought, at once, and almost at once rejected it. He didn't want her name associated with the things that ship would do in the Old Federation. *Revenge*, *Avenger*, *Retribution*, *Vendetta;* none appealed to him. A news-commentator, turgidly eloquent about the nemesis which the criminal Dunnan had invoked against himself, supplied it; *Nemesis* it was.

Now he was studying his new profession of interstellar robbery and murder against which he had once inveighed. Otto Harkaman's handful of followers became his teachers. Vann Larch, guns-and-missiles, who was also a painter; Guatt Kirbey, sour and pessimistic, the hyperap-

tial astrogator who tried to express his science in music;
Sharll Renner, the normal-space astrogator, and Alvyn
Karffard, the exec., who had been with Harkaman longest
of all. And Sir Paytrik Morland, a local recruit, formerly
guard-captain to Count Lionel of Newhaven, who commanded the ground fighters and the combat contragravity.
They were using the farms and villages of Traskon for drill
and practice, and he noticed that while the *Nemesis* would
carry only five hundred ground and air fighters, over a
thousand were being trained.

He commented to Rovard Grauffis.

"Yes. Don't mention it outside," the Duke's henchman said. "You and Sir Paytrik and Captain Harkaman
will pick the five hundred best. The Duke will take the rest
into his service. Some of these days, Omfray of Glaspyth
will find out what a Space Viking raid is really like."

And Duke Angus would tax his new subjects of Glaspyth to redeem the pledges on his new barony of Traskon.
Some old Pre-Atomic writer Harkaman was fond of quot-
ing had said, "Gold will not always get you good soldiers,
but good soldiers can always get you gold."

The *Nemesis* came back to the Gorram yards and settled
onto her curved landing-legs like a monstrous spider. The
Enterprise had borne the Ward sword and atom-symbol;
the *Nemesis* should bear his own badge, but the bisonoid
head, tawny on green, of Traskon, was no longer his. He
chose a skull impaled on an upright sword, and it was
blazoned on the ship when he and Harkaman took her out
for her shakedown cruise.

When they landed again at the Gorram yards, two
hundred hours later, they learned that a tramp freighter
from Morglay had come into Bigglersport in their absence
with news of Andray Dunnan. Her captain had come to

Wardshaven at Duke Angus' urgent invitation and was waiting for them at the Ducal Palace.

They sat, a dozen of them, around a table in the Duke's private apartments. The freighter captain, a small, precise man with a graying beard, alternately puffed at a cigarette and sipped from a beaker of brandy.

"I spaced out from Morglay two hundred hours ago," he was saying. "I'd been there twelve local days, three hundred Galactic Standard hours, and the run from Curtana was three hundred and twenty. This ship, the *Enterprise,* spaced out from there several days before I did. I'd say she's twelve hundred hours out of Windsor, on Curtana, now."

The room was still. The breeze fluttered curtains at the open windows; from the garden below, winged night-things twittered among the trees.

"I never expected it," Harkaman said. "I thought he'd take the ship out to the Old Federation at once." He poured wine for himself. "Of course, Dunnan's crazy. A crazy man has an advantage, sometimes, like a left-handed knife-fighter. He does unexpected things."

"That wasn't such a crazy move," Rovard Grauffis said. "We have very little direct trade with Curtana. It's only an accident we heard about this when we did."

The freighter captain's beaker was half empty. He filled it to the brim from the decanter.

"She was the first Gram ship there for years," he agreed. "That attracted notice, of course. And his having the blazonry changed, from the sword-and-atom symbol to the blue crescent. And the ill-feeling on the part of other captains and planet-side employers about the men he'd lured away from them."

"Just how many men, and what kind?"

The man with the gray beard shrugged. "I was too busy getting a cargo together for Morglay, to pay much attention. Almost a full spaceship complement, officers and spacemen of every kind. And a lot of industrial engineers and technicians."

"Then he is going to use that equipment that was aboard, and put in a base somewhere," somebody said.

"If he left Curtana twelve hundred hours ago, he's still in hyperspace," Guatt Kirbey said. "It's over two thousand from Curtana to the nearest Old Federation planet."

"How far to Tanith?" Duke Angus asked. "I'm sure that's where he's gone. He'd expect me to finish the other ship and equip her like the *Enterprise* and send her out; he'd want to get there first."

"I'd thought that Tanith would be the last place he'd go," Harkaman said, "but this changes the whole outlook. He could have gone to Tanith."

"He's crazy, and you're trying to apply sane logic to him," Guatt Kirbey said. "You're figuring what you'd do, and you aren't crazy. Of course, I've had my doubts, at times, but—"

"Yes, he's crazy, and Captain Harkaman's allowing for that," Rovard Grauffis said. "Dunnan hates all of us. He hates his Grace, here. He hates Lord Lucas, and Sesar Karvall; of course, he may think he killed both of them. He hates Captain Harkaman. So how could he score all of us off at once? By taking Tanith."

"You say he was buying supplies and ammunition?"

"That's right. Gun ammunition, ship's missiles, and a lot of ground-defense missiles."

"What was he buying them with? Trading machinery?"

"No. Gold."

"Yes. Lothar Ffayle found out that a lot of gold was transferred to Dunnan from banks in Glaspyth and Didreksburg," Grauffis said. "He got that aboard when he took the ship, evidently."

"All right," Trask said. "We can't be sure of anything, but we have some reasons for thinking he went to Tanith, and that's more than we have for any other planet in the Old Federation. I won't try to estimate the odds against our finding him there, but they're a good deal bigger anywhere else. We'll go there, first."

VII

THE OUTSIDE viewscreen, which had been vacantly gray for over three thousand hours, was now a vertiginous swirl of color, the indescribable color of a collapsing hyperspatial field. No two observers ever saw it alike, and no imagination could vision the actuality. Trask found that he was holding his breath. So, he noticed, was Otto Harkaman, beside him. It was something, evidently, that nobody got used to. Even Guatt Kirbey, the astrogator, was sitting with his pipe clenched in his mouth, staring at the screen.

Then, in an instant, the stars, which had literally not been there before, filled the screen with a blaze of splendor against the black velvet backdrop of normal space. Dead in the center, brighter than all the rest, Ertado's Star, the sun of Tanith, burned yellowly. The light from it was ten hours old.

"Pretty good, Guatt," Harkaman said, picking up his coffee cup.

"Good, Gehenna; it was perfect," somebody else said.

Kirbey was relighting his pipe. "Oh, I suppose it'll have to do," he grudged, around the stem. He had gray hair and an untidy mustache, and nothing was ever quite good enough to satisfy him. "I could have made it a little closer. Need three microjumps, now, and I'll have to cut the last one pretty fine. Now don't bother me." He began punching buttons for data and fiddling with setscrews and verniers.

For a moment, in the screen, Trask could see the face of Andray Dunnan. He blinked it away, reached for his cigarettes, and put one in his mouth wrong-end-to. When he reversed it and snapped his lighter, he saw that his hand was trembling. Otto Harkaman must have seen that, too.

"Take it easy, Lucas," he whispered. "Keep your optimism under control. We only think he might be here."

"I'm sure he is. He has to be."

No; that was the way Dunnan, himself, thought. Let's be sane about this.

"We have to assume he is. If we do, and he isn't, it's a disappointment. If we don't, and he is, it's a disaster."

Others, it seemed, thought the same way. The battle-stations board was a solid blaze of red light for full combat readiness.

"All right," Kirbey said. "Jumping."

Then he twisted the red handle to the right and shoved it in viciously. Again the screen boiled with colored turbulence; again dark and mighty forces stalked through the ship like demons in a sorcerer's tower. The screen turned featureless gray as the pickups stared blindly into some dimensionless noplace. Then it convulsed with color again, and this time Ertado's Star, still in the center, was a coin-sized disc, with the little sparks of its seven planets scattered around it. Tanith was the third—the inhabitable planet of a G-class system usually was. It had a single moon, barely visible in the telescopic screen, five hundred miles in diameter and fifty thousand off-planet.

"You know," Kirbey said, as though he was afraid to admit it, "that wasn't too bad. I think we can make it in one more microjump."

Sometime, Trask supposed, he'd be able to use the expression "micro" about a distance of fifty-five million miles, too.

"What do you think about it?" Harkaman asked him, as deferentially as though seeking expert guidance instead of examining his apprentice. "Where should Guatt put us?"

"As close as possible, of course." That would be a lightsecond at the least; if the Nemesis came out of hyperspace any closer to anything the size of Tanith, the collapsing field itself would kick her back. "We have to assume Dunnan's been there at least nine hundred hours. By that time, he could have put in a detection-station, and maybe missile-launchers, on the moon. The Enterprise carries four pinnaces, the same as the Nemesis; in his place, I'd have at least two of them on off-planet patrol. So let's accept it that we'll be detected as soon as we come out of the last jump, and come out with the moon directly between us and the planet. If it's occupied, we can knock it off on the way in."

"A lot of captains would try to come out with the moon masked off by the planet," Harkaman said.

"Would you?"

The big man shook his tousled head. "No. If they have launchers on the moon, they could launch at us in a curve around the planet, by data relayed from the other side, and we'd be at a disadvantage replying. Just go straight in. You hearing this, Guatt?"

"Yeah. It makes sense. Sort of. Now, stop pestering me. Sharll, look here a minute."

The normal-space astrogator conferred with him; Alvyn Karffard, the executive officer, joined them. Finally Kirbey pulled out the big red handle, twisted it, and said, "All right, jumping." He shoved it in. "I suppose I cut it too fine; now we'll get kicked back half a million miles."

The screen convulsed again; when it cleared the third planet was directly in the center; its small moon, looking almost as large, was a little above and to the right, sunlit on one side and planetlit on the other. Kirbey locked the red handle, gathered up his tobacco and lighter and things from the ledge, and pulled down the cover of the instrument-console, locking it.

"All yours, Sharll," he told Renner.

"Eight hours to atmosphere," Renner said. "That's if we don't have to waste a lot of time shooting up Junior, there."

Vann Larch was looking at the moon in the six hundred power screen.

"I don't see anything to shoot. Five hundred miles; one planetbuster, or four or five thermonuclears," he said.

It wasn't right, Trask thought indignantly. Minutes ago, Tanith had been six and a half billion miles away. Seconds ago, fifty-odd million. And now, a quarter of a million, and looking close enough to touch in the screen, it would take them eight hours to reach it. Why, on hyper-drive you could go forty-eight trillion miles in that time.

Well, it took a man just as long to walk across a room today as it had taken Pharoah the First, or Homo Sap, the First, for that matter.

In the telescopic screen Tanith looked like any picture of any Terra-type planet from space, with cloud-blurred contours of seas and continents and a vague mottling of gray and brown and green, topped at the pole by an icecap. None of the surface features, not even the major mountain ranges or rivers, were yet distinguishable, but Harkaman and Sharll Renner and Alvyn Karffard and the other old hands seemed to recognize it. Karffard was talking by phone to Paul Koreff, the signals-and-detection officer, who could detect nothing from the moon and nothing that was getting through the Van Allen belt from the planet.

Maybe they'd guessed wrong, at that. Maybe Dunnan hadn't gone to Tanith at all.

Harkaman, who had the knack of putting himself to sleep at will, with some sixth or nth sense posted as a sentry, leaned back in his chair and closed his eyes. Trask wished he could, too. It would be hours before anything happened, and until then he needed all the rest he could get. He drank more coffee, chain-smoked cigarettes; he rose and prowled about the command room, looking at screens. Signals-and-detection was getting a lot of routine stuff—Van Allen count, micrometeor count, surface temperature, gravitation-field strength, radar and scanner echoes. He went back to his chair and sat down, staring at the screen-image. The planet didn't seem to be getting any closer at all, and it ought to; they were approaching it at better than escape velocity. He sat and stared at it . . .

He woke with a start. The screen-image was much larger, now. River courses and the shadow-lines of mountains were clearly visible. It must be early autumn in the northern hemisphere; there was snow down to the sixtieth parallel and a belt of brown was pushing south against the green. Harkaman was sitting up, eating lunch. By the clock, it was four hours later.

"Have a good nap?" he asked. "We're picking up some stuff, now. Radio and screen signals. Not much, but some. The locals wouldn't have learned enough for that in the five years since I was here. We didn't stay long enough, for one thing."

On decivilized planets that were visited by Space Vikings, the locals picked up bits and scraps of technology very quickly. In the four months of idleness and long conversations while they were in hyperspace he had heard many stories confirming that. But from the level to which Tanith had sunk, radio and screen communication in five years was a little too much of a jump.

"You didn't lose any men, did you?"

That happened frequently—men who took up with local women, men who had made themselves unpopular with their shipmates, men who just liked the planet and wanted to stay. They were always welcomed by the locals for what they could do and teach.

"No, we weren't there long enough for that. Only three hundred and fifty hours. This we're getting is outside stuff; somebody's there beside the locals."

Dunnan. He looked again at the battle-stations board; it was still uniformly red-lighted. Everything was on full combat ready. He summoned a mess-robot, selected a couple of dishes, and began to eat. After the first mouthful, he called to Alvyn Karffard:

"Is Paul getting anything new?"

Karffard checked. A little contragravity-field distortion effect. It was still too far to be sure. He went back to his lunch. He had finished it and was lighting a cigarette over his coffee when a red light flashed and a voice from one of the speakers shouted.

"Detection! Detection from planet! Radar, and microray!"

Karffard began talking rapidly into a hand-phone; Harkaman unhooked one beside him and listened.

"Coming from a definite point, about twenty fifty north parallel," he said, aside. "Could be from a ship hiding against the planet. There's nothing at all on the moon."

They seemed to be approaching the planet more and more rapidly. Actually, they weren't, the ship was decelerating to get into an orbit, but the decreasing distance created the illusion of increasing speed. The red lights flashed again.

"*Ship detected!* Just outside atmosphere, coming around the planet from the west."

"Is she the *Enterprise?*"

"Can't tell, yet," Karffard said, and then cried: "There she is, in the screen! That spark, about thirty degrees north, just off the west side."

Aboard her, too, voices from speakers would be shouting, "Ship detected!" and the battle station board would be blazing red. And Andray Dunnan, at the command-desk . . .

"She's calling us." That was Paul Koreff's voice, out of the squawk-box on the desk. "Standard Sword-World impulse-code. Interrogative: What ship are you? Informative: her screen combination. Request: Please communicate."

"All right," Harkaman said. "Let's be polite and communicate. What's her screen-combination?"

Koreff's voice gave it, and Harkaman punched it out. The communication screen in front of them lit at once; Trask shoved over his chair beside Harkaman's, his hands tightening on the arms. Would it be Dunnan himself, and what would his face show when he saw who confronted him out of his own screen?

It took him an instant to realize that the other ship was not the *Enterprise* at all. The *Enterprise* was the *Nemesis'* twin; her command-room was identical with his own. This one was different in arrangements and fittings. The *Enterprise* was a new ship; this one was old, and had suffered for years at the hands of a slack captain and a slovenly crew.

And the man who sat facing him in the screen was not Andray Dunnan, or any man he had ever seen before. A dark-faced man, with an old scar that ran down one cheek from a little below the eye; he had curly black hair, on his head and on a V of chest exposed by an open shirt. There was an ashtray in front of him, and a thin curl of smoke rose from a cigar in it, and coffee steamed in an ornate but battered silver cup beside it. He was grinning gleefully.

"Well! Captain Harkaman, of the *Enterprise*, I believe! Welcome to Tanith. Who's the gentleman with you? He isn't the Duke of Wardshaven, is he?"

TANITH

I

HE GLANCED quickly at the showback over the screen, to assure himself that his face was not betraying him. Beside him, Otto Harkaman was laughing.

"Why, Captain Valkanhayn; this is an unexpected pleasure. That's the *Space-Scourge* you're in, I take it? What are you doing here on Tanith?"

A voice from one of the speakers shouted that a second ship had been detected coming over the north pole. The dark-faced man in the screen smirked complacently.

"That's Garvan Spasso, in the *Lamia*," he said. "And what we're doing here, we've taken this planet over. We intend keeping it, too."

"Well! So you and Garvan have teamed up. You two were just made for one another. And you have a little planet, all your very own. I'm so happy for both of you. What are you getting out of it—beside poultry?"

The other's self-assurance started to slip. He slapped it back into place.

"Don't kid me; we know why you're here. Well, we got here first. Tanith is our planet. You think you can take it away from us?"

"I know we could, and so do you," Harkaman told him. "We outgun you and Spasso together; why, a couple of our pinnaces could knock the *Lamia* apart. The only question is, do we want to bother?''

By now, he had recovered from his surprise, but not from his disappointment. If this fellow thought the *Nemesis* was the *Enterprise* . . . Before he could check himself, he had finished the thought aloud.

''Then the *Enterprise* didn't come here, at all!''

The man in the screen started. ''Isn't that the *Enterprise* you're in?''

''Oh, no. Pardon my remissness, Captain Valkanhayn,'' Harkaman apologized. ''This is the *Nemesis*. The gentleman with me, Lord Lucas Trask, is owner-aboard, for whom I am commanding. Lord Trask, Captain Boake Valkanhayn, of the *Space-Scourge*. Captain Valkanhayn is a Space Viking.'' He said that as though expecting it to be disputed. ''So, I am told, is his associate, Captain Spasso, whose ship is approaching. You mean to tell me that the *Enterprise* hasn't been here?''

Valkanhayn was puzzled, slightly apprehensive.

''You mean the Duke of Wardshaven has two ships?''

''As far as I know, the Duke of Wardshaven hasn't any ships,'' Harkaman replied. ''This ship is the property and private adventure of Lord Trask. The *Enterprise*, for which we are looking, is owned and commanded by one Andray Dunnan.''

The man with the scarred face and hairy chest had picked up his cigar and was puffing on it mechanically. Now he took it out of his mouth as though he wondered how it had gotten there in the first place.

''But isn't the Duke of Wardshaven sending a ship here to establish a base? That was what we'd heard. We heard you'd gone from Flamberge to Gram to command for him.''

"Where did you hear this? And when?"

"On Hoth. That'd be about two thousand hours ago; a Gilgamesher brought the news from Xochitl."

"Well, considering it was fifth or sixth hand, your information was good enough, when it was fresh. It was a year and a half old when you got it, though. How long have you been here on Tanith?"

About a thousand hours. Harkaman clucked sadly at that.

"Pity you wasted all that time. Well, it was nice talking to you, Boake. Say hello to Garvan for me when he comes up."

"You mean you're not staying?" Valkanhayn was horrified, an odd reaction for a man who had just been expecting a bitter battle to drive them away. "You're just spacing right out again?"

Harkaman shrugged. "Do we want to waste time here, Lord Trask? The *Enterprise* has obviously gone somewhere else. She was still in hyperspace when Captain Valkanhayn and his accomplice arrived here."

"Is there anything worth staying for?" That seemed to be the reply Harkaman was expecting. "Beside poultry that is?"

Harkaman shook his head. "This is Captain Valkanhayn's planet; his and Captain Spasso's. Let them be stuck with it."

"But, look; this is a good planet. There's a big local city, maybe ten or twenty thousand people; temples and palaces and everything. Then, there are a couple of Old Federation cities. The one we're at is in good shape, and there's a big spaceport. We've been doing a lot of work on it. And the locals won't give you any trouble. All they have is spears and a few crossbows and matchlocks . . ."

"I know. I've been here."

"Well, couldn't we make some kind of a deal?" Valkanhayn asked. A mendicant whine was beginning to creep into his voice. "I can get Garvan on screen and switch him over to your ship . . ."

"Well, we have a lot of Sword-World merchandise aboard," Harkaman said. "We could make you good prices on some of it. How are you fixed for robotic equipment?"

"But aren't you going to stay here?" Valkanhayn was almost in a panic. "Listen, suppose I talk to Garvan, and we all get together on this. Just excuse me for a minute . . ."

As soon as he had blanked out, Harkaman threw back his head and guffawed as though he had just heard the funniest and bawdiest joke in the Galaxy. Trask, himself, didn't feel like laughing.

"The humor escapes me," he admitted. "We came here on a fools' errand."

"I'm sorry, Lucas," Harkaman was still shaking with mirth. "I know it's a letdown, but that pair of chiseling chicken-thieves! I could almost pity them, if it weren't so funny." He laughed again. "You know what their idea was?"

Trask shook his head. "Who are they?"

"What I called them, a couple of chicken-thieves. They raid planets like Set and Hertha and Melkarth, where the locals haven't anything to fight with—or anything worth fighting for. I didn't know they'd teamed up, but that figures. Nobody else would team up with either of them. What must have happened, this story of Duke Angus' Tanith adventure must have filtered out to them, and they thought that if they got here first, I'd think it was cheaper to take them in than run them out. I probably would have, too. They do have ships, of a sort, and they do raid, after a fashion. But now, there isn't going to be any Tanith base, and they have a no-good planet and they're stuck with it.''

"Can't they make anything out of it themselves?"

"Like what?" Harkaman hooted. "They have no equipment, and they have no men. Not for a job like that. The only thing they can do is space out and forget it."

"We could sell them equipment."

"We could if they had anything to use for money. They haven't. One thing, we do want to let down and give the men a chance to walk on ground and look at a sky for a while. The girls here aren't too bad, either," Harkaman said. "As I remember, some of them even take a bath, now and then."

"That's the kind of news of Dunnan we're going to get. By the time we'd get to where he's been reported, he'd be a couple of thousand light-years away," he said disgustedly. "I agree; we ought to give the men a chance to get off the ship, here. We can stall this pair along for a while and we won't have any trouble with them."

The three ships were slowly converging toward a point fifteen thousand miles off-planet and over the sunset line. The *Space-Scourge* bore the device of a mailed fist clutching a comet by the head; it looked more like a wisk-broom than a scourge. The *Lamia* bore a coiled snake with the head, arms and bust of a woman. Valkanhayn and Spasso were taking their time about screening back, and he began to wonder if they weren't maneuvering the *Nemesis* into a cross-fire position. He mentioned this to Harkaman and Alvyn Karffard; they both laughed.

"Just holding ship's meetings," Karffard said. "They'll be yacking back and forth for a couple of hours, yet."

"Yes, Valkanhayn and Spasso don't own their ships," Harkaman explained. "They've gone in debt to their crews for supplies and maintenance till everybody owns everything in common. The ships look like it, too. They don't even command, really; they just preside over elected command-councils."

Finally, they had both of the more or less commanders on screen. Valkanhayn had zipped up his shirt and put on a jacket. Garvan Spasso was a small man, partly bald. His eyes were a shade too close together, and his thin mouth had a bitterly crafty twist. He began speaking at once:

"Captain, Boake tells me you say you're not here in the service of the Duke of Wardshaven at all." He said it aggrievedly, almost accusingly.

"That's correct," Harkaman said. "We came here because Lord Trask thought another Gram ship, the *Enterprise*, would be here. Since she isn't, there's no point in our being here. We do hope, though, that you won't make any difficulty about our letting down and giving our men a couple of hundred hours' liberty. They've been in hyperspace for three thousand hours."

"See!" Spasso clamored. "He wants to trick us into letting him land . . ."

"Captain Spasso," Trask cut in. "Will you please stop insulting everybody's intelligence, your own included." Spasso glared at him, belligerently but hopefully. "I understand what you thought you were going to do here. You expected Captain Harkaman here to establish a base for the Duke of Wardshaven, and you thought, if you were

54

here ahead of him and in a posture of defense, that he'd take you into the Duke's service rather than waste ammunition and risk damage and casualties wiping you out. Well, I'm very sorry, gentlemen. Captain Harkaman is in my service, and I'm not in the least interested in establishing a base on Tanith.''

Valkanhayn and Spasso looked at each other. At least, in the two side-by-side screens, their eyes shifted, each to the other's screen on his own ship.

"I get it!'' Spasso cried suddenly. "There's two ships, the *Enterprise* and this one. The Duke of Wardshaven fitted out the *Enterprise,* and somebody else fitted out this one. They both want to put in a base here!''

That opened a glorious vista. Instead of merely capitalizing on their nuisance-value, they might find themselves holding the balance of power in a struggle for the planet. All sorts of profitable perfidies were possible.

"Why, sure you can land, Otto,'' Valkanhayn said. "I know what it's like to be three thousand hours in hyper, myself.''

"You're at this old city with the two tall tower-buildings, aren't you?'' Harkaman asked. He looked up at the viewscreen. "Ought to be about midnight there now. How's the spaceport? When I was here, it was pretty bad.''

"Oh, we've been fixing it up. We got a big gang of locals working for us . . .''

The city was familiar, from Otto Harkaman's descriptions and from the pictures Vann Larch had painted during the long jump from Gram. As they came in, it looked impressive, spreading for miles around the twin buildings that spired almost three thousand feet above it, with a great spaceport like an eight pointed star at one side. Whoever had built it, in the sunset splendor of the old Terran Federation, must have done so confident that it would become the metropolis of a populous and prospering world. Then the sun of the Federation had gone down. Nobody knew what had happened on Tanith after that, but evidently none of it had been good.

At first, the two towers seemed as sound as when they had been built; gradually it became apparent that one was broken at the top. For the most part, the smaller buildings scattered widely around them were standing, though here and there mounds of brush-grown rubble showed where some had fallen in. The spaceport looked good—a central octagon mass of buildings, the landing-berths, and, beyond, the triangular areas of airship docks and warehouses. The central building was outwardly intact, and the ship-berths seemed clear of wreckage and rubble.

By the time the *Nemesis* was following the *Space-Scourge* and the *Lamia* down, towed by her own pinnaces, the illusion that they were approaching a living city had vanished. The interspaces between the buildings were choked with forest growth, broken by a few small fields and garden plots. At one time, there had been three of the high buildings, literally vertical cities in themselves. Where the third had stood was a glazed crater, with a ridge of fallen rubble lying away from it. Somebody must have landed a medium missile, about twenty kilotons, against its base. Something of the same sort had scored on the far edge of the spaceport, and one of the eight arrowheads of docks and warehouses was an indistinguishable slagpile.

The rest of the city seemed to have died of neglect rather than violence. It certainly hadn't been bombed out. Harkaman thought most of the fighting had been done with subneutron bombs or Omega-ray bombs, that killed the people without damaging the real estate. Or bio-weapons; a manmade plague that had gotten out of control and all but depopulated the planet.

"It takes an awful lot of people, working together at an awful lot of jobs, to keep a civilization running. Smash the installations and kill the top technicians and scientists, and the masses don't know how to rebuild. They go back to stone hatchets. Kill off enough of the masses and even if the plant and the know-how is left, there's nobody to do the work. I've seen planets that decivilized both ways. Tanith, I think, is one of the latter."

That had been during one of the long after-dinner bull sessions on the way out from Gram. Somebody, one of the noble gentlemen-adventurers who had joined the company after the piracy of the *Enterprise* and the murder, had asked;

"But some of them survived. Don't they know what happened?"

" 'In the old times, there were sorcerers. They built the old buildings by wizard arts. Then the sorcerers fought among themselves and went away,' " Harkaman said. "That's all they know about it."

You could make any kind of an explanation out of that.

As the pinnaces pulled and nudged the *Nemesis* down to her berth, he could see people, far down on the spaceport floor, at work. Either Valkanhayn and Spasso had more men than the size of their ships indicated, or they had gotten a lot of locals to work for them. More than the population of the moribund city, at least as Harkaman remembered it.

There had been about five hundred in all; they lived by

mining the old buildings for metal, and trading metalwork for food and textiles and powder and other things made elsewhere. It was accessible only by oxcarts traveling a hundred miles across the plains; it had been built by a contragravity-using people with utter disregard for natural travel and transportation routes.

"I don't envy the poor buggers," Harkaman said, looking down at the antlike figures on the spaceport floor. "Boake Valkanhayn and Garvan Spasso have probably made slaves of the lot of them. If I really were going to put in a base here, I wouldn't thank that pair for the kind of public realtions work they've been doing among the locals."

II

THAT WAS just about the situation. Spasso and Valkanhayn and some of their officers met them on the landing-stage of the big building in the middle of the spaceport, where they had established quarters. Entering and going down a long hallway, they passed a dozen men and women gathering up rubbish from the floor with shovels and with their hands and putting it into a lifter-skid. Both sexes wore shapeless garments of coarse cloth, like ponchos, and flat-soled sandals. Watching them was another local in a kilt, buskins and a leather jerkin; he wore a short sword on his belt and carried a wickedly thonged whip. He also wore a Space Viking combat helmet, painted with the device of Spasso's *Lamia*. He bowed as they approached, putting a hand to his forehead. After they had passed, they could hear him shouting at the others, and the sound of whip blows.

You make slaves out of people, and some will always be slave-drivers; they will bow to you, and then take it out on the others. Harkaman's nose was twitching as though he had a bit of rotten fish caught in his mustache.

"We have about eight hundred of them. There were only three hundred that were any good for work here; we gathered the rest up at villages along the big river," Spasso was saying.

"How do you get food for them?" Harkaman asked. "Or don't you bother?"

"Oh, we gather that up all over," Valkanhayn told him. "We send parties out with landing craft. They'll let down on a village, run the locals out, gather up what's around and bring it here. Once in a while they put up a fight, but the best they have is a few crossbows and some muzzle-loading muskets. When they do, we burn the village and machine-gun everybody we see."

"That's the stuff," Harkaman approved. "If the cow doesn't want to be milked, just shoot her. Of course, you don't get much milk out of her again, but—"

The room to which their hosts guided them was at the far end of the hall. It had probably been a conference room or something of the sort, and originally it had been panelled, but the panelling had long ago vanished. Holes had been dug here and there in the walls, and he remembered having noticed that the door was gone and the metal groove in which it had slid had been pried out.

There was a big table in the middle, and chairs and couches covered with colored spreads. All the furniture was hand-made, cunningly pegged together and highly polished. On the walls hung trophies of weapons —thrusting-spears and throwing-spears, crossbows and quarrels, and a number of heavy guns, crude things but carefully made.

"Pick all this stuff up off the locals?" Harkaman asked.

"Yes, we got most of it at a big town down at the forks of the river," Valkanhayn said. "We shook it down a couple of times. That's where we recruited the fellows we're using to boss the workers."

Then he picked up a stick with a leather-covered knob and beat on a gong, bawling for wine. A voice, some-where, replied, "Yes, master; I come!" In a few moments a woman entered, carrying a jug in either hand. She was wearing a blue bathrobe several sizes too large for her, instead of the poncho things the slaves in the hallway wore. She had dark brown hair and gray eyes; if she had not been so obviously frightened she would have been beautiful. She set the jugs on the table and brought silver cups from a chest against the wall; when Spasso dismissed her, she went out hastily.

"I suppose it's silly to ask if you're paying these people anything for the work they do or for the things you take from them," Harkaman said. From the way the *Space-Scourge* and *Lamia* people laughed it evidently was. Harkaman shrugged. "Well, it's your planet. Make any kind of a mess out of it you want to."

"You think we *ought* to pay them?" Spasso was in-credulous. "Damn bunch of savages!"

"They aren't as savage as the Xochitl locals were when Haulteclere took it over. You've been there; you've seen what Prince Viktor does with them now."

"We haven't got the men or equipment they have on Xochitl," Valkanhayn said. "We can't afford to coddle the locals."

"You can't afford not to," Harkaman told him. "You have two ships, here. You can only use one for raiding; the other will have to stay here to hold the planet. If you take them both away, the locals, whom you have been studiously antagonizing, will swamp whoever you leave behind. And if you don't leave anybody behind, what's the use of having a planetary base?"

"Well, why don't you join us," Spasso finally came out with it. "With our three ships we could have a real thing, here."

Harkaman looked at him inquiringly. "The gentlemen," Trask said, "are putting this wrongly. They mean, why don't we let them join us?"

"Well, if you want to put it like that," Valkanhayn conceded. "We'll admit, your Nemesis would be the big end of it. But why not? Three ships, we could have a real base here. Nicky Gratham's father only had two when he started on Jaganath, and look what the Grathams got there now."

"Are we interested?" Harkaman asked.

"Not very, I'm afraid. Of course, we've just landed; Tanith may have great possibilities. Suppose we reserve decision for a while and look around a little."

There were stars in the sky, and, for good measure, a sliver of moon on the eastern horizon. It was only a small moon, but it was close. He walked to the edge of the observation deck, and Elaine was walking with him. The noise from inside, where the Nemesis crew were feasting with those of the *Lamia* and *Space-Scourge* grew fainter. To the south, a star moved; one of the pinnaces they had left on off-planet watch. There was firelight far below, and he could hear singing. Suddenly he realized that it was the poor devils of locals whom Valkanhayn and Spasso had enslaved. Elaine went away quickly.

"Have your fill of Space Viking glamor, Lucas?"

He turned. It was Baron Rathmore, who had come along to serve for a year or so and then hitch a ride home from some base planet and cash in politically on having been with Lucas Trask.

"For the moment. I'm told that this lot aren't typical."

"I hope not. They're a pack of sadistic brutes, and piggish along with it."

"Well, brutality and bad manners I can condone, but Spasso and Valkanhayn are a pair of ignominious little crooks, and stupid along with it. If Andray Dunnan had gotten here ahead of us, he might have done one good thing in his wretched life. I can't understand why he didn't come here."

"I think he still will," Rathmore said. "I knew him and I knew Nevil Ormm. Ormm's ambitious, and Dunnan is insanely vindictive—" He broke off with a sour laugh. "I'm telling *you* that!"

"Why didn't he come here directly, then?"

"Maybe he doesn't want a base on Tanith. That would be something constructive; Dunnan's a destroyer. I think he took that cargo of equipment somewhere and sold it. I think he'll wait till he's fairly sure the other ship is finished. Then he'll come in and shoot the place up, the way—" He bit that off abruptly.

"The way he did my wedding; I think of it all the time."

The next morning, he and Harkaman took an aircar and went to look at the city at the forks of the river. It was completely new, in the sense that it had been built since the collapse of Federation civilization and the loss of civilized technologies. It was huddled on a long, irregularly triangular mound, evidently to raise it above flood-level. Generations of labor with spades and ox-carts must have gone into it. To the eyes of a civilization using contragravity and powered equipment it wasn't at all impressive. Fifty to a hundred men with adequate equipment could have gotten the thing up in a summer. It was only by forcing himself to think in terms of spadeful after spadeful of earth, cartload after cartload creaking behind straining beasts, timber after timber cut with axes and dressed with adzes, stone after stone and brick after brick, that he could appreciate it. They even had it walled, with a palisade of tree-trunks behind which earth and rocks had been banked, and along the river were docks, at which boats were moored. The locals simply called it Tradetown.

As they approached, a big gong began booming, and a white puff of smoke was followed by the thud of a signal-gun. The boats, long canoe-like craft and round-bowed, many-oared barges, put out hastily into the river; through binoculars they could see people scattering from the surrounding fields, driving cattle ahead of them. By the time they were over the city, nobody was in sight. They seemed to have developed a pretty fair air-raid warning system in the nine-hundred-odd hours in which they had been exposed to the figurative mercies of Boake Valkanhayn and Garvan Spasso. It hadn't saved them entirely; a section of the city·had been burned, and there were evidences of shelling. Light chemical-explosive stuff; this city was too

63

good a cow for even those two to kill before the milking was over.

They circled slowly over it at a thousand feet. When they turned away, black smoke began rising from what might have been pottery works or brick-kilns on the out-skirts; something resinous had evidently been fed to the fires. Other columns of black smoke began rising across the countryside on both sides of the river.

"You know, these people are civilized, if you don't limit the term to contragravity and nuclear energy," Harkaman said. "They have gunpowder, for one thing, and I can think of some rather impressive Old Terran civilizations that didn't have that much. They have an organized society, and anybody who has that is starting toward civilization."

"I hate to think of what'll happen to this planet if Spasso and Valkanhayn stay here long."

"Might be a good thing, in the long run. Good things in the long run are often tough while they're happening. I know what'll happen to Spasso and Valkanhayn, though. They'll start decivilizing, themselves. They'll stay here for a while, and when they need something they can't take from the locals they'll go chicken-stealing after it, but most of the time they'll stay here lording it over their slaves, and finally their ships will wear out and they won't be able to fix them. Then, some time, the locals'll jump them when they aren't watching and wipe them out. But in the meantime, the locals'll learn a lot from them."

They turned the aircar west again and along the river. They looked at a few villages. One or two dated from the Federation period; they had been plantations before what-ever it was had happened. More had been built within the past five centuries. A couple had recently been destroyed, in punishment for the crime of self-defense.

"You know," he said, at length. "I'm going to do everybody a favor. I'm going to let Spasso and Valkanhayn persuade me to take this planet away from them."

Harkaman, who was piloting, turned sharply. "You crazy or something?"

" 'When somebody makes a statement you don't understand, don't tell him he's crazy. Ask him what he means.' Who said that?"

"On target," Harkaman grinned. " 'What *do* you mean, Lord Trask?' "

"I can't catch Dunnan by pursuit; I'll have to get him by interception. You know the source of that quotation, too. This looks to me like a good place to intercept him. When he learns I have a base here, he'll hit it, sooner or later. And even if he doesn't, we can pick up more information on him, when ships start coming in here, than we would batting around all over the Old Federation."

Harkaman considered for a moment, then nodded. "Yes, if we could set up a base like Nergal or Xochitl," he agreed. "There'll be four or five ships, Space Vikings, traders, Gilgameshers and so on, on either of those planets all the time. If we had the cargo Dunnan took to space in the *Enterprise*, we could start a base like that. But we haven't anything near what we need, and you know what Spasso and Valkanhayn have."

"We can get it from Gram. As it stands, the investors in the Tanith Adventure, from Duke Angus down, lost everything they put into it. If they're willing to throw some good money after bad, they can get it back, and a handsome profit to boot. And there ought to be planets above the rowboat and ox-cart level not too far away that could be raided for a lot of things we'd need.''

"That's right; I know of half a dozen within five hundred light-years. They won't be the kind Spasso and Valkanhayn are in the habit of raiding, though. And beside machinery, we can get gold, and valuable merchandise that could be sold on Gram. And if we could make a go of it, you'd go farther hunting Dunnan by sitting here on Tanith than by going looking for him. That was the way we used to hunt marsh-pigs on Colada, when I was a kid; just find a good place and sit down and wait.''

They had Valkanhayn and Spasso aboard the *Nemesis* for dinner; it didn't take much guiding to keep the conversation on the subject of Tanith and its resources, advantages and possibilities. Finally, when they had reached brandy and coffee, Trask said idly:

"I believe, together, we could really make something out of this planet.''

"That's what we've been telling you, all along,'' Spasso broke in eagerly. "This is a wonderful planet . . .''

"It could be. All it has now is possibilities. We'd need a spaceport, for one thing.''

"Well, what's this, here?'' Valkanhayn wanted to know.

"It was a spaceport,'' Harkaman told him. "It could be one again. And we'd need a shipyard, capable of any kind of heavy repair work. Capable of building a complete ship, in fact. I never saw a ship come into a Viking base planet with any kind of a cargo worth dickering over that hadn't taken some damage getting it. Prince Viktor of Xochitl makes a good half of his money on ship repairs, and so do Nicky Gratham on Jaganath and the Everrards on Hoth.''

"And engine-works, hyperdrive, normal-space and pseudograv,'' Trask added. "And a steel mill, and a collapsed-matter plant. And robotic-equipment works, and . . .''

"Oh, that's out of all reason!'' Valkanhayn cried. "It would take twenty trips with a ship the size of this one to get all that stuff here, and how'd we ever be able to pay for it?''

"That's the sort of base Duke Angus of Wardshaven planned. The *Enterprise*, practically a duplicate of the *Nemesis*, carried everything that would be needed to get it started, when she was pirated.''

"When she was . . .?''

"Now you're going to have to tell the gentlemen the truth,'' Harkaman chuckled.

"I intend to.'' He laid his cigar down, sipped some of his brandy, and explained about Duke Angus' Tanith Adventure. "It was part of a larger plan; Angus wanted to gain economic supremacy for Wardshaven to forward his political ambitions. It was, however, an entirely practical business proposition. I was opposed to it, because I thought it would be too good a proposition for Tanith and work to the disadvantage of the home planet in the end.'' He told them about the *Enterprise*, and the cargo of industrial and construction equipment she carried, and then told them how Andray Dunnan had pirated her.

"That wouldn't have annoyed me at all; I had no money invested in the project. What did annoy me, to put it mildly, was that just before he took the ship out, Dunnan shot up my wedding, wounded me and my father-in-law, and killed the lady to whom I had been married for less than half an hour. I fitted out this ship at my own expense, took on Captain Harkaman, who had been left without a command when the *Enterprise* was pirated, and came out here to hunt Dunnan down and kill him. I believe that I can do that best by establishing a base on Tanith myself. The base will have to be operated at a profit, or it can't be operated at all." He picked up the cigar again and puffed slowly. "I am inviting you gentlemen to join me as partners."

"Well, you still haven't told us how we're going to get the money to finance it," Spasso insisted.

"The Duke of Wardshaven, and the others who invested in the original Tanith Adventure will put it up. It's the only way they can recover what they lost on the *Enterprise.*"

"But then, this Duke of Wardshaven will be running it, not us," Valkanhayn objected.

"The Duke of Wardshaven," Harkaman reminded him, "is on Gram. We are here on Tanith. There are three thousand light-years between."

That seemed a satisfactory answer. Spasso, however, wanted to know who would run things here on Tanith.

"We'll have to hold a meeting of all three crews," he began.

"We will do nothing of the kind," Trask told him. "I will be running things here on Tanith. You people may allow your orders to be debated and voted on, but I don't. You will inform your respective crews to that effect. Any orders you give them in my name will be obeyed without argument."

"I don't know how the men'll take that," Valkanhayn said.

"I know how they'll take it if they're smart," Harkaman told him. "And I know what'll happen if they aren't. I know how you've been running your ships, or how your ships' crews have been running you. Well, we don't do it that way. Lucas Trask is owner, and I'm captain. I obey his orders on what's to be done, and everybody else obeys mine on how to do it."

Spasso looked at Valkanhayn, then shrugged. "That's how the man wants it, Boake. You want to give him an argument? I don't."

"The first order," Trask said, "is that these people you have working here are to be paid. They are not to be beaten by these plug-uglies you have guarding them. If any of them want to leave, they may do so; they will be given presents and furnished transportation home. Those who wish to stay will be issued rations, furnished with clothing and bedding and so on as they need it, and paid wages. We'll work out some kind of a pay-token system and set up a commissary where they can buy things."

"Discs of plastic or titanium or something, stamped and uncounterfeitable. Get Alvyn Karffard to see about that. Organize work-gangs, and promote the best and most intelligent to foremen. And those guards could be taken in hand by some ground-fighter sergeant and given Sword-World weapons and tactical training; use them to train others; they'd need a sepoy army of some sort. Even the best of good will is no substitute for armed force, conspicuously displayed and unhesitatingly used when necessary.

"And there'll be no more of this raiding villages for food or anything else. We will pay for anything we get from any of the locals."

"We'll have trouble about that," Valkanhayn predicted. "Our men think anything a local has belongs to anybody who can take it."

"So do I," Harkaman said. "On a planet I'm raiding. This is our planet, and our locals. We don't raid our own planet or our own people. You'll just have to teach them that."

III

IT TOOK Valkanhayn and Spasso more time and argument to convince their crews than Trask thought necessary. Harkaman seemed satisfied, and so was Baron Rathmore, the Wardshaven politician.

"It's like talking a lot of uncommitted small landholders into taking somebody's livery-and-maintenance," the latter said. "You can't use too much pressure; make them think it's their own idea."

There were meetings of both crews, with heated arguments; Baron Rathmore made frequent speeches, while Lord Trask of Tanith and Admiral Harkaman—the titles were Rathmore's suggestion—remained loftily aloof. On both ships, everybody owned everything in common, which meant that nobody owned anything. They had taken over Tanith on the same basis of diffused ownership, and nobody in either crew was quite stupid enough to think that they could do anything with the planet by themselves. By joining the *Nemesis*, it appeared that they were getting something for nothing. In the end, they voted to place themselves under the authority of Lord Trask and Admiral

Harkaman. After all, Tanith would be a feudal lordship, and the three ships together a fleet.

Admiral Harkaman's first act of authority was to order a general inspection of fleet-units. He wasn't shocked by the condition of the two ships, but that was only because he had expected much worse. They were spaceworthy; after all, they had gotten here from Hoth under their own power. They were only combat-worthy if the combat weren't too severe. His original estimate that the *Nemesis* could have knocked both of them to pieces was, if anything, overconservative. The engines were only in fair shape, and the armament was bad.

"We aren't going to spend our time sitting here on Tanith," he told the two captains. "This planet is a raiding base, and 'raiding' is the operative word. And we are not going to raid easy planets. A planet that can be raided with impunity isn't worth the time it takes getting to it. We are going to have to fight on every planet we hit, and I am not going to jeopardize the lives of the men under me, which includes your crews as well as mine, because of under-powered and under-armed ships."

Spasso tried to argue. "We've been getting along."

Harkaman cursed. "Yes. I know how you've been getting along; chicken-stealing on planets like Set and Xipototec and Melkarth. Not making enough to cover maintenance expenses; that's why your ship's in the shape she is. Well, those days are over. Both ships ought to have a full overhaul, but we'll have to skip that till we have a shipyard of our own. But I will insist, at least, that your guns and launchers are in order. And your detection equipment; you didn't get a fix on the *Nemesis,* till we were less than twenty thousand miles off-planet."

"We had better get the *Lamia* in condition first," Trask said. "We can put her on off-planet watch, instead of that pair of pinnaces."

Work on the *Lamia* started the next day, and considerable friction-heat was generated between her officers and the engineers sent over from the *Nemesis*. Baron Rathmore went aboard, and came back laughing.

"You know how that ship's run?" he asked. "There's a sort of soviet of officers; chief engineer, exec, guns-and-missiles, astrogator and so on. Spasso's just an animated ventriloquist's dummy. I talked to all of them. None of them can pin me down to anything, but they think we're going to heave Spasso out of command and appoint one of them, and each one thinks he'll be it. I don't know how long that'll last, it's a string-and-tape job like the one we're having to do on the ship. It'll hold till we get something better."

"We'll have to get rid of Spasso," Harkaman agreed. "I think we'll put one of our own people in his place. Valkanhayn can stay in command of the *Space-Scourge;* he's a spaceman. But Spasso's no good for anything."

The local problem was complicated, too. The locals spoke Lingua Terra of a sort, like every descendant of the race that had gone out from the Sol system in the Third Century, but it was a barely comprehensible sort. On civilized planets, the language had been frozen unalterably in microbooks and voice-tapes. But microbooks can only be read and sound-tapes heard with the aid of electricity, and Tanith had lost that long ago.

Most of the people Spasso and Valkanhayn had kidnapped and enslaved came from villages within a radius of five hundred miles. About half of them wanted to be repatriated; they were given gifts of knives, tools, blankets, and bits of metal which seemed to be the chief standard of value and medium of exchange, and shipped home. Finding their proper village was not easy. At each such village, the news was spread that the Space Vikings would hereafter pay for what they received.

The *Lamia* was overhauled as rapidly as possible. She was still far from being a good ship, but she was much closer being one than before. She was fitted with the best detection equipment that could be assembled, and put on orbit; Alvyn Karffard took command of her, with some of Spasso's officers, some of Valkanhayn's, and a few from the *Nemesis*. Harkaman was intending to use her for retraining of all the *Lamia* and *Space-Scourge* officers, and rotated them back and forth.

The labor-guards, a score in number, were relieved of their duties, issued Sword-World firearms, and given intensive training. The trade-tokens, stamped of colored plastic, were introduced, and a store was set up where they could be exchanged for Sword-World items. After a while, it dawned on the locals that the tokens could also be used for trading among themselves; money seemed to have been one of the adjuncts of civilization that had been lost along Tanith's downward path. A few of them were able to use contragravity hand-lifters and hand-towed lifter-skids; several were even learning to operate things like bulldozers, at least to the extent of knowing which lever or button did what. Give them a little time, Trask thought, watching a gang at work down on the spaceport floor. It won't be many years before half of them will be piloting aircars.

As soon as the *Lamia* was on orbital watch, the

Space-Scourge was set down at the spaceport and work started on her. It was decided that Valkanhayn would take her to Gram; enough *Nemesis* people would go along to insure good faith on his part, and to talk to Duke Angus and the Tanith investors. Baron Rathmore, and Paytrik Morland, and several other Wardshaven gentlemen-adventurers for the latter function; Alvyn Karffard to act as Valkanhayn's exec, with private orders to supersede him in command if necessary, and Guatt Kirbey to do the astrogating.

"We'll have to take the *Nemesis* and the *Space-Scourge* out, first, and make a big raid," Harkaman said. "We can't send the *Space-Scourge* back to Gram empty. When Baron Rathmore and Lord Valpry and the rest of them talk to Duke Angus and the Tanith investors, they'll have to have a lot more than some travel-films of Tanith. They'll have to be able to show that Tanith is producing. We ought to have a little money of our own to invest, too."

"But, Otto; both ships?" That worried him. "Suppose Dunnan comes and finds nobody here but Spasso and the *Lamia?*"

"Chance we'll have to take. Personally, I think we have a year to a year and a half before Dunnan shows up here. I know, we were fooled trying to guess what he'd do before. But the sort of raid I have in mind, we'll need two ships, and in any case, I don't want to leave both those ships here while we're gone, even if you do."

"When it comes to that, I don't think I do, either. But we can't trust Spasso here alone, can we?"

"We'll leave enough of our people to make sure. We'll leave Alvyn—that'll mean a lot of work for me that he'd otherwise do, on the ship. And Baron Rathmore, and young Valpry, and the men who've been training our sepoys. We can shuffle things around and leave some of Valkanhayn's men in place of some of Spasso's. We might even talk Spasso into going along. That'll mean having to endure him at our table, but it would be wise."

"Have you picked a place to raid?"

"Three of them. First, Khepera. That's only thirty light-years from here. That won't amount to much; just chicken-stealing. It'll give our green hands some relatively safe combat-training, and it'll give us some idea of how Spasso's and Valkanhayn's people behave, and give them confidence for the next job."

"And then?"

"Amaterasu. My information about Amaterasu is about twenty years old. A lot of things can happen in twenty years. As I know of it—I was never there myself—it's fairly civilized. About like Terra just before the beginning of the Atomic Era. No nuclear energy, they lost that, and of course nothing beyond it, but they have hydro-electric and solar-electric power, and non-nuclear jet aircraft, and some very good chemical-explosive weapons, which they use very freely on each other. It was last known to have been raided by a ship from Excalibur twenty years ago."

"That sounds promising. And the third planet?"

"Beowulf. We won't take enough damage on Amaterasu to make any difference there, but if we saved Amaterasu for last, we might be needing too many repairs."

"It's like that?"

"Yes. They have nuclear energy. I don't think it would be wise to mention Beowulf to Captains Spasso and Valkanhayn. Wait till we've hit Khepera and Amaterasu. They may be feeling like heroes, then."

IV

KHEPERA LEFT a bad taste in his mouth. He was still tasting it when the colored turbulence died out of the screen and left the gray nothingness of hyperspace. Garvan Spasso—they had had no trouble in inducing him to come along—was staring avidly at the screen as though he could still see the ravished planet they had left.

"That was a good one; that was a good one!" he was crowing. He'd said that a dozen times since they had lifted out. "Three cities in five days, and all the stuff we gathered up around them. We took over two million stellars."

And did ten times as much damage getting it, and there was no scale of values by which to compute the death and suffering.

"Knock it off, Spasso. You said that before."

There was a time when he wouldn't have spoken to the fellow, or anybody else, like that. Gresham's law, extended: Bad manners drive out good manners. Spasso turned on him indignantly.

"Who do you think you are . . .?"

"He thinks he's Lord Trask of Tanith," Harkaman said. "He's right, too; he is." He looked searchingly at Trask for a moment, then turned back to Spasso. "I'm just as tired as he is of hearing you pop your mouth about a lousy two million stellars. Nearer a million and a half, but two million's nothing to pop about. Maybe it would be for the *Lamia*, but we have a three-ship fleet and a planetary base to meet expenses on. Out of this raid, a ground-fighter or an able spaceman will get a hundred and fifty stellars. We'll get about a thousand, ourselves. How long do you think we can stay in business doing this kind of chicken-stealing.''

"You call this chicken-stealing?"

"I call it chicken-stealing, and so'll you before we get back to Tanith. If you live that long.''

For a moment, Spasso was still affronted. Then, temporarily, his vulpine face showed avaricious hope, and then apprehension. Evidently he knew Otto Harkaman's reputation, and some of the things Harkaman had done weren't his idea of an easy way to make money.

Khepera had been easy; the locals hadn't had anything to fight with. Smallarms, and light cannon which hadn't been able to fire more than a few rounds. Wherever they had attempted resistance, the combat-cars had swooped in, dropping bombs and firing machine guns and auto-cannon. Yet they had fought, bitterly and hopelessly —just as he would have, defending Traskon.

He busied himself getting coffee and a cigarette from one of the robots. When he looked up, Spasso had gone away, and Harkaman was sitting on the edge of the desk, loading his short pipe.

"Well, you saw the elephant, Lucas,'' he said. You don't seem to have liked it.''

"Elephant?"

"Old Terran expression I read somewhere. All I know is that an elephant was an animal about the size of one of your Gram megatheres. The expression means, experiencing something for the first time which makes a great impression. Elephants must have been something to see. This was your first Viking raid. You've seen it, now.''

He'd been in combat before; he'd led the fighting-men of Traskon during the boundary dispute with Baron Manniwel, and there were always bandits and cattle-rustlers. He'd thought it would be like that. He remembered, five days, or was it five ages, ago, his excited anticipation as the city grew and spread in the screen and the *Nemesis* came dropping down toward it. The pinnaces, his four and the two from the *Space-Scourge*, had gone spiraling out a hundred miles beyond the city; the *Space-Scourge* had gone into a tighter circle twenty miles from its center; the *Nemesis* had continued her relentless descent until she was ten miles from the ground, before she began spewing out landing-craft, and combat cars, and the little egg-shaped one-man air cavalry mounts. It had been thrilling. Everything had gone perfectly; not even Valkanhayn's gang had goofed.

Then the screen-views had begun coming in. The brief and hopeless fight in the city. He could still see that silly little field-gun, it must have been around seventy or eighty millimeter, on a high-wheeled carriage, drawn by six shaggy, bandy-legged beasts. They had gotten it unlimbered and were trying to get it on a target when a rocket from an aircar landed directly under the muzzle. Gun, caisson, crew, even the draft-team fifty yards behind, had simply vanished.

Or the little company, some of them women, trying to defend the top of a tall and half-ruinous building with rifles and pistols. One air-cavalryman wiped them all out with his machine guns.

"They don't have a chance," he'd said, half-sick. "But they keep on fighting."

"Yes; stupid of them, isn't it?" Harkaman, beside him, had said.

"What would you do in their place?"

"Fight. Try to kill as many Space Vikings as I could before they got me. Terro-humans are all stupid like that. That's why we're human."

If the taking of the city had been a massacre, the sack that had followed had been a man-made Hell. He had gone down, along with Harkaman, while the fighting, if it could be so called, was still going on. Harkaman had suggested that the men ought to see him moving about among them; for his own part, he had felt a compulsion to share their guilt.

He and Sir Paytrik Morland had been on foot together in one of the big hollow buildings that had stood since Khepera had been a Member Republic of the Terran Federation. The air was acrid with smoke, powder-smoke and the smoke of burning. It was surprising, how much would burn, in this city of concrete and vitrified stone. It was surprising, too, how well-kept everything was, at least on the ground level. These people had taken pride in their city.

They found themselves alone, in a great empty hallway; the noise and horror of the sack had moved away from them, or they from it, and then, when they entered a side hall, they saw a man, one of the locals, squatting on the floor with the body of a woman cradled on his lap. She was dead, half her head had been blown off, but he was clasping her tightly, her blood staining his shirt, and sobbing heartbrokenly. A carbine lay forgotten on the floor beside him.

"Poor devil," Morland said, and started forward.

"No."

Trask stopped him with his left hand. With his right, he drew his pistol and shot the man dead. Morland was horrified.

"Great Satan, Lucas! Why did you do that?"

"I wish Andray Dunnan had done that for me." He thumbed the safety on and holstered the pistol. "None of this would be happening if he had. How many more happinesses do you think we've smashed here today? And we don't even have Dunnan's excuse of madness."

The next morning, with everything of value collected and sent aboard, they had started cross-country for five hundred miles to another city, the first hundred over a countryside asmoke from burning villages Valkanhayn's men had pillaged the night before. There was no warning; Khepera had lost electricity and radio and telegraph, and the spread of news was at the speed of one of the beasts the locals insisted on calling horses. By mid-afternoon, they had finished with that city. It had been as bad as the first one.

One thing, it was the center of a considerable cattle country. The cattle were native to the planet, heavy-bodied unicorns the size of a Gram bisonoid or one of the slightly mutated Terran carabaos on Tanith, with long hair like a Terran yak. He had detailed a dozen of the *Nemesis* ground-fighters who had been vaqueros on his Traskon ranches to collect a score of cows and four likely bulls, with enough fodder to last them on the voyage. The odds were strongly against any of them living to acclimate themselves to Tanith, but if they did, they might prove to be one of the most valuable pieces of loot from Khepera.

The third city was at the forks of a river, like Tradetown on Tanith. Unlike it, this was a real metropolis. They should have gone there first of all. They spent two days systematically pillaging it. The Kheperans carried on considerable river-traffic, with stern-wheel steamboats, and the waterfront was lined with warehouses crammed with every sort of merchandise. Even better, the Kheperans had money, and for the most part it was gold specie, and the bank-vaults were full of it.

Unfortunately, the city had been built since the fall of the Federation and the climb up from the barbarism that had followed, and a great deal of it was of wood. Fires started almost at once, and it was almost completely on fire by the end of the second day. It had been visible in the telescopic screen even after they were out of atmosphere, a black smear until the turning planet carried it into darkness and then a lurid glow.

"It was a filthy business."

Harkaman nodded. "Robbery and murder always are. You don't have to ask me who said that Space Vikings are professional robbers and murderers, but who was it said that he didn't care how many planets were raided and how many innocents massacred in the Old Federation?"

"A dead man. Lucas Trask of Traskon. He didn't know what he was talking about."

"You wish, now, that you'd kept Traskon and stayed on Gram?"

"No. If I had, I'd have spent every hour wishing I was doing what I'm doing now. I can get used to this, I suppose."

"I think you will. At least, you kept your rations down. I puked myself empty on my first raid, and had bad dreams about it for a year.'' He gave his coffee-cup back to the robot and got to his feet. ''Get a little rest, for a couple of hours. Then draw some alcodote-vitimine pills from the medic. As soon as things are secured, there'll be parties all over the ship, and we'll be expected to look in on every one of them, have a drink, and say 'Well done, boys!' ''

Elaine came to him, while he was resting. She looked at him in horror, and he tried to hide his face from her, and then realized that he was trying to hide it from himself.

V

THEY CAME straight down on Eglonsby, on Amaterasu, the *Nemesis* and the *Space-Scourge* side by side. The radar had picked them up at point-five light-seconds; by this time the whole planet knew they were coming, and nobody was wondering why. Paul Koreff was monitoring at least twenty radio stations, assigning somebody to each one as it was identified. What was coming in was uniformly excited, some panicky, and all in fairly standard Lingua Terra.

Garvan Spasso was perturbed. So, in the communication screen from the *Space-Scourge*, was Boake Valkanhayn.

''They got radio, and they got radar,'' he clamored.

''Well, so what?'' Harkaman asked. ''They had radio and radar twenty years ago, when Rock Morgan was here in the *Coalsack*. But they don't have nuclear energy, do they?''

"Well, no. I'm picking up a lot of industrial electrical discharge, but nothing nuclear."

"All right. A man with a club can lick a man with his fists. A man with a gun can lick half a dozen with clubs. And two ships with nuclear weapons can lick a whole planet without them. Think it's time, Lucas?"

He nodded. "Paul, can you cut in on that Eglonsby station yet?"

"What are you going to do?" Valkanhayn wanted to know, against it in advance.

"Summon them to surrender. If they don't, we will drop a hellburner, and then we will pick out another city and summon it to surrender. I don't think the second one will refuse. If we are going to be murderers, we'll do it right, this time."

Valkanhayn was aghast, probably at the idea of burning an unlooted city. Spasso was sputtering something about, ". . . teach the dirty Neobarbs a lesson . . ." Koreff told him he was switched on. He picked up a hand-phone.

"Space Vikings *Nemesis* and *Space-Scourge*, calling the city of Eglonsby, Space Vikings . . ."

He repeated it for over a minute; there was no reply.

"Vann," he called Guns-and-Missiles. "A subcrit display job, about four miles over the city."

He laid the phone down and looked to the underside from the ship's south pole. The telescopic screen went off, and the unmagnified screen darkened as the filters went on. Valkanhayn, aboard the other ship, was shouting a warning about his own screens. The only unfiltered screen aboard the *Nemesis* was the one tuned to the falling missile. The city of Eglonsby rushed upward in it, and then it went suddenly dark. There was an orange-yellow blaze in the other screens. After a while, the filters went off and the telescopic screen went on again. He picked up the phone.

"Space Vikings calling Eglonsby; this is your last warning. Communicate at once."

Less than a minute later, a voice came out of one of the speakers:

"Eglonsby calling Space Vikings. Your bomb has done great damage. Will you hold your fire until somebody in authority can communicate with you? This is the chief operator at the central State telecast station; I have no authority to say anything to you, or discuss anything."

"Oh, good, that sounds like a dictatorship," Harkaman was saying. "Grab the dictator and shove a pistol in his face and you have everything."

"There is nothing to discuss. Get somebody who has authority to surrender the city to us. If this is not done within the hour, the city and everybody in it will be obliterated."

Only minutes later, a new voice said:

"This is Gunsalis Jan, secretary to Pedrosan Pedro, President of the Council of Syndics. We will switch President Pedrosan over as soon as he can speak directly to the personage in supreme command of your ships."

"That is myself; switch him to me at once."

After a delay of less than fifteen seconds they had President Pedrosan Pedro:

"We are prepared to resist, but we realize what this would cost in lives and destruction of property," he began.

"You don't begin to. Do you know anything about nuclear weapons?"

"From history; we have no nuclear power of any sort. We can find no fissionables on this planet."

"The cost, as you put it, would be everything and everybody in Eglonsby and for a radius of almost a hundred miles. Are you still prepared to resist?"

The President of the Council of Syndics wasn't and said so. Trask asked him how much authority his position gave him.

"I have all powers in any emergency. I think," the voice added tonelessly, "that this is an emergency. The Council will automatically ratify any decision I make."

Harkaman depressed a button in front of him. "What I said; dictatorship, with parliamentary false front."

"If he isn't a false-front dictator for some oligarchy." He motioned to Harkaman to take his thumb off the button. "How large is this Council?"

"Sixteen, elected by the Syndicates they represent. There is the Syndicate of Labor, the Syndicate of Manufacturers, the Syndicate of Small Businesses, the . . ."

"Corporate State, First Century Pre-Atomic on Terra. Benny the Moose," Harkaman said. "Let's all go down and talk to them."

When they were sure that the public had been warned to make no resistance, the *Nemesis* went down to two miles, bulking over the center of the city. The buildings were low by the standards of a contragravity-using people, the highest barely a thousand feet and few over five hundred, and they were more closely set than Sword-Worlders were accustomed to, with broad roadways between. In several places there were queer arrangements of crossed roadways, apparently leading nowhere. Harkaman laughed when he saw them.

"Airstrips. I've seen them on other planets where they've lost contragravity. For winged aircraft powered by chemical fuel. I hope we have time for me to look around, here. I'll bet they even have railroads here."

The "great damage" caused by the bomb was about equal to the effect of a medium hurricane; he had seen worse from high winds at Traskon. Mostly it had been moral, which had been the kind intended.

They met President Pedrosan and the Council of Syndics in a spacious and well-furnished chamber near the top of one of the medium-high buildings. Valkanhayn was surprised; in a loud aside he considered that these people must be almost civilized. They were introduced. Amaterasun surnames preceded personal names, which hinted at a culture and a political organization making much use of registration by alphabetical list. They all wore garments which had the indefinable but unmistakable appearance of uniforms. When they had all seated themselves at a large oval table, Harkaman drew his pistol and used the butt for a gavel.

"Lord Trask, will you deal with these people directly?" he asked, stiffly formal.

"Certainly, Admiral." He spoke to the President, ignoring the others. "We want it understood that we control this city, and we expect complete submission. As long as you remain submissive to us, we will do no damage beyond removal of the things we wish to take from it, and there will be no violence to any of your people, or any indiscriminate vandalism. This visit we are paying you will cost you heavily, make no mistake about that, but whatever the cost, it will be a cheap price for avoiding what we might otherwise do."

The President and the Syndics exchanged relieved glances. Let the taxpayers worry about the cost; they'd come out of it with whole skins.

"You understand, we want maximum value and minimum bulk," he continued. "Jewels, objects of art, furs, the better grades of luxury goods of all kinds. Rare-element metals. And monetary metals, gold and platinum. You have a metallic-based currency, I suppose?"

"Oh, no!" President Pedrosan was slightly scandalized. "Our currency is based on services to society. Our monetary unit is simply called a credit."

Harkaman snorted impolitely. Evidently he'd seen economic systems like that before. Trask wanted to know if they used gold or platinum at all.

"Gold, to some extent, for jewelry." Evidently they weren't complete economic puritans. "And platinum in industry, of course."

"If they want gold, they should have raided Stolgoland," one of the Syndics said. "They have a gold-standard currency." From the way he said it, he might have been accusing them of eating with their fingers, and possibly of eating their own young.

"I know, the maps we're using for this planet are a few centuries old; Stolgoland doesn't seem to appear on them."

"I wish it didn't appear on ours, either." That was a General Dagró Ector, Syndic for State Protection.

"It would have been a good thing for this whole planet if you'd decided to raid them instead of us," somebody else said.

"It isn't too late for these gentlemen to make that decision," Pedrosan said. "I gather that gold is a monetary metal among your people?'' When Trask nodded, he continued: ''It is also the basis of the Stolgonian currency. The actual currency is paper, theoretically redeemable in gold. In actuality, the circulation of gold has been prohibited, and the entire gold wealth of the nation is concentrated in vaults at three depositories. We know exactly where they are.''

''You begin to interest me, President Pedrosan.''

''I do? Well, you have two large spaceships and six smaller craft. You have nuclear weapons, something nobody on this planet has. You have contragravity, something that is hardly more than a legend here. On the other hand, we have a million and a half ground-troops, jet aircraft, armored ground-vehicles, and chemical weapons. If you will undertake to attack Stolgoland, we will place this entire force at your disposal; General Dagró will command them as you direct. All that we ask is that, when you have loaded the gold hoards of Stolgoland aboard your ships, you will leave our troops in possession of the country.''

That was all there was to that meeting. There was a second one; only Trask, Harkaman and Sir Paytrik Morland represented the Space Vikings, and the Eglonsby government was represented by President Pedrosan and General Dagró. They met more intimately, in a smaller and more luxurious room in the same building.

''If you're going to declare war on Stolgoland, you'd better get along with it,'' Morland advised. ''We aren't going to stay here forever.''

''What?'' Pedrosan seemed to have only the vaguest idea of what he was talking about. ''You mean, warn them? Certainly not. We will attack them by surprise. It will be nothing but plain self-defense," he added righteously. "The oligarchic capitalists of Stolgoland have been plotting to attack us for years."

"Yes. If you had carried out your original intention of looting Eglonsby, they would have invaded us the moment your ships lifted out. It's exactly what I'd do in their place."

"But you maintain nominally friendly relations with them?"

"Of course. We are civilized. The peace-loving government and people of Eglonsby . . ."

"Yes, Mr. President; I understand. And they have an embassy here?"

"They call it that!" cried Dagró. "It is a nest of vipers, a plague-spot of espionage and subversion . . .!"

"We'll grab that ourselves, right away," Harkaman said. "You won't be able to round up all their agents outside it, and if we tried to, it would cause suspicion. We'll have to put up a front to deceive them."

"Yes. You will go on the air at once, calling on the people to collaborate with us, and you will specifically order your troops mobilized to assist us in collecting the tribute we are levying on Eglonsby," Trask said. "In that way, if any Stolgonian spies see your troops concentrated around our landing-craft, they'll think it's to help us load our loot."

"And we'll announce that a large part of the tribute will consist of military equipment," Dagró added. "That will explain why our guns and tanks are being loaded on your contragravity vehicles."

When the Stolgonian embassy was seized by the Space Vikings, the ambassador asked to be taken at once to their leader. He had a proposition: If the Space Vikings would completely disable the army of Eglonsby and admit Stolgonian troops when they were ready to leave, the invaders would bring with them ten thousand kilos of gold. Trask affected to be very hospitable to the offer.

Stolgoland lay across a narrow and shallow sea from the State of Eglonsby; it was dotted with islands, and every one of them was, in turn, dotted with oil-wells. Petroleum was what kept the aircraft and ground-vehicles of Amaterasu in operation; oil, rather than ideology, was at the root of the enmity between the two nations. Apparently the Stolgonian espionage in Eglonsby was completely deceived, and the reports Trask allowed the captive ambassador to make confirmed the deception. Hourly the Eglonsby radio stations poured out exhortations to the people to cooperate with the Space Vikings, with an occasional lamentation about the masses of war-materials being taken. Eglonsby espionage in Stolgoland was similarly active. The Stolgonian armies were being massed at four seaports on the coast facing Eglonsby, and there was a frantic gathering of every sort of ship available. By this time, any sympathy that Trask might have felt for either party had evaporated.

The invasion of Stolgoland started the fifth morning after their arrival over Eglonsby. Before dawn, the six pinnaces went in, making a wide sweep around the curvature of the planet and coming in from the north, two to each of the three gold-troves. They were detected by radar, eventually but too late for any effective resistance to be organized. Two were even taken without a shot; by mid-morning all three had been blown open and the ingots and specie were being removed.

The four seaports from whence the Stolgonian-invasion of Eglonsby was to have been launched were neutralized by nuclear bombing. Neutralized was a nice word, Trask thought; there was no echo in it of the screams of the still-living, maimed and burned and blinded, around the fringes of ground-zero. The *Nemesis* and the *Space-Scourge*, from landing-craft and from the ships themselves, landed Eglonsby troops on Stolgonopolis. While they were sacking the city, with all the usual atrocities, the Space Vikings were loading the gold, and anything else that was of more than ordinary value, aboard the ships.

They were still at it the next morning when President Pedrosan arrived at the newly conquered capital, announcing his intention of putting the Stolgonian chief of state and his cabinet on trial as war-criminals. Before sunset, they were back over Eglonsby. The loot might run as high as a half-billion Excalibur stellars. Boake Valkanhayn and Garvan Spasso were simply beyond astonishment and beyond words.

The looting of Eglonsby then began.

They gathered up machinery, and stocks of steel and light-metal alloys. The city was full of warehouses, and the warehouses were crammed with valuables. In spite of the socialistic and egalitarian verbiage behind which the government operated, there seemed to be a numerous elite class and if gold were not a monetary metal it was not despised for purposes of ostentation. There were several large art museums. Van Larch, their nearest approach to an art specialist, took charge of culling the best from them.

And there was a vast public library. Into this Otto Harkaman vanished, with half a dozen men and a contragravity scow. Its historical section would be much poorer in the future.

President Pedro Pedrosan was on the radio from Stolgonopolis that night.

"Is this how you Space Vikings keep faith?" he demanded indignantly. "You've abandoned me and my army here in Stolgoland, and you're sacking Eglonsby. You promised to leave Eglonsby alone if I helped you get the gold of Stolgoland."

"I promised nothing of the kind. I promised to help you take Stolgoland. You've taken it," Trask told him. "I promised to avoid unnecessary damage or violence. I've already hanged a dozen of my own men for rape, murder and wanton vandalism. Now, we expect to be out of here in twenty-four hours. You'd better be back here before then. Your own people are starting to loot. We did not promise to control them for you."

That was true. What few troops had been left behind, and the police, were unable to cope with the mobs that were pillaging in the wake of the Space Vikings. Everybody seemed to be trying to grab what he could and let the Vikings be blamed for it. He had been able to keep his own people in order. There had been at least a dozen cases of rape and wanton murder, and the offenders had been promptly hanged. None of their shipmates, not even the *Space-Scourge* company, seemed resentful. They felt the culprits had deserved what they'd gotten; not for what they'd done to the locals, but for disobeying orders.

A few troops had been flown in from Stolgoland by the time they had gotten their vehicles stowed and were lifting out. They didn't seem to be making much headway. Harkaman, who had gotten his load of microbooks stowed and was at the command-desk, laughed heartily.

"I don't know what Pedrosan'll do. Gehenna, I don't even know what I'd do, if I'd gotten myself into a mess like that. He'll probably bring half his army back, leave the other half in Stolgoland, and lose both. Suppose we drop in, in about three or four years, just out of curiosity. If we make twenty percent of what we did this time, the trip would pay for itself."

After they went into hyperspace and had the ship secured, the parties lasted three Galactic Standard days, and nobody was at all sober. Harkaman was drooling over the mass of historical material he had found. Spasso was jubilant. Nobody could call this chicken-stealing. He kept repeating that as long as he was able to say anything. Khepera, he conceded, had been. Lousy two or three million stellars; poo!

VI

BEOWULF WAS BAD.

Valkanhayn and Spasso had both been opposed to the raid. Nobody raided Beowulf; Beowulf was too tough. Beowulf had nuclear energy and nuclear weapons and contragravity and normal-space craft, they even had colonies on a couple of other planets of their system. They had everything but hyperdrive. Beowulf was a civilized planet, and you didn't raid civilized planets, not and get away with it.

And besides, hadn't they gotten enough loot on Amaterasu?

"No, we did not," Trask told them. "If we're going to

make anything out of Tanith, we're going to need power, and I don't mean windmills and waterwheels. As you've remarked, Beowulf has nuclear energy. That's where we get our plutonium and our power-units.''

So they went to Beowulf. They came out of hyperspace eight light-hours from the F-7 star of which Beowulf was the fourth planet, and twenty light-minutes apart. Guatt Kirbey made a microjump that brought the ships within practical communicating distance, and they began making plans in an intership screen conference.

"There are, or were, three chief sources of fissionable ores," Harkaman said. "The last ship to raid here and get away was Stafan Kintour's *Princess of Lyonesse*, sixty years ago. He hit one on the Antarctic continent; according to his account, everything there was fairly new. He didn't mess things up too badly, and it ought to be still operating. We'll go in from the south pole, and we'll have to go in fast."

They shifted personnel and equipment. They would go in bunched, the pinnaces ahead; they and the *Space-Scourge* would go down to the ground, while the better-armed *Nemesis* would hover above to fight off local contragravity, shoot down missiles, and generally provide overhead cover. Trask transferred to the *Space-Scourge*, taking with him Morland and two hundred of the *Nemesis* ground-fighters. Most of the single-mounts, landing-craft and manipulators and heavy-duty lifters went with him, jamming the decks around the vehicle-ports of Valkanhayn's ship.

They jumped in to six light-minutes, and while Valkanhayn's astrogator was still fiddling with his controls they began sensing radar and microray detection.

When they came out again, they were two light-seconds off the south pole, and half a dozen ships were either in orbit or coming up from the planet. All normal-space craft, of course, but some were almost as big as the *Nemesis*.

From there on, it was a nightmare.

Ships pounded at them with guns, and they pounded back. Missiles went out, and counter-missiles stopped them in rapidly expanding and quickly vanishing globes of light. Red lights flashed on the damage-board, and sirens howled and klaxons squawked. In the outside-view screens, they saw the *Nemesis* vanish in a blaze of radiance, and then, while their hearts were still in their throats, come out of it again. Red lights went off on the board as damage-control crews and their robots sealed the breaches in the hull and pumped air back into evacuated areas, and then more red lights came on.

Occasionally, he would glance toward Boake Valkanhayn, who sat motionless in his chair, chewing a cigar that had gone out long ago. He wasn't enjoying it, but he wasn't showing fear. Once a Beowulfer vanished in a supernova flash, and when the ball of incandescence widened to nothing the ship was gone. All Valkanhayn said was: "Hope one of our boys did that."

They fought their way in and down, toward the atmosphere. Another Beowulf ship blew up, a craft about the size of Spasso's *Lamia*. A moment later, another; Valkanhayn was pounding the desk in front of him with his fist and yelling: "That was one of ours! Find out who launched it; get his name!"

Missiles were coming up from the planet, now. Valkanhayn's detection officer was trying to locate the source. While he was trying, a big melon-shaped thing fell away from the *Nemesis*, and in the jiggling, radiation-distorted intership screen Harkaman's image was laughing.

"Hellburner just went off; target about 50° South, 25° East of the sunrise line. That's where those missiles are coming from."

Counter-missiles sped toward the big metal melon; defense missiles, robot-launched, met them. The hellburner's track was marked first by expanding red and orange globes in airless space and then by fire-puffs after it entered atmosphere. It vanished into the darkness beyond the sunset, and then made sunlight of its own. It *was* sunlight; a Bethe solar-phoenix reaction, and it would sustain itself for hours. He hoped it hadn't landed within a thousand miles of their objective.

The ground operation was a nightmare of a different sort. He went down in a command-car, with Paytrik Morland and a couple of others. There were missiles and gun-batteries. There were darting patterns of flights of combat-vehicles, blazing gunfire, and single vehicles that shot past or blew up in front of them. Robots on contragravity—military robots, with missiles to launch, and working robots with only their own mass to hurl, flung themselves mindlessly at them. Screens that went crazy from radiation; speakers that jabbered contradictory orders. Finally, the battle, which had raged in the air over two thousand square miles of mines and refineries and reaction-plants, became two distinct and concentrated battles, one at the packing-plant and storage vaults and one at the power-unit cartridge factory.

Three pinnaces came down to form a triangle over each;

the *Space-Scourge* hung midway between, poured out a swarm of vehicles and big claw-armed manipulators; armored lighters and landing-craft shuttled back and forth. The command-car looped and dodged from one target to the other; at one, keglike canisters of plutonium, collapsium-plated and weighing tons apiece, were coming out of the vaults, and at the other lifters were bringing out loads of nuclear-electric power-unit cartridges, some as big as a ten-liter jar, to power a spaceship engine, and some small as a round of pistol ammunition, for things like flashlights.

Every hour or so, he looked at his watch, and it would be three or four minutes later.

At last, when he was completely convinced that he had really been killed, and was damned and would spend all eternity in this fire-riven chaos, the *Nemesis* began firing red flares and the speakers in all the vehicles were signalling recall. He got aboard the *Space-Scourge* somehow, after assuring himself that nobody who was still alive was being left behind.

There were twenty-odd who weren't, and the sick-bay was full of wounded who had gone up with cargo, and more were being helped off the vehicles as they were berthed. The car in which he had been riding had been hit several times, and one of the gunners was bleeding under his helmet and didn't seem aware of it. When he got to the command-room, he found Boake Valkanhayn, his face drawn and weary, getting coffee from a robot and lacing it with brandy.

"That's it," he said, blowing on the steaming cup. It was the battered silver one that had been in front of him when he had first appeared in the *Nemesis'* screen. He nodded toward the damage-screen; everything had been patched up, or the outer decks around breached portions of the hull sealed. "Ship secure." He set down the silver mug and lit a cigar. "To quote Garvan Spasso, 'Nobody can call that chicken-stealing.' "

"No. Not even if you count Tizona giraffe-birds as chickens. That Gram gum-pear brandy you're putting in that coffee? I'll have the same. Just leave out the coffee."

VII

THE *Lamia's* detection picked them up as soon as they were out of the last microjump; Trask's gnawing fear that Dunnan might attack in their absence had been groundless. Incredibly, he realized, they had been gone only thirty-odd Galactic Standard days, and in that time Alvyn Karffard had done an incredible amount of work.

He had gotten the spaceport completely cleared of rubble and debris, and he had the woods cleared away from around it and the two tall buildings. The locals called the city Rivvin; a few inscriptions found here and there in it indicated that the original name had been Rivington. He had done considerable mapping, in some detail of the continent on which it was located and, in general, of the rest of the planet. And he had established friendly relations with the people of Tradetown and made friends with their king.

Nobody, not even those who had collected it, quite believed their eyes when the loot was unloaded. The little herd of long haired unicorns—the Khepera locals had called them kreggs, probably a corruption of the name of some naturalist who had first studied them—had come through the voyage and even the Battle of Beowulf in good shape. Trask and a few of his former cattlemen from Traskon watched them anxiously, and the ship's doctor, acting veterinarian, made elaborate tests of vegetation they would be likely to eat. Three of the cows proved to be with calf; these were isolated and watched over with especial solicitude.

The locals were inclined to take a poor view of the kreggs, at first. Cattle ought to have two horns, one on either side, curved back. It wasn't right for cattle to have only one horn, in the middle, slanting forward.

Both ships had taken heavy damage. The *Nemesis* had one pinnace-berth knocked open, and everybody was glad the Beowulfers hadn't noticed that and gotten a missile inside. The *Space-Scourge* had taken a hit directly on her south pole while lifting out from the planet, and a good deal of the southern part of the ship was sealed off when she came in. The *Nemesis* was repaired as far as possible and put on off-planet patrol, then they went to work on the *Space-Scourge*, transferring much of her armament to ground defense, clearing out all the available cargo space, and repairing her hull as far as possible. To repair her completely was a job for a regular shipyard, like Alex Gorram's on Gram. That was precisely where the work would be done.

Boake Valkanhayn would command her on the voyage to and from Gram. Since Beowulf, Trask had not only ceased to dislike the man, but was beginning to admire him. He had been a good man once, before ill fortune

99

which had been only partly of his own making had over-taken him. He'd just let himself go and stopped caring. Now he had taken hold of himself again. It had started showing after they had landed on Amaterasu. He had begun to dress more neatly and speak more grammatically; to look and act more like a spaceman and less like a barfly. His men had begun to jump to obey when he gave an order. He had opposed the raid on Beowulf, but that had been the dying struggle of the chicken-thief he had been. He had been scared, going in; well, who hadn't been, except a few greenhorns brave with the valor of ignorance. But he had gone in, and fought his ship well, and had held his station over the fissionables plant in a hell of bombs and missiles, and he had made sure everybody who had gone down and who was still alive was aboard before he lifted out.

He was a Space Viking again.

Garvan Spasso wasn't, and never would be. He was outraged when he heard that Valkanhayn would take his ship, loaded with much of the loot of the three planets, to Gram. He came to Trask, fairly spluttering about it.

"You know what'll happen?" he demanded. "He'll space out with that cargo, and that'll be the last any of us'll hear of him again. He'll probably take it to Joyeuse or Excalibur and buy himself a lordship with it."

"Oh, I doubt that, Garvan. A number of our people are going along—Guatt Kirbey will be the astrogator; you'd trust him, wouldn't you? And Sir Paytrik Morland, and Baron Rathmore, and Lord Valpry, and Rolve Hemmerding . . ." He was silent for a moment, struck by an idea. "Would you be willing to make the trip in the *Space-Scourge*, too?"

Spasso would, very decidedly. Trask nodded.

"Good. Then we'll be sure nothing crooked is pulled," he said seriously.

After Spasso was gone, he got in touch with Baron Rathmore.

"See to it that he gets as much money that's due him as possible, when you get to Gram. And ask Duke Angus, as a favor to give him some meaningless position with a suitably impressive title, Lord Chamberlain of the Ducal Washroom, or something. Then he can prime him with misinformation and give him an opportunity to sell it to Omfray of Glaspyth. Then, of course, he could be contacted to sell Omfray out to Angus. A couple of times around and somebody'll stick a knife in him, and then we'll be rid of him for good."

They loaded the *Space-Scourge* with gold from Stolgoland, and paintings and statues from the art museums and fabrics and furs and jewels and porcelains and plate from the markets of Eglonsby. They loaded sacks and kegs of specie from Khepera. Most of the Khepera loot wasn't worth hauling to Gram, but it was far enough in advance of their own technologies to be priceless to the Tanith locals.

Some of these were learning simple machine operations, and a few were able to handle contragravity vehicles that had been fitted with adequate safety devices. The former slave guards had all become sergeants and lieutenants in an infantry regiment that had been formed, and the King of Tradetown borrowed some to train his own army. Some genius in the machine-shop altered a matchlock musket to flintlock and showed the local gunsmiths how to do it.

The kreggs continued to thrive, after the *Space-Scourge*

departed. Several calves were born, and seemed to be doing well; the biochemistry of Tanith and Khepera were safely alike. Trask had hopes for them. Every Viking ship had its own carniculture vats, but men tired of carniculture meat, and fresh meat was always in demand. Some day, he hoped, kregg-beef would be an item of sale to ships putting in on Tanith, and the long-haired hides might even find a market in the Sword-Worlds. They had contragravity scows plying between Rivington and Tradetown regularly, now, and airlorries were linking the villages. The boatmen of Tradetown rioted occasionally against this unfair competition. And in Rivington itself, bulldozers and power-shovels and manipulators labored, and there was always a rising cloud of dust over the city.

There was so much to do, and only a trifle under twenty-five Galactic Standard hours in a day to do it. There were whole days in which he never thought once of Andray Dunnan.

A hundred and twenty-five days to Gram, and a hundred and twenty-five days back. They had long ago passed. Of course, there would be the work of repairing the *Space-Scourge*, the conferences with the investors in the original Tanith Adventure, the business of gathering the needed equipment for the new base. Even so, he was beginning to worry a little. Worry about something as far out of his control as the *Space-Scourge* was useless, he knew. He couldn't help it, though. Even Harkaman, usually imperturbable, began to be fretful, after two hundred and seventy days had passed.

They were relaxing in the living quarters they had fitted out at the top of the spaceport building before retiring, both sprawled wearily in chairs that had come from one of the better hotels of Eglonsby, their drinks between them on a low table, the top of which was inlaid with something that looked like ivory but wasn't. On the floor beside it lay the plans for a reaction-plant and mass-energy converter they would build as soon as the *Space-Scourge* returned with equipment for producing collapsium-plated shielding.

"Of course, we could go ahead with it, now," Harkaman said. "We could tear enough armor off the *Lamia* to shield any kind of a reaction-plant."

That was the first time either of them had gotten close to the possibility that the ship mightn't return. Trask laid his cigar in the ashtray—it had come from President Pedrosan Pedro's private office—and splashed a little more brandy into his glass.

"She'll be coming before long. We have enough of our people aboard to make sure nobody else tries to take the ship. And I really believe, now, that Valkanhayn can be trusted."

"I do, too. I'm not worried about what might happen on the ship. But we don't know what's been happening on Gram. Glaspyth and Didreksburg could have teamed up and jumped Wardshaven before Duke Angus was ready to invade Glaspyth. Boake might be landing the ship in a trap at Wardshaven."

"Be a sorry looking trap after it closed on him. That would be the first time in history that a Sword-World was raided by Space Vikings." Harkaman looked at his half-empty glass, then filled it to the top. It was the same drink he had started with, just as a regiment that has been decimated and recruited up to strength a few times is still the same regiment.

The buzz of the communication screen—one of the few things in the room that hadn't been looted somewhere —interrupted him. They both rose; Harkaman, still carrying his drink, went to put it on. It was a man on duty in the control-room, overhead, reporting that two emergencies had just been detected at twenty light-minutes due north of the planet. Harkaman gulped his drink and set down the empty glass.

"All right. You put out a general alert? Switch anything that comes in over to this screen." He got out his pipe and was packing tobacco into it mechanically. "They'll be out of the last microjump and about two light-seconds away in a few minutes."

Trask sat down again, saw that his cigarette had burned almost to the tip, and lit a fresh one from it, wishing he could be as calm about it as Harkaman. Three minutes later, the control-tower picked up two emergencies at a light second and a half, a thousand or so miles apart. Then the screen flickered, and Boake Valkanhayn was looking out of it, from the desk in the newly refurbished command-room of the *Space-Scourge*.

He was a newly refurbished Boake Valkanhayn, too. His heavily braided captain's jacket looked like the work of one of the better tailors on Gram, and on the breast was a large and ornate knight's star, of unfamiliar design, bearing, among other things, the sword and atom-symbol of the house of Ward.

"Prince Trask; Count Harkaman," he greeted. "*Space-Scourge*, Tanith; thirty-two hundred hours out of Wardshaven on Gram, Baron Valkanhayn commanding, accompanied by chartered freighter *Rozinante*, Durendal, Captain Morbes. Requesting permission and instructions to orbit in."

"Baron Valkanhayn?" Harkaman asked.

"That's right," Valkanhayn grinned. "And I have a vellum scroll the size of a blanket to prove it. I have a whole cargo of scrolls. One says you're Otto, Count Harkaman, and another says you're Admiral of the Royal Mardukan Navy."

"He did it!" Trask cried. "He made himself King of Gram!"

"That's right. And you're his trusty and well-loved Lucas, Prince Trask, and Viceroy of his Majesty's Realm of Tanith."

Harkaman bristled at that. "The Gehenna you say. This is *our* Realm of Tanith."

"Is his Majesty making it worth while to accept his sovereignty?" Trask asked. "That is, beside vellum scrolls?"

Valkanhayn was still grinning. "Wait till we start sending cargo down. And wait till you see what's crammed into the other ship."

"Did Spasso come back with you?" Harkaman asked.

"Oh, no. Sir Garvan Spasso entered the service of his Majesty, King Angus. He is Chief of Police at Glaspyth, now, and nobody can call what he's doing there chicken-stealing, either. Any chickens he steals, he steals the whole farm to get them."

That didn't sound good. Spasso could make King Angus' name stink all over Glaspyth. Or maybe he'd allow Spasso to crush the adherents of Omfray, and then hang him for his oppression of the people. He'd read about somebody who'd done something like that, in one of Harkaman's Old Terran history books.

Baron Rathmore had stayed on Gram; so had Rolve Hemmerding. The rest of the gentlemen-adventurers, all with shiny new titles of nobility, had returned. From them, as the two ships were getting into orbit, he learned what had happened on Gram since the *Nemesis* had spaced out.

Duke Angus had announced his intention of carrying on with the Tanith Adventure, and had started construction of a new ship at the Gorram yards. This had served plausibly to explain all the activities of preparation for the invasion of Glaspyth, and had deceived Duke Omfray completely. Omfray had already started a ship of his own; the entire resources of his duchy were thrown into an effort to get her finished and to space ahead of the one Angus was building. Work was going on frantically on her when the Wardshaven invaders hit Glaspyth; she was now nearing completion as a unit of the Royal Navy. Duke Omfray had managed to escape to Didreksburg; when Angus' troops moved in on the latter duchy, he had escaped again, this time off-planet. He was now eating the bitter bread of exile at the court of his wife's uncle, the King of Haulteclere.

The Count of Newhaven, the Duke of Bigglersport, and the Lord of Northport, all of whom had favored the establishment of a planetary monarchy, had immediately acknowledged Angus as their sovereign. So, with a knife at his throat, had the Duke of Didreksburg. Many other feudal magnates had refused to surrender their sovereignty. That might mean fighting, but Paytrik, now Baron Morland, doubted it.

"The *Space-Scourge* stopped that," he said. "When they heard about the base here, and saw what we'd shipped to Gram, they started changing their minds. Only subjects of King Angus will be allowed to invest in the Tanith Adventure. It's too good a thing to stay out of."

As for accepting King Angus' annexation of Tanith and accepting his sovereignty, that would also be advisable. They would need a Sword-World outlet for the loot they took or obtained by barter from other Space Vikings, and until they had adequate industries of their own, they would be dependent on Gram for many things which could not be gotten by raiding.

"I suppose the King knows I'm not out here for my health, or his profit?" he asked Lord Valpry, during one of the screen conversations as the *Space-Scourge* was getting into orbit. "My business out here is Andray Dunnan."

"Oh, yes," the Wardshaven noble replied. "In fact, he told me, in so many words, that he would be most happy if you sent him his nephew's head in a block of lucite. What Dunnan did touched his honor, too. Sovereign princes never see any humor in things like that."

"I suppose he knows that sooner or later Dunnan will try to attack Tanith?"

"If he doesn't, it isn't because I didn't tell him often enough. When you see the defense armament we're bringing, you'll think he does."

It was impressive, but nothing to the engineering and industrial equipment. Mining robots for use on the iron Moon of Tanith, and normal-space transports for the fifty thousand mile run between planet and satellite. A collapsed-matter producer; now they could collapsium-plate their own shielding. A small, fully robotic, steel mill that could be set up and operated on the satellite. Industrial robots, and machinery to make machinery. And, best of all, two hundred engineers and highly skilled technicians.

Quite a few industrial baronies on Gram would realize, before long, what they had lost in those men. He wondered what Lord Trask of Traskon would have thought about that.

The Prince of Tanith was no longer interested in what happened to Gram. Maybe, if things prospered for the next century or so, his successors would be ruling Gram by viceroy from Tanith.

VIII

AS SOON AS the *Space-Scourge* was unloaded, she was put on off-planet watch; Harkaman immediately spaced out in the *Nemesis*, while Trask remained behind. They began unloading the *Rozinante*, after setting her down at Rivington Spaceport. After that was done, her officers and crew took a holiday which lasted a month, until the *Nemesis* returned. Harkaman must have made quick raids on half a dozen planets. None of the cargo he brought back was spectacularly valuable, and he dismissed the whole thing as chicken-stealing, but he had lost some men and the ship showed a few fresh scars. A good deal of what was transshipped to the *Rozinante* was manufactured goods which would compete with merchandise produced on Gram.

"That load will be a come-down, after what the *Space-Scourge* took back, but we didn't want to send the *Rozinante* back empty," he said. "One thing, I had time to do a little reading, between stops."

"The books from the Eglonsby library?"

"Yes. I learned a curious thing about Amaterasu. Do

you know why that planet was so extensively colonized by the Federation, when there don't seem to be any fissionable ores? The planet produced gadolinium.''

Gadolinium was essential to hyperdrive engines; the engines of a ship the size of the *Nemesis* required fifty pounds of it. On the Sword-Worlds, it was worth several times its weight in gold. If they still mined it, Amaterasu would repay a second visit.

When he mentioned it, Harkaman shrugged. ''Why should they mine it? There's only one thing it's good for, and you can't run a spaceship on diesel-oil. I suppose the mines could be reopened, and new refineries built, but . . .''

''We could trade plutonium for gadolinium. They have none of their own. We could charge our own prices for it, and we wouldn't need to tell them what gadolinium sells for on the Sword-Worlds.''

''We could, if we could do business with anybody there, after what we did to Eglonsby and Stolgoland. Where would we get plutonium?''

''Why do you think the Beowulfers don't have hyperships, when they have everything else?''

Harkaman snapped his fingers. ''By Satan, that's it!'' Then he looked at Trask in alarm. ''Hey, you're not thinking of selling Amaterasu plutonium and Beowulf gadolinium, are you?''

''Why not? We could make a big profit on both ends of the deal.''

''You know what would happen next, don't you? There'd be ships from both planets all over the place in a few years. We want that like we want a hole in the head.''

He couldn't see the objection. Tanith and Amaterasu

and Beowulf could work up a very good triangular trade; all three would profit. It wouldn't cost men and ship-damage and ammunition, either. Maybe a mutual defense alliance, too. Think about it later; there was too much to do here on Tanith at present.

There had been mines on the Moon of Tanith before the collapse of the Federation; they had been stripped of their equipment afterward, while Tanith was still fighting a rear-guard battle against barbarism, but the underground chambers and man-made caverns could still be used, and in time the mines were reopened and the steel-mill put in, and eventually ingots of finished steel were coming down by shuttle-craft. In the meantime, the shipyard had been laid out and was taking shape.

The Gram ship *Queen Flavia*—she had been the one found unfinished at Glaspyth—came in three months after the *Rozinante* started back; she must have been finished while Valkanhayn was still in hyperspace. She carried considerable cargo, some of it superfluous but all of it useful; everybody was investing in the Tanith Adventure now, and the money had to be spent for something. Better, she brought close to a thousand men and women; the leakage of brains and ability from the Sword-Worlds was turning into a flood. Among them was Basil Gorram. Trask remembered him as an insufferable young twerp, but he seemed to be a good shipyard man. He very frankly predicted that in a few years his father's yards at Wardshaven would be idle and all the Tanith ships would be Tanith-built. A junior partner of Lothar Ffayle's also came out, to establish a branch of the Bank of Wardshaven at Rivington.

As soon as the *Queen Flavia* had discharged her cargo

and passengers, she took on five hundred ground-fighters from the *Lamia, Nemesis* and *Space-Scourge* companies and spaced out on a raiding voyage. While she was gone, the second ship, the one Duke Angus had started at Wardshaven and King Angus had finished, the *Black Star*, came in.

Trask was slightly incredulous at realizing that she had spaced out from Gram almost exactly two years after the *Nemesis* had departed. He still hadn't any idea where Andray Dunnan was, or what he was doing, or how to find him.

The news of the Gram base on Tanith spread slowly, first by the scheduled liners and tramp freighters that linked the Sword-Worlds, and then by trading ships and outbound Space Vikings to the Old Federation. Two years and six months after the *Nemesis* had come out of hyperspace to find Boake Valkanhayn and Garvan Spasso on Tanith, the first independent Space Viking came in, to sell a cargo and get repairs. They bought his loot—he had been raiding some planet rather above the level of Khepera and below that of Amaterasu—and healed the wounds his ship had taken getting it. He had been dealing with the Everrard family on Hoth, and professed himself much more satisfied with the bargains he had gotten on Tanith and swore to return.

He had never even heard of Andray Dunnan or the *Enterprise*.

It was a Gilgamesher that brought the first news.

He had first heard of Gilgameshers—the word was used indiscriminately for a native of or a ship from Gilgamesh—on Gram, from Harkaman and Karffard and Vann Larch and the others. Since coming to Tanith, he had heard about them from every Space Viking, never in complimentary and rarely in printable terms.

Gilgamesh was rated, with reservations, as a civilized planet though not on a level with Odin or Isis or Baldur or Marduk or Aton or any of the other worlds which had maintained the culture of the Terran Federation uninterruptedly. Perhaps Gilgamesh deserved more credit; its people had undergone two centuries of darkness and pulled themselves out of it by their bootstraps. They had recovered all the old techniques, up to and including the hyperdrive.

They didn't raid; they traded. They had religious objections to violence, though they kept these within sensible limits, and were able and willing to fight with fanatical ferocity in defense of their home planet. About a century before, there had been a five-ship Viking raid on Gilgamesh; one ship had returned and had been sold for scrap after reaching a friendly base. Their ships went everywhere to trade, and wherever they traded a few of them usually settled, and where they settled they made money, sending most of it home. Their society seemed to be a loose theo-socialism, and their religion an absurd potpourri of most of the major monotheisms of the Federation period, plus doctrinal and ritualistic innovations of their own. Aside from their propensity for sharp trading, their bigoted refusal to regard anybody not of their creed as more than half human, and the maze of dietary and other taboos in which they hid from social contact with others, made them generally disliked.

After their ship had gotten into orbit, three of them came down to do business. The captain and his exec. wore long coats, almost knee-length, buttoned to the throat, and small white caps like forage-caps; the third, one of their priests, wore a robe with a cowl, and the symbol of their religion, a blue triangle in a white circle, on his breast. They all wore beards that hung down from their cheeks, with their chins and upper lips shaved. They all had the same righteous, disapproving faces, they all refused refreshments of any sort, and they sat uneasily as though fearing contamination from the heathens who had sat in their chairs before them. They had a mixed cargo of general merchandise picked up here and there on sub-civilized planets, in which nobody on Tanith was interested. They also had some good stuff—vegetable-amber and flame-bird plumes from Irminsul; ivory or something very like it from somewhere else; diamonds and Uller organic opals and Zarathustra sunstones. They also had some platinum. They wanted machinery, especially contragravity engines and robots.

The trouble was, they wanted to haggle. Haggling, it seemed, was the Gilgamesh planetary sport.

"Have you ever heard of a Space Viking ship named the *Enterprise?*" he asked them, at the seventh or eighth impasse in the bargaining. "She bears a crescent, light blue on black. Her captain's name is Andray Dunnan."

"A ship so named, with such a device, raided Chermosh more than a year ago," the priest-supercargo said. "Some of our people tarry on Chermosh to trade. This ship sacked the city in which they were; some of them lost heavily in world's goods."

"That's a pity."

The Gilgamesh priest shrugged. "It is as Yah the Almighty wills," he said, then brightened slightly. "The Chermoshers are heathens and worshipers of false gods.

The Space Vikings looted their temple and destroyed it utterly; they carried away the graven images and abominations. Our people bore witness that there was much wailing and lamentation among the idolators.''

So that was the first entry on the Big Board. It covered, optimistically, the whole of one wall in his office, and for some time that one chalked note about the raid on Chermosh, and the date, as nearly as it could be approximated, looked very lonely on it. The captain of the *Black Star* brought back material for a couple more. He had put in on several planets known to be temporarily occupied by Space Vikings, to barter loot, give his men some time off-ship, and make inquiries, and he had names for a couple of planets raided by the blue crescent ship. One was only six months old.

The way news filtered about in the Old Federation, that was practically hot off the stove.

The owner-captain of the *Alborak* had something to add, when he brought his ship in six months later. He sipped his drink slowly, as though he had limited himself to one and wanted to make it last as long as possible.

''Almost two years ago, on Jagannath,'' he said. ''The *Enterprise* was on orbit there, getting some light repairs. I met the man a few times. Looks just like those pictures, but he's wearing a small pointed beard, now. He'd sold a lot of loot. General merchandise, precious and semi-precious stones, a lot of carved and inlaid furniture that looked as though it had come from some Neobarb king's palace, and some temple stuff. Buddhist; there were a couple of big gold Dai-Butsus. His crew were standing drinks for all comers. Some of them were pretty dark above the collar, as though they'd been on a hot-star planet not too long before. And he had a lot of Imhotep furs to sell, simply fabulous stuff.''

''What kind of repairs? Combat damage?''

''That was my impression. He spaced out a little over a hundred hours after I came in, in company with another ship. The *Starhopper*, Captain Teodor Vaghn. The talk was that they were making a two-ship raid somewhere.'' The captain of the *Alborak* thought for a moment. ''One other thing. He was buying ammunition, everything from pistol cartridges to hellburners. And he was buying all the air-and-water recycling equipment, and all the carniculture and hydroponic equipment, he could get.''

That was something to know. He thanked the Space Viking, and then asked:

''Did he know, at the time, that I'm out here hunting for him?''

''If he did, nobody else on Jagannath did. I didn't hear about it, myself, till six months afterward.''

That evening he played off the recording he had make of the conversation for Harkaman and Valkanhayn and Karffard and some of the others. Somebody instantly said:

''That temple stuff came from Chermosh. They're Buddhists, there. That checks with the Gilgamesher's story.''

''He got the furs on Imhotep; he traded for them,'' Harkaman said. ''Nobody gets anything off Imhotep by raiding. The planet's in the middle of a glaciation, the land surface down to the fiftieth parallel is iced over solid. There is one city, ten or fifteen thousand, and the rest of the population is scattered around in settlements of a couple of hundred all along the face of the glaciers. They're all hunters and trappers. They have some contragravity, and when a ship comes in, they spread the news by radio and everybody brings his furs to town. They use telescope sights, and everybody over ten years old can hit a man in the head at five hundred yards. And big weapons are no good; they're too well dispersed. So the only way to get anything out of them is to trade for it.''

"I think I know where all he was," Alvyn Karffard said. "On Imhotep, silver is a monetary metal. On Agni, they use silver for sewer-pipe. Agni is a hot-star planet, class B-3 sun. And on Agni they are tough, and they have good weapons. That could be where the *Enterprise* took that combat damage.''

That started an argument as to whether he'd gone to Chermosh first. It was sure that he had gone to Agni and then Imhotep. Guatt Kirbey tried to figure both courses.

"It doesn't tell us anything, either way," he said at length. "Chermosh is away off to the side from Agni and Imhotep in either case.''

"Well, he does have a base, somewhere, and it's not on any Terra-type planet," Valkanhayn said. "Otherwise, what would he want with all that air-and-water and hydroponic and carniculture stuff.''

The Old Federation area was full of non-Terra-type planets, and why should anybody bother going to any of them? Any planet that wasn't oxygen-atmosphere, six to eight thousand miles in diameter, and within a narrow surface-temperature range, wasn't worth wasting time on. But a planet like that, if one had the survival equipment, would make a wonderful hideout.

"What sort of a captain is this Teodor Vaghn?" he asked.

"A good one," Harkaman said promptly. "He has a

nasty streak—sadistic—but he knows his business and he has a good ship and a well-trained crew. You think he and Dunnan have teamed up?''

''Don't you? I think, now that he has a base, Dunnan is getting a fleet together.''

''He'll know we're after him by now,'' Vann Larch said. ''And he knows where we are, and that puts him one up on us.''

IX

SO ANDRAY DUNNAN was haunting him again. Tiny bits of information came in—Dunnan's ship had been on Hoth, on Nergal, selling loot. Now he sold for gold or platinum, and bought little, usually arms and ammunition. Apparently his base, wherever it was, was fully self-sufficient. It was certain, too, that Dunnan knew he was being hunted. One Space Viking who had talked with him quoted him as saying: ''I don't want any trouble with Trask, and if he's smart he won't look for any with me.'' This made him all the more positive that somewhere Dunnan was building strength for an attack on Tanith. He made it a rule that there should always be at least two ships in orbit off Tanith in addition to the *Lamia,* which was on permanent patrol, and he installed more missile-launching stations both on the moon and on the planet.

There were three ships bearing the Ward sword and atom-symbol, and a fourth building on Gram. Count Lionel of Newhaven was building one of his own, and three big freighters shuttled across the three thousand light-years between Tanith and Gram. Sesar Karvall, who had never recovered from his wounds, had died; Lady Lavina had turned the barony and the business over to her brother, Burt Sandrasan, and gone to live on Excalibur. The shipyard at Rivington was finished, and now they had built the landing-legs of Harkaman's *Corisande II*, and were putting up the skeleton.

And they were trading with Amaterasu, now. Pedrosan Pedo had been overthrown and put to death by General Dagró Ector during the disorders following the looting of Eglonsby; the troops left behind in Stolgoland had mutinied and made common cause with their late enemies. The two nations were in an uneasy alliance, with several other nations combining against them, when the *Nemesis* and the *Space-Scourge* returned and declared peace against the whole planet. There was no fighting; everybody knew what had happened to Stolgoland and Eglonsby. In the end, all the governments of Amaterasu joined in a loose agreement to get the mines reopened and resume production of gadolinium, and to share in the fissionables being imported in exchange.

It had been harder, and had taken a year longer, to do business with Beowulf. The Beowulfers had a single planetary government, and they were inclined to shoot first and negotiate afterward, a natural enough attitude in view of experiences of the past. However, they had enough old Federation-period textbooks still in microprint to know what could be done with gadolinium. They decided to write off the past as fair fight and no bad blood, and start over again.

It would be some years before either planet had hyperships of their own. In the meantime, both were good customers, and rapidly becoming good friends. A number of young Amaterasuans and Beowulfers had come to Tanith to study various technologies.

The Tanith locals were studying, too. In the first year, Trask had gathered the more intelligent boys of ten to twelve from each community and begun teaching them. In the past year, he had sent the most intelligent of them off to Gram to school. In another five years, they'd be coming home to teach; in the meantime, he was bringing teachers to Tanith from Gram. There was a school at Tradetown, and others in some of the larger villages, and at Rivington there was something that could almost be called a college. In another ten years or so, Tanith would be able to pretend to the status of civilization.

If only Andray Dunnan and his ships didn't come too soon. They would be beaten off, he was confident of that, but the damage Tanith would take, in the defence, would set back his work for years. He knew all too well what Space Viking ships could do to a planet. He'd have to find Dunnan's base, smash it, destroy his ships, kill the man himself, first. Not to avenge that murder six years ago on Gram; that was long ago and far away, and Elaine was vanished, and so was the Lucas Trask who had loved and lost her. What mattered now was planting and nurturing civilization on Tanith.

But where would he find Dunnan, in two hundred billion cubic light-years? Dunnan had no such problem. He knew where his enemy was.

And Dunnan was gathering strength. The *Yo-Yo*, Captain Vann Humfort; she had been reported twice, once in company with the *Starhopper*, and once with the

Enterprise. She bore a blazon of a feminine hand dangling a planet by a string from one finger; a good ship, and an able, ruthless captain. The *Bolide,* she and the *Enterprise* had made a raid on Ithunn. The Gilgameshers had settled there and one of their ships had brought that story in.

And he recruited two ships at once on Melkarth, and there was a good deal of mirth about that among the Tanith Space Vikings.

Melkarth was strictly a poultry planet. Its people had sunk to the village-peasant level; they had no wealth worth taking or carrying away. It was, however, a place where a ship could be set down, and there were women, and the locals had not lost the art of distillation, and made potent liquors. A crew could have fun there, much less expensively than on a regular Viking base planet, and for the last eight years a Captain Nial Burrik, of the *Fortuna,* had been occupying it, taking his ship out for occasional quick raids and spending most of the time living from day to day almost on the local level. Once in a while, a Gilgamesher would come in to see if he had anything to trade. It was a Gilgamesher who brought the story to Tanith, and it was almost two years old when he told it.

"We heard it from the people of the planet, the ones who live where Burrik had his base. First, there was a trading ship came in. You may have heard of her; she is the one called the *Honest Horris.*"

Trask laughed at that. Her captain, Horris Sasstroff, called himself "Honest Horris," a misnomer which he had also bestowed on his ship. He was a trader of sorts. Even the Gilgameshers despised him, and not even a Gilgamesher would have taken a wretched craft like the *Honest Horris* to space.

"He had been to Melkarth before," the Gilgamesher said. "He and Burrik are friends." He pronounced that like a final and damning judgment of both of them. "The story the locals told our brethren of the *Fairdealer* was that the *Honest Horris* was landed beside Burrik's ship for ten days, when two other ships came in. They said one had the blue crescent badge, and the other bore a green monster leaping from one star to another."

The *Enterprise* and the *Starhopper*. He wondered why they'd gone to a planet like Melkarth. Maybe they knew in advance whom they'd find there.

"The locals thought there would be fighting, but there was not. There was a great feast, of all four crews. Then everything of value was loaded aboard the *Fortuna,* and all four ships lifted and spaced out together. They said Burrik left nothing of any worth whatever behind; they were much disappointed at that."

"Have any of them been back since?"

All three Gilgameshers, captain, exec. and priest, shook their heads.

"Captain Gurrash of the *Fairdealer* said it had been over a year before his ship put in there. He could still see where the landing-legs of the ships had pressed into the ground, but the locals said they had not been back."

That made two more ships about which inquiries must be made. He wondered, for a moment, why in Gehenna Dunnan would want ships like that; they must make the *Space-Scourge* and the *Lamia* as he had first seen them look like units of the Royal Navy of Excalibur. Then he became frightened, with an irrational retrospective fright at what might have happened. It could have, too, at any time in the last year and a half; either or both of those ships could have come in on Tanith completely unsuspected. It was only by the sheerest accident that he had found out, even now, about them.

Everybody else thought it was a huge joke. They thought it would be a bigger joke if Dunnan sent those ships to Tanith now, when they were warned and ready for them.

There were other things to worry about. One was the altering attitude of his Majesty Angus I. When the *Space-Scourge* returned, the newly-titled Baron Valkanhayn brought with him, along with the princely title and the commission of Viceroy of Tanith, a most cordial personal audiovisual greeting, warm and friendly. Angus had made it seated at his desk, bare headed and smoking a cigarette. The one which had come on the next ship out was just as cordial, but the King was not smoking and wore a small gold-circled cap-of-maintenance. By the time they had three ships in service on scheduled three-month arrivals, a year and a half later, he was speaking from his throne, wearing his crown and employing the first person plural for himself and finally the third person singular for Trask. By the end of the fourth year, there was no audiovisual message from him in person, and a stiff complaint from Rovard Grauffis to the effect that his Majesty felt it unseemly for a subject to address his sovereign while seated, even by audiovisual. This was accompanied by a rather apologetic personal message from Grauffis—now Prime Minister—to the effect that his Majesty felt compelled to stand on his royal dignity at all times, and that, after all, there was a difference between the position and dignity of the Duke of Wardshaven and that of the Planetary King of Gram.

Prince Trask of Tanith couldn't quite see it. The King

was simply the first nobleman of the planet. Even kings like Rodolf of Excalibur or Napolyon of Flamberge didn't try to be anything more. Thereafter, he addressed his greetings and reports to the Prime Minister, always with a personal message, to which Grauffis replied in kind.

Not only the form but also the content of the messages from Gram underwent change. His Majesty was most dissatisfied. His Majesty was deeply disappointed. His Majesty felt that his Majesty's colonial realm of Tanith was not contributing sufficiently to the Royal Exchequer. And his Majesty felt that Prince Trask was placing entirely too much emphasis upon trade and not enough upon raiding; after all, why barter with barbarians when it was possible to take what you wanted from them by force?

And there was the matter of the *Blue Comet,* Count Lionel of Newhaven's ship. His Majesty was most displeased that the Count of Newhaven was trading with Tanith from his own spaceport. All goods from Tanith should pass through the Wardshaven spaceport.

"Look, Rovard," he told the audiovisual camera which was recording his reply to Grauffis. "You saw the *Space-Scourge* when she came in, didn't you? That's what happens to a ship that raids a planet where there's anything worth taking. Beowulf is lousy with fissionables; they'll give us all the plutonium we can load, in exchange for gadolinium, which we sell them at about twice Sword-World prices. We trade plutonium on Amaterasu for gadolinium, and get it for about half Sword-World prices." He pressed the stop-button, until he could remember the ancient formula. "You may quote me as saying that whoever has advised his Majesty that that isn't good business is no friend to his Majesty or to the Realm.

"As for the complaint about the *Blue Comet*; as long as she is owned and operated by the Count of Newhaven, who is a stockholder in the Tanith Adventure, she has every right to trade here."

He wondered why his Majesty didn't stop Lionel of Newhaven from sending the *Blue Comet* out from Gram. He found out from her skipper, the next time she came in.

"He doesn't dare, that's why. He's King as long as the great lords like Count Lionel and Joris of Bigglersport and Alan of Northport want him to be. Count Lionel has more men and more guns and contragravity than he has, now, and that's without the help he'd get from everybody else. Everything's quiet on Gram now, even the war on South-main Continent's stopped. Everybody wants to keep it that way. Even King Angus isn't crazy enough to do anything to start a war. Not yet, anyhow."

"Not *yet?*"

The captain of the *Blue Comet*, who was one of Count Lionel's vassal barons, was silent for a moment.

"You ought to know, Prince Trask," he said. "Andray Dunnan's grandmother was the King's mother. Her father was old Baron Zarvas of Blackcliffe. He was what was called an invalid, the last twenty years of his life. He was always attended by two male nurses about the size of Otto Harkaman. He was also said to be slightly eccentric."

The unfortunate grandfather of Duke Angus had always been a subject nice people avoided. The unfortunate grandfather of King Angus was probably a subject everybody who valued their necks avoided.

Lothar Ffayle had also come out on the *Blue Comet*. He was just as outspoken.

"I'm not going back. I'm transferring most of the funds

124

of the Bank of Wardshaven out here; from now on, it'll be a branch of the Bank of Tanith. This is where the business is being done. It's getting impossible to do business at all in Wardshaven. What little business there is to do.''

''Just what's been happening?''

''Well, taxation, first. It seems the more money came in from here, the higher taxes got on Gram. Discriminatory taxes, too; pinched the small landholding and industrial barons and favored a few big ones. Baron Spasso and his crowd.''

''Baron Spasso, now?''

Ffayle nodded. ''Of about half of Glaspyth. A lot of the Glaspyth barons lost their baronies—some of them their heads—after Duke Omfray was run out. It seems there was a plot against the life of his Majesty. It was exposed by the zeal and vigilance of Sir Garvan Spasso, who was elevated to the peerage and rewarded with the lands and estates of these conspirators.''

''You said business was bad, as business?''

Ffayle nodded again. ''The big Tanith boom has busted. It got oversold; everybody wanted in on it. And they should never have built those two last ships, the *Speedwell* and the *Goodhope*; the return on them didn't justify it. Then, you're creating your own industries and building your own equipment and armament here; that's caused a slump in industry on Gram. I'm glad Lavina Karvall has enough money invested to live on. And finally, the consumers' goods market is getting flooded with stuff that's coming in from here and competing with Gram industry.''

Well, that was understandable. One of the ships that made the shuttle-trip to Gram would carry enough in her strong-rooms, in gold and jewels and the like, to pay a handsome profit on the voyage. The bulk-goods that went into the cargo holds were practically taking a free ride, so anything on hand, stuff that nobody would ordinarily think of shipping in interstellar trade, went aboard. A two thousand foot freighter had a great deal of cargo-space.

Baron Trask of Traskon hadn't even begun to realize what Tanith base was going to cost Gram.

X

AS MIGHT BE expected, the Beowulfers finished their hypership first. They had started with everything but a little know-how which had been quickly learned. Amaterasu had had to begin by creating the industry they needed to create the industry they needed to build a ship. The Beowulf ship—she was named *Viking's Gift*—came in on Tanith five and a half years after the *Nemesis* and the *Space-Scourge* had raided Beowulf; her skipper had fought a normal-drive ship in that battle. Beside plutonium and radioactive isotopes, she carried a general cargo of the sort of luxury-goods unique to Beowulf which could always find a market in interstellar trade.

After selling the cargo and depositing the money in the Bank of Tanith, the skipper of the *Viking's Gift* wanted to know where he could find a good planet to raid. They gave him a list, none too tough but all slightly above the chicken-stealing level, and another list of planets he was *not* to raid; planets with which Tanith was trading.

Six months later they learned that he had showed up on Khepera, with which they were now trading, and had flooded the market there with plundered textiles, hardware, ceramics and plastics. He had bought kregg-meat and hides.

"You see what you did, now?" Harkaman clamored. "You thought you were making a customer; what you made was a competitor."

"What I made was an ally. If we ever do find Dunnan's planet, we'll need a fleet to take it. A couple of Beowulf ships would help. You know them; you fought them, too."

Harkaman had other worries. While cruising in *Corisande II*, he had come in on Vitharr, one of the planets where Tanith ships traded, to find it being raided by a Space Viking ship based on Xochitl. He had fought a short but furious ship-action, battering the invader until he was glad to hyper out. Then he had gone directly to Xochitl, arriving on the heels of the ship he had beaten, and had had it out both with the captain and Prince Viktor, serving them with an ultimatum to leave Tanith trade planets alone in the future.

"How did they take it?" Trask asked, when he returned to report.

"Just about the way you would have. Viktor said his people were Space Vikings, not Gilgameshers. I told him we weren't Gilgameshers, either, as he'd find out on Xochitl the next time one of his ships raided one of our planets. Are you going to back me up? Of course, you can always send Prince Viktor my head, and an apology . . ."

"If I have to send him anything, I'll send him a sky full

of ships and a planet full of hellburners. You did perfectly right, Otto; exactly what I'd have done in your place."

There the matter rested. There were no more raids by Xochitl ships on any of their trade-planets. No mention of the incident was made in any of the reports sent back to Gram. The Gram situation was deteriorating rapidly enough. Finally, there was an audiovisual message from Angus himself; he was seated on his throne, wearing his crown, and he began speaking from the screen abruptly:

"We, Angus, King of Gram and Tanith, are highly displeased with our subject, Lucas, Prince and Viceroy of Tanith; we consider ourselves very badly served by Prince Trask. We therefore command him to return to Gram, and render to us account of his administration of our colony and realm of Tanith."

After some hasty preparations, Trask recorded a reply. He was sitting on a throne, himself, and he wore a crown just as ornate as King Angus', and robes of white and black Imhotep furs.

"We, Lucas, Prince of Tanith," he began, "are quite willing to acknowledge the suzerainty of the King of Gram, formerly Duke of Wardshaven. It is our earnest desire, if possible, to remain at peace and friendship with the King of Gram, and to carry on trade relations with him and with his subjects.

"We must, however, reject absolutely any efforts on his part to dictate the internal policies of our realm of Tanith. It is our earnest hope,"—dammit, he'd said "earnest," he should have thought of some other word—"that no act on the part of his Majesty the King of Gram will create any breach in the friendship existing between his realm and ours."

Three months later, the next ship, which had left Gram

while King Angus' summons was still in hyperspace, brought Baron Rathmore. Shaking hands with him as he left the landing-craft, Trask wanted to know if he'd been sent out as the new Viceroy. Rathmore started to laugh and ended by cursing vilely.

"No. I've come out to offer my sword to the King of Tanith," he said.

"Prince of Tanith, for the time being," Trask corrected. "The sword, however, is most acceptable. I take it you've had all of our blessed sovereign you can stomach?"

"Lucas, you have enough ships and men here to take Gram," Rathmore said. "Proclaim yourself King of Tanith and then lay claim to the throne of Gram and the whole planet would rise for you."

Rathmore had lowered his voice, but even so the open landing stage was no place for this sort of talk. He said so, ordered a couple of the locals to collect Rathmore's luggage, and got him into a hall-car, taking him down to his living quarters. After they were in private, Rathmore began again:

"It's more than anybody can stand! There isn't one of the old great nobility he hasn't alienated, or one of the minor barons, the landholders and industrialists, the people who were always the backbone of Gram. And it goes from them down to the commonfolk. Assessments on the lords, taxes on the people, inflation to meet the taxes, high prices, debased coinage. Everybody's being beggared except this rabble of new lords he has around him, and that slut of a wife and her greedy kinfolk . . ."

Trask stiffened. "You're not speaking of Queen Flavia, are you?" he asked softly.

Rathmore's mouth opened slightly. "Great Satan,

don't you know? No, of course not; the news would have come on the same ship I did. Why, Angus divorced Flavia. He claimed that she was incapable of giving him an heir to the throne. He remarried immediately."

The girl's name meant nothing to Trask; he did know of her father, a Baron Valdive. He was lord of a small estate south of the Ward lands and west of Newhaven. Most of his people were out-and-out bandits and cattle-rustlers, and he was as close to being one himself as he could get.

"Nice family he's married into. A credit to the dignity of the throne."

"Yes. You wouldn't know this Lady-Demoiselle Evita; she was only seventeen when you left Gram, and hadn't begun to acquire a reputation outside her father's lands. She's made up for lost time since, though. And she has enough uncles and aunts and cousins and ex-lovers and what-not to fill out an infantry regiment, and every one of them's at court with both hands out to grab everything they can."

"How does Duke Joris like this?" The Duke of Bigglersport was Queen Flavia's brother. "I daresay he's less than delighted."

"He's hiring mercenaries, is what he's doing, and buying combat contragravity. Lucas, why don't you come back? You have no idea what a reputation you have on Gram, now. Everybody would rally to you."

He shook his head. "I have a throne, here on Tanith. On Gram I want nothing. I'm sorry for the way Angus turned out; I thought he'd make a good King. But since he's made an intolerable King, the lords and people of Gram will have to get rid of him for themselves. I have my own tasks, here."

Rathmore shrugged. "I was afraid that would be it," he

said. "Well, I offered my sword; I won't take it back. I can help you in what you're doing on Tanith."

The captain of the free Space Viking *Damnthing* was named Roger-fan-Morvill Esthersan, which meant that he was some Sword-Worlder's acknowledged bastard by a woman of one of the Old Federation planets. His mother's people could have been Nergalers; he had coarse black hair, a mahogany-brown skin, and red-brown, almost maroon, eyes. He tasted the wine the robot poured for him and expressed appreciation, then began unwrapping the parcel he had brought in.

"Something I found while raiding on Tetragrammaton," he said. "I thought you might like to have it. It was made on Gram."

It was an automatic pistol, with a belt and holster. The leather was bisonoid-hide; the buckle of the belt was an oval enameled with a crescent, pale blue on black. The pistol was a plain 10-mm military model with grooved plastic grips; on the receiver it bore the stamp of the House of Hoylbar, the firearms manufacturers of Glaspyth. Evidently it was one of the arms Duke Omfray had provided for Andray Dunnan's original mercenary company.

"Tetragrammaton?" He glanced over to the Big Board; there was no previous report from that planet. "How long ago?"

"I'd say about three hundred hours. I came from there directly, less than two hundred and fifty hours. Dunnan's ships had left the planet three days before I got there."

That was practically sizzling hot. Well, something like that had to happen, sooner or later. The Space Viking was asking him if he knew what sort of a place Tetragrammaton was.

Neobarbarian, trying to recivilize in a crude way. Small population, concentrated on one continent; farming and fisheries. A little heavy industry, in a small way, at a couple of towns. They had some nuclear power, introduced a century or so ago by traders from Marduk, one of the really civilized planets. They still depended on Marduk for fissionables; their export product was an abominable-smelling vegetable oil which furnished the base for delicate perfumes, and which nobody was ever able to synthesize properly.

"I heard they had steel mills in operation, now," the half-breed Space Viking said. "It seems that somebody on Rimmon has just re-invented the railroad, and they need more steel than they can produce for themselves. I thought I'd raid Tetragrammaton for steel and trade it on Rimmon for a load of heaven-tea. When I got there, though, the whole planet was in a mess; not raiding, plain wanton destruction. The locals were just digging themselves out of it when I landed. Some of them, who didn't think they had anything at all left to lose, gave me a fight. I captured a few of them, to find out what had happened. One of them had that pistol; he said he'd taken it off a Space Viking he'd killed. The ships that raided them were the *Enterprise* and the *Yo-Yo*. I knew you'd want to hear about it. I got some of the locals' stories on tape, and then came here directly."

"Well, thank you. I'll want to hear those tapes. Now, you say you want steel?"

"Well, I haven't any money. That's why I was going to raid Tetragrammaton."

"Nifflheim with the money; your cargo's paid for already. This," he said, touching the pistol, "and whatever's on the tapes."

They played off the tapes that evening. They weren't particularly informative. The locals who had been interrogated hadn't been in actual contact with Dunnan's people except in combat. The man who had been carrying the 10-mm Hoylbar was the best witness of the lot, and he knew little. He had caught one of them alone, shot him from behind with a shotgun, taken his pistol, and then gotten away as quickly as he could. They had sent down landing-craft, it seemed, and said they wanted to trade; then something must have happened, nobody knew what, and they had begun a massacre and sacked the town. After returning to their ships, they had opened fire with nuclear missiles.

"Sounds like Dunnan," Hugh Rathmore said in disgust. "He just went kill-crazy. The bad blood of Blackcliffe."

"There are funny things about this," Boake Valkanhayn said. "I'd say it was a terror-raid, but who in Gehenna was he trying to terrorize?"

"I wondered about that, too." Harkaman frowned. "This town where he landed seems, such as it was, to have been the planetary capital. They just landed, pretending friendship, which I can't see why they needed to pretend, and then began looting and massacring. There wasn't anything of real value there; all they took was what the men could carry themselves or stuff into their landing-craft, and they did that because they have what amounts to a religious taboo against landing anywhere and leaving without stealing something. The real loot was at these two other towns; a steel mill and big stocks of steel at one, and all that skunkapple oil at the other. So what did they do? They dropped a five-megaton bomb on each one, and blew both of them to Em-See-Square. That was a terror-raid pure and simple, but as Boake inquires, just who were they terrorizing? If there were big cities somewhere else on the planet, it would figure. But there aren't. They blew out the two biggest cities, and all the loot in them.''

"Then they wanted to terrorize somebody off the planet.''

"But nobody'd hear about it off-planet,'' somebody protested.

"The Mardukans would; they trade with Tetragrammaton,'' the acknowledged bastard of somebody named Morvill said. ''They have a couple of ships a year there.''

"That's right,'' Trask agreed. ''Marduk.''

"You mean, you think Dunnan's trying to terrorize *Marduk?*'' Valkanhayn demanded. ''Great Satan, even he isn't crazy enough for that!''

Baron Rathmore started to say something about what Andray Dunnan was crazy enough to do, and what his uncle was crazy enough to do. It was just one of the cracks he had been making since he'd come to Tanith and didn't have to look over his shoulder while he was making them.

"I think he is, too,'' Trask said. ''I think that is exactly what he is doing. Don't ask me why; as Otto is fond of remarking, he's crazy and we aren't, and that gives him an advantage. But what have we gotten, since those Gilgameshers told us about his picking up Burrik's ship and the *Honest Horris?* Until today, we've heard nothing from any other Space Viking. What we have gotten were stories from Gilgameshers about raids on planets where they trade, and every one of them is also a planet where Marduk ships trade. And in every case, there has been little or nothing reported about valuable loot taken. The stories are all about wanton and murderous bombings. I think Andray Dunnan is making war on Marduk.''

"Then he's crazier than his grandfather and his uncle both!" Rathmore cried.

"You mean, he's making a string of terror-raids on their trade planets, hoping to pull the Mardukan space-navy away from the home planet?" Harkaman had stopped being incredulous. "And when he gets them all lured away, he'll make a fast raid?"

"That's what I think. Remember our fundamental postulate: Dunnan is crazy. Remember how he convinced himself that he was the rightful heir to the ducal crown of Wardshaven?" And remember his insane passion for Elaine; he pushed that thought hastily from him. "Now, he's convinced that he's the greatest Space Viking in history. He has to do something worthy of that distinction. When was the last time anybody attacked a civilized planet? I don't mean Gilgamesh, I mean a planet like Marduk."

"A hundred and twenty years ago; Prince Havilgar of Haulteclere, six ships, against Aton. Two ships got back. He didn't. Nobody's tried it since," Harkaman said.

"So Dunnan the Great will do it. I hope he tries," he surprised himself by adding. "That's provided I find out what happened. Then I could stop thinking about him."

There was a time when he had dreaded the possibility that somebody else might kill Dunnan before he could.

XI

SESHAT, Obidicut, Lugaluru, Audhumla.

The young man elevated by his father's death in the Dunnan raid to the post of hereditary President of the democratic Republic of Tetragrammaton had been sure that the Marduk ships which came to his planet traded also on those. There had been some difficulty about making contact, and the first face-to-face meeting had begun in an atmosphere of bitter distrust on his part. They had met out of doors; around them, spread wrecked and burned buildings, and hastily constructed huts and shelters, and wide spaces of charred and slagged rubble.

"They blew up the steel mill here, and the oil-refinery at Jannsboro. They bombed and strafed the little farm-towns and villages. They scattered radioactives that killed as many as the bombing. And after they had gone away, this other ship came."

"The *Damnthing?* She bore the head of a beast with three horns?"

"That's the one. They did a little damage, at first. When the captain found out what had happened to us, he left some food and medicines for us." Roger-fan-Morvill Esthersan hadn't mentioned that.

"Well, we'd like to help you, if we can. Do you have nuclear power? We can give you a little equipment. Just remember it of us, when you're back on your feet; we'll be back to trade later. But don't think you owe us anything.

The man who did this to you is my enemy. Now, I want to talk to every one of your people who can tell me anything at all . . ."

Seshat was the closest; they went there first. They were too late. Seshat had had it already, and on the evidence of the radioactivity counters, not too long ago. Four hundred hours at most. There had been two hellburners; the cities on which they had fallen were still-smoking pits literally burned into the ground and the bedrock below, at the center of five hundred mile radii of slag and lava and scorched earth and burned forests. There had been a planetbuster; it had started a major earthquake. And half a dozen thermonuclears. There were probably quite a few survivors—a human planetary population is extremely hard to exterminate completely—but within a century or so they'd be back to the loincloth and the stone hatchet.

"We don't even know Dunnan did it, personally," Paytrik Morland said. "For all we know, he's down in an airtight cave city on some planet nobody ever heard of, sitting on a golden throne, surrounded by a harem."

He had begun to suspect that Dunnan was doing something of just the sort. The Greatest Space Viking of History would naturally found a Space Viking empire.

"An emperor goes out to look his empire over, now and then; I don't spend all my time on Tanith. Say we try Audhumla next. It's the farthest away. We might get there while he's still shooting up Obidicut and Lugaluru. Guatt, figure us a jump for it."

When the colored turbulence washed away and the screen cleared, Audhumla looked like Tanith or Khepera or Amaterasu or any other Terra-type planet, a big disc brilliant with reflected sunlight and glowing with starlit and moonlit atmosphere on the other side. There was a single rather large moon, and, in the telescopic screen, the usual markings of seas and continents and rivers and mountain-ranges. But there was nothing to show . . .

Oh, yes; lights on the darkened side, and from the size they must be vast cities. All the available data for Audhumla was long out of date; a considerable civilization must have developed in the last half dozen centuries.

Another light appeared, a hard blue-white spark that spread into a larger, less brilliant yellow light. At the same time, all the alarm-devices in the command-room went into a pandemonium of jangling and flashing and squawking and howling and shouting. Radiation. Energy-release. Contragravity distortion effects. Infra-red output. A welter of indecipherable radio and communication-screen signals. Radar and scanner-ray beams from the planet.

Trask's fist began hurting; he found that he had been pounding the desk in front of him with it. He stopped it.

"We caught him, we caught him!" he was yelling hoarsely. "Full speed in, continuous acceleration, as much as we can stand. We'll worry about decelerating when we're in shooting distance."

The planet grew steadily larger; Karffard was taking him at his word about continuous acceleration. There'd be a Gehenna of a bill to pay when they started decelerating. On the planet, more bombs were going off just outside atmosphere beyond the sunset line.

"Ship observed. Altitude about a hundred to five hundred miles—hundreds, not thousands—35° North Latitude, 15° west of the sunset line. Ship is under fire, bomb explosions near her," a voice whooped.

Somebody else was yelling that the city lights were

really burning cities, or burning forests. The first voice, having stopped, broke in again:

"Ship is visible in telescopic screen, just at the sunset line. And there's another ship detected but not visible, somewhere around the equator, and a third one somewhere out of sight, we can just get the fringe of her contragravity field around the planet."

That meant there were two sides, and a fight. Unless Dunnan had picked up a third ship, somewhere. The telescopic view shifted; for a moment the planet was completely off-screen, and then its curvature came into the screen against a star-scattered background. They were almost in to two thousand miles now; Karffard was yelling to stop acceleration and trying to put the ship into a spiral orbit. Suddenly they caught a glimpse of one of the ships.

"She's in trouble." That was Paul Koreff's voice. "She's leaking air and water vapor like crazy."

"Well, is she a good guy or a bad guy?" Morland was yelling back, as though Koreff's spectroscopes could distinguish. Koreff ignored that.

"Another ship making signal," he said. "She's the one coming up over the equator. Sword-World impulse code; her communication-screen combination, and an identify-yourself."

Karffard punched out the combination as Koreff furnished it. While Trask was desperately willing his face into immobility, the screen lighted. It wasn't Andray Dunnan; that was a disappointment. It was almost as good, though. His henchman, Sir Nevil Ormm.

"Well, Sir Nevil! A pleasant surprise," he heard himself saying. "We last met on the terrace at Karvall House, did we not?"

For once, the paper-white face of Andray Dunnan's *âme damnée* showed expression, but whether it was fear, surprise, shock, hatred, anger, or what combination of them, Trask could no more than guess.

"Trask! Satan curse you . . . !"

Then the screen went blank. In the telescopic screen, the other ship came on unfalteringly. Paul Koreff, who had gotten more data on mass, engine energy-output and dimensions, was identifying her as the *Enterprise*.

"Well, go for her! Give her everything!"

They didn't need the order; Vann Larch was speaking rapidly into his hand-phone, and Alvyn Karffard was hurling his voice all over the *Nemesis*, warning of sudden deceleration and direction change, and while he was speaking, things in the command-room began sliding. In the telescopic screen, the other ship was plainly visible; he could see the oval patch of black with the blue crescent, and in his screen Dunnan would be seeing the sword-impaled skull of the *Nemesis*.

If only he could be sure Dunnan was there to see it. If it had only been Dunnan's face, instead of Ormm's, that he had seen in the screen. As it was, he couldn't be sure, and if one of the missiles that were already going out made a lucky hit, he might never be sure. He didn't care who killed Dunnan, or how. All he wanted was to know that Dunnan's death had set him free from a self-assumed obligation that was now meaningless to him.

The *Enterprise* launched counter-missiles; so did the *Nemesis*. There were momentarily unbearable flashes of pure energy and from them globes of incandescence spread and vanished. Something must have gotten through; red lights flashed on the damage board. It had been something heavy enough even to jolt the huge mass of the *Nemesis*. At the same time, the other ship took a hit from something that would have vaporized her had she not been armored in collapsium. Then, as they passed close together, guns hammered back and forth along with missiles, and then the *Enterprise* was out of sight around the horizon.

Another ship, the size of Otto Harkaman's *Corisande II*, was approaching; she bore a tapering, red-nailed feminine hand dangling a planet by a string. They rushed toward each other, planting a garden of evanescent fireflowers between them; they pounded one another with guns, and then they sped apart. At the same time, Paul Koreff was picking up an impulse-code signal from the third, crippled, ship; a screen combination. Trask punched it out as he received it.

A man in space-armor was looking out of the screen. That was bad, if they had to suit up in the command-room. They still had air; his helmet was off, but it was attached and hinged back. On his breastplate was a device of a dragonlike beast perched with its tail around a planet, and a crown above. He had a thin, high-cheeked face, with a vertical wrinkle between his eyes, and a clipped blond mustache.

"Who are you, stranger. You're fighting my enemies; does that make you a friend."

"I'm a friend of anybody who owns Andray Dunnan his enemy. Sword-World ship *Nemesis*; I'm Prince Lucas Trask of Tanith, commanding."

"Royal Mardukan ship *Victrix*." The thin-faced man gave a wry laugh. "Not been living up to her name so well. I'm Prince Simon Bentrik, commanding."

"Are you still battle-worthy?"

"We can fire about half our guns; we still have a few missiles left. Seventy percent of the ship's sealed off, and we've been holed in a dozen places. We have power enough for lift and some steering-way. We can't make lateral way except at the expense of lift."

Which made the *Victrix* practically a stationary target. He yelled over his shoulder at Karffard to cut speed all he could without tearing things apart.

"When that cripple comes into view, start circling around her. Get into a tight circle above her." He turned back to the man in the screen. "If we can get ourselves slowed down enough, we'll do all we can to cover you."

"All you can is all you can; thank you, Prince Trask."

"Here comes the *Enterprise!*" Karffard shouted, with obscenely blasphemous embellishments. "She hairpinned on us."

"Well, do something about her!"

Vann Larch was already doing it. The *Enterprise* had taken damage in the last exchange; Koreff's spectroscopes showed her halo-ed with air and water vapor. Her instruments would be getting the same story from the *Nemesis;* wedge-shaped segments extending six to eight decks in were sealed off in several places. Then the only thing that could be seen with certainty was the blaze of mutually destroying missiles between. The short-range gun duel began and ended as they passed.

In the screen, he had seen a fat round-nosed thing come up from the *Victrix*, curving far out ahead of the passing *Enterprise*. She was almost out of sight around the planet when she ran head-on into it, and vanished in an awesome blaze. For a moment, he thought she had been destroyed, then she lurched into sight and went around the curvature of Audhumla.

Trask and the Mardukan were shaking hands with themselves at each other in their screens; everybody in the *Nemesis* command-room was screaming: "Well shot, *Victrix!* Well shot!"

Then the *Yo-Yo* was coming around again, and Vann Larch was saying, "Gehenna with this fooling around! I'll fix the expurgated unprintability!"

He yelled orders—a jumble of code letters and numbers—and things began going out. Most of them blew up in space. Then the *Yo-Yo* blew up, very quietly, as things do where there is no air to carry shock- and sound-waves, but very brilliantly. There was brief daylight all over the night side of the planet.

"That was our planetbuster," Larch said. "I don't know what we'll use on Dunnan."

"I didn't know we had one," Trask admitted.

"Otto had a couple built on Beowulf. The Beowulfers are good nuclear weaponeers."

The *Enterprise* came back, hastily, to see what had blown up. Larch put off another entertainment of small stuff, with a fifty megaton thermonuclear, viewscreen-piloted, among them. It had its own arsenal of small missiles, and it got through. In the te'escopic screen, a jagged hole was visible just below the equator of the *Enterprise*, the edges curling outward. Something, possibly a heavy missile in an open tube, ready for launching, had gone off inside her. What the inside of the ship was like, or how many of her company were still alive, was hard to guess.

There were some, and her launchers were still spewing

out missiles. They were intercepted and blew up. The hull of the *Enterprise* bulked huge in the guidance-screen of the missile and filled it; the jagged crater that had obliterated the bottom of Dunnan's blue crescent blazon spread to fill the whole screen. The screen went milky white as the pickup went off.

All the other screens blazed briefly, until their filters went on. Even afterward, they glared like the cloud-veiled sun of Gram at high noon. Finally, when the light-intensity had dropped and the filters went off, there was nothing left of the *Enterprise* but an orange haze.

Somebody—Paytrik, Baron Morland, he saw—was pounding him on the back and screaming inarticulately in his ear. A dozen space-armored officers with planet-perched dragons on their breasts were crowding beside Prince Bentrik in the screen from the *Victrix*, whooping like drunken bisonoid-herders on payday night.

"I wonder," he said, almost inaudibly, "if I'll ever know if Andray Dunnan was on that ship?"

MARDUK

I

PRINCE TRASK of Tanith and Prince Simon Bentrik were dining together on an upper terrace of what had originally been the mansion-house of a Federation period plantation. It had been a number of other things since; now it was the municipal building of a town that had grown around it, which had, somehow escaped undamaged from the Dunnan blitz. Normally about five or ten thousand, the place was now jammed with almost fifty thousand homeless refugees from half a dozen other towns that had been destroyed, overflowing the buildings and crowding into a sprawling camp of hastily built huts and shelters, and already permanent buildings were going up to accommodate them. Everybody, locals, Mardukans and Space Vikings, had been busy with the work of relief and reconstruction; this was the first meal the two commanders had been able to share in any leisure at all. Prince Bentrik's enjoyment of it was somewhat impaired by the fact that from where he sat he could see, in the distance, the sphere of his grounded and disabled ship.

"I doubt we can get her off-planet again, let alone into hyperspace."

"Well, we'll get you and your crew to Marduk in the

Nemesis, then.'' They were both speaking loudly, above the clank and clatter of machinery below. "I hope you didn't think I'd leave you stranded here."

"I don't know how either of us will be received. Space Vikings haven't been exactly popular on Marduk, lately. They may thank you for bringing me back to stand trial,'' Bentrik said bitterly. "Why, I'd have anybody shot who let his ship get caught as I did mine. Those two were down in atmosphere before I knew they'd come out of hyperspace."

"I think they were down on the planet before your ship arrived."

"Oh, that's ridiculous, Prince Trask!" the Mardukan cried. "You can't hide a ship on a planet. Not from the kind of instruments we have in the Royal Navy."

"We have pretty fair detection ourselves," Trask reminded him. "There's one place where you can do it. At the bottom of an ocean, with a thousand or so feet of water over her. That's where I was going to hide the *Nemesis*, if I got here ahead of Dunnan."

Prince Bentrik's fork stopped half way to his mouth. He lowered it slowly to his plate. That was a theory he'd like to accept, if he could.

"But the locals. They didn't know about it."

"They wouldn't. They have no off-planet detection of their own. Come in directly over the ocean, out of the sun, and nobody'd see the ship."

"Is that a regular Space Viking trick?"

"No. I invented it myself, on the way from Seshat. But if Dunnan wanted to ambush your ship, he'd have thought of it, too. It's the only practical way to do it."

Dunnan, or Nevil Ormm; he wished he knew, and was afraid he would go on wishing all his life.

Bentrik started to pick up his fork again, changed his mind, and sipped from his wineglass instead.

"You may find you're quite welcome on Marduk, at that," he said. "These raids have only been a serious problem in the last four years. I believe, as you do, that this enemy of yours is responsible for all of them. We have half the Royal Navy out now, patrolling our trade-planets. Even if he wasn't aboard the *Enterprise* when you blew her up, you've put a name on him and can tell us a good deal about him." He set down the wineglass. "Why, if it weren't so utterly ridiculous, one might even think he was making war on Marduk."

From Trask's viewpoint, it wasn't ridiculous at all. He merely mentioned that Andray Dunnan was psychotic and left it at that.

The *Victrix* was not completely unrepairable, although quite beyond the resources they had at hand. A fully equipped engineer-ship from Marduk could patch her hull and replace her Dillinghams and her Abbot lift-and-drive engines and make her temporarily spaceworthy, until she could be gotten to a shipyard. They concentrated on repairing the *Nemesis*, and in another two weeks she was ready for the voyage.

The six hundred hour trip to Marduk passed pleasantly enough. The Mardukan officers were good company, and found their Space Viking opposite numbers equally so. The two crews had become used to working together on Audhumla, and mingled amicably off watch, interesting themselves in each other's hobbies and listening avidly to tales of each other's home planets. The Space Vikings were surprised and disappointed at the somewhat lower intellectual level of the Mardukans. They couldn't understand that; Marduk was supposed to be a civilized planet, wasn't it? The Mardukans were just as surprised, and inclined to be resentful, that the Space Vikings all acted and talked like officers. Hearing of it, Prince Bentrik was also puzzled. Fo'c'sle hands on a Mardukan ship belonged definitely to the lower orders.

"There's still too much free land and free opportunity on the Sword-Worlds," Trask explained. "Nobody does much bowing and scraping to the class above him; he's too busy trying to shove himself up into it. And the men who ship out as Space Vikings are the least class-conscious of the lot. Think my men may have trouble on Marduk about that? They'll all insist on doing their drinking in the swankiest places in town."

"No. I don't think so. Everybody will be so amazed that Space Vikings aren't twelve feet tall, with three horns like a Zarathustra damnthing and a spiked tail like a Fafnir mantichore that they won't even notice anything less. Might do some good, in the long run. Crown Prince Edvard will like your Space Vikings. He's much opposed to class distinctions and caste prejudices. Says they have to be eliminated before we can make democracy really work."

The Mardukans talked a lot about democracy. They thought well of it; their government was a representative democracy. It was also a hereditary monarchy, if that made any kind of sense. Trask's efforts to explain the political and social structure of the Sword-Worlds met the same incomprehension from Bentrik.

"Why, it sounds like feudalism to me!"

"That's right; that's what it is. A king owes his position to the support of his great nobles; they owe theirs to their barons and landholding knights; they owe theirs to their people. There are limits beyond which none of them can go; after that, their vassals turn on them."

"Well, suppose the people of some barony rebel? Won't the king send troops to support the baron?"

"What troops? Outside a personal guard and enough men to police the royal city and hold the crown lands, the king has no troops. If he wants troops, he has to get them from his great nobles; they have to get them from their vassal barons, who raise them by calling out their people." That was another source of dissatisfaction with King Angus of Gram; he had been augmenting his forces by hiring off-planet mercenaries. "And the people won't help some other baron oppress his people; it might be their turn next."

"You mean, the people are armed?" Prince Bentrik was incredulous.

"Great Satan, aren't yours?" Prince Trask was equally surprised. "Then your democracy's a farce, and the people are only free on sufferance. If their ballots aren't secured by arms, they're worthless. Who has the arms on your planet?"

"Why, the Government."

"You mean the King?"

Prince Bentrik was shocked. Certainly not; horrid idea. That would be . . . why, it would be *despotism!* Beside, the King wasn't the Government, at all; the Government ruled in the King's name. There was the Assembly; the Chamber of Representatives, and the Chamber of Delegates. The people elected the Representatives, and the Representatives elected the Delegates, and the Delegates elected the Chancellor. Then, there was the Prime Minister; he was appointed by the King, but the King had to appoint him from the party holding the most seats in the Chamber of Representatives, and he appointed the Ministers, who handled the executive work of the Government, only their subordinates in the different Ministries were career-officials who were selected by competitive examination for the bottom jobs and promoted up the bureaucratic ladder from there.

This left Trask wondering if the Mardukan constitution hadn't been devised by Goldberg, the legendary Old Terran inventor who always did everything the hard way. It also left him wondering just how in Gehenna the Government of Marduk ever got anything done.

Maybe it didn't. Maybe that was what saved Marduk from having a real despotism.

"Well, what prevents the Government from enslaving the people? The people can't; you just told me that they aren't armed, and the Government is."

He continued, pausing now and then for breath, to catalogue every tyranny he had ever heard of, from those practised by the Terran Federation before the Big War to those practised at Eglonsby on Amaterasu by Pedrosan Pedro. A few of the very mildest were pushing the nobles and people of Gram to revolt against Angus I.

"And in the end," he finished, "the Government would be the only property owner and the only employer on the planet, and everybody else would be slaves, working at assigned tasks, wearing Government-issued clothing and eating Government food, their children educated as the Government prescribes and trained for jobs selected for them by the Government, never reading a book or seeing a play or thinking a thought that the Government had not approved . . ."

Most of the Mardukans were laughing, now. Some of them were accusing him of being just too utterly ridiculous.

"Why, the people *are* the Government. The people would not legislate themselves into slavery."

He wished Otto Harkaman were there. All he knew of history was the little he had gotten from reading some of Harkaman's books, and the long, rambling conversations aboard ship in hyperspace or in the evenings at Rivington. But Harkaman, he was sure, could have furnished hundreds of instances, on scores of planets and over ten centuries of time, in which people had done exactly that and hadn't known what they were doing, even after it was too late.

"They have something like that on Aton," one of the Mardukan officers said.

"Oh, Aton; that's a dictatorship, pure and simple. That Planetary Nationalist gang got into control fifty years ago, during the crisis after the war with Baldur . . . "

"They were voted into power by the people, weren't they?"

"Yes; they were," Prince Bentrik said gravely. "It was an emergency measure, and they were given emergency powers. Once they were in, they made the emergency permanent."

"That couldn't happen on Marduk!" a young nobleman declared.

"It could if Zaspar Makann's party wins control of the

Assembly at the next election," somebody else said.

"Oh, then Marduk's safe! The sun'll go nova first," one of the junior Royal Navy officers said.

After that, they began talking about women, a subject any spaceman will drop any other subject to discuss.

Trask made a mental note of the name of Zaspar Makann, and took occasion to bring it up in conversation with his shipboard guests. Every time he talked about Makann to two or more Mardukans, he heard at least three or more opinions about the man. He was a political demagogue; on that everybody agreed. After that, opinions diverged.

Makann was a raving lunatic, and all the followers he had were a handful of lunatics like him. He might be a lunatic, but he had a dangerously large following. Well, not so large; maybe they'd pick up a seat or so in the Assembly, but that was doubtful—not enough of them in any representative district to elect an Assemblyman. He was just a smart crook, milking a lot of half-witted plebeians for all he could get out of them. Not just plebes, either; a lot of industrialists were secretly financing him, in hope that he would help them break up the labor-unions. You're nuts; everybody knew the labor-unions were backing him, hoping he'd scare the employers into granting concessions. You're both nuts; he was backed by the mercantile interests; they were hoping he'd run the Gilgameshers off the planet.

Well, that was one thing you had to give him credit for. He wanted to run out the Gilgameshers. Everybody was in favor of that.

Now, Trask could remember something he'd gotten from Harkaman. There had been Hitler, back at the end of the First Century Pre-Atomic; hadn't he gotten into power because everybody was in favor of running out the Christians, or the Moslems, or the Albigensians, or somebody?

II

MARDUK HAD three moons; a big one, 1500 miles in diameter, and two insignificant twenty-mile chunks of rock. The big one was fortified, and a couple of ships were in orbit around it. The *Nemesis* was challenged as she emerged from her last hyperjump; both ships broke orbit and came out to meet her, and several more were detected lifting away from the planet.

Prince Bentrik took the communication-screen, and immediately encountered difficulties. The commandant, even after the situation had been explained twice to him, couldn't understand. A Royal Navy fleet unit knocked out in a battle with Space Vikings was bad enough, but being rescued and brought to Marduk by another Space Viking simply didn't make sense. He then screened the Royal Palace at Malverton, on the planet; first he was icily polite to somebody several echelons below him in the peerage, and then respectfully polite to somebody he addressed as Prince Vandarvant. Finally, after some minutes' wait, a frail, white-haired man in a little black cap-of-maintenance appeared in the screen. Prince Bentrik instantly sprang to his feet. So did all the other Mardukans in the command-room.

"Your Majesty! I am deeply honored!"

"Are you all right, Simon?" the old gentleman asked solicitously. "They haven't done anything to you, have they?"

"Saved my life, and my men's, and treated me like a friend and a comrade, your Majesty. Have I your permission to present, informally, their commander, Prince Trask of Tanith?"

"Indeed you may, Simon. I owe the gentleman my deepest thanks."

"His majesty, Mikhyl the Eighth, Planetary King of Marduk," Prince Bentrik said. "His Highness, Lucas, Prince Trask, planetary Viceroy of Tanith for his Majesty Angus the First of Gram."

The elderly monarch bowed his head slightly; Trask bowed a little more deeply, from the waist.

"I am very happy, Prince Trask, first, I confess, at the safe return of my kinsman Prince Bentrik, and then at the honor of meeting one in the confidence of my fellow sovereign King Angus of Gram. I will never be ungrateful for what you did for my cousin and for his officers and men. You must stay at the Palace while you are on this planet; I am giving orders for your reception, and I wish you to be formally presented to me this evening." He hesitated briefly. "Gram; that is one of the Sword-Worlds, is it not?" Another brief hesitation. "Are you really a Space Viking, Prince Trask?"

Maybe he'd expected Space Vikings to have three horns and a spiked tail and stand twelve feet tall, himself.

It took several hours for the Nemesis to get into orbit. Bentrik spent most of them in a screen-booth, and emerged visibly relieved.

"Nobody's going to be sticky about what happened on

154

Audhumla," he told Trask. "There will be a Board of Inquiry. I'm afraid I had to mix you up in that. It's not only about the action on Audhumla; everybody from the Space Minister down wants to hear what you know about this fellow Dunnan. Like yourself, we all hope he went to Em-See-Square along with his flagship, but we can't take it for granted. We have over a dozen trade-planets to protect, and he's hit more than half of them already."

The process of getting into orbit took them around the planet several times, and it was a more impressive spectacle at each circuit. Of course, Marduk had a population of almost two billion, and had been civilized, with no hiatus of Neobarbarism, since it had first been colonized in the Fourth Century. Even so, the Space Vikings were amazed—and stubbornly refusing to show it—at what they saw in the telescopic screens.

"Look at that city!" Paytrik Morland whispered. "We talk about the civilized planets, but I never realized they were anything like this. Why, this makes Excalibur look like Tanith!"

The city was Malverton, the capital; like any city of a contragravity-using people, it lay in a rough circle of buildings towering out of green interspaces, surrounded by the smaller circles of spaceports and industrial suburbs. The difference was that any of these were as large as Camelot on Excalibur or four Wardshavens on Gram, and Malverton itself was almost half the size of the whole barony of Traskon.

"They aren't any more civilized than we are, Paytrik. There are just more of them. If there were two billion people on Gram—which I hope there will be —Gram would have cities like this, too."

One thing; the government of a planet like Marduk would have to be something more elaborate than the loose feudalism of the Sword-Worlds. Maybe this Goldberg-ocracy of theirs had been forced upon them by the sheer complexity of the population and its problems.

Alvyn Karffard took a quick look around him to make sure none of the Mardukans were in earshot.

"I don't care how many people they have," he said. "Marduk can be had. A wolf never cares how many sheep there are in a flock. With twenty ships, we could take this planet like we took Eglonsby. There'd be losses coming in, sure, but after we were in and down, we'd have it."

"Where would we get twenty ships?"

Tanith, at a pinch, could muster five or six, counting the free Space Vikings who used the base facilities; they would have to leave a couple to hold the planet. Beowulf had one, and another almost completed, and now there was an Amaterasu ship. But to assemble a Space Viking armada of twenty . . . He shook his head. The real reason why Space Vikings had never raided a civilized planet successfully had always been their inability to combine under one command in sufficient strength.

Beside, he didn't want to raid Marduk. A raid, if successful, would yield immense treasures, but cause a hundred, even a thousand, times as much destruction, and he didn't want to destroy anything civilized.

The landing-stages of the palace were crowded when he and Prince Bentrik landed, and, at a discreet distance, swarms of air-vehicles circled, creating a control-problem for the police. Parting from Bentrik, he was escorted to the suite prepared for him; it was luxurious in the extreme but scarcely above Sword-World standards. There were a surprising number of human servants, groveling and fawning and getting underfoot and doing work robots could have been doing better. What robots there were were inefficient, and much work and ingenuity had been lavished on efforts to copy human form to the detriment of function.

After getting rid of most of the superfluous servants, he put on a screen and began sampling the newscasts. There were telescopic views of the *Nemesis* from some craft on orbit nearby, and he watched the officers and men of the *Victrix* being disembarked; there were other views of their landing at some naval installation on the ground, and he could see reporters being chivied away by Navy ground-police. And there was a wide range of commentary opinion.

The Government had already denied that, (1) Prince Bentrik had captured the *Nemesis* and brought her in as a prize, and, (2) the Space Vikings had captured Prince Bentrik and were holding him for ransom. Beyond that, the Government was trying to sit on the whole story, and the Opposition was hinting darkly at corrupt deals and sinister plots. Prince Bentrik arrived in the midst of an impassioned tirade against pusillanimous traitors surrounding his Majesty who were betraying Marduk to the Space Vikings.

"Why doesn't your Government publish the facts and put a stop to that nonsense?" Trask asked.

"Oh, let them rave," Bentrik replied. "The longer the Government waits, the more they'll be ridiculed when the facts are published."

Or, the more people will be convinced that the Government had something to hush up, and had to take time to

construct a plausible story. He kept the thought to himself
It was their government; how they mismanaged it was
their own business. He found that there was no bartending
robot; he had to have a human servant bring drinks. He
made up his mind to have a few of the *Nemesis* robots sent
down to him.

The formal presentation would be in the evening; there
would be a dinner first, and because Trask had not yet
been formally presented, he couldn't dine with the King
but because he was, or claimed to be, Viceroy of Tanith
he ranked as a chief of state and would dine with the
Crown Prince, to whom there would be an informal introduction first.

This took place in a small antechamber off the
banquet-hall; the Crown Prince and Crown Princess and
Princess Bentrik were there when they arrived. The
Crown Prince was a man of middle age, graying at the
temples, with the glassy stare that betrayed contact lenses
The resemblance between him and his father was apparent; both had the same studious and impractical expression, and might have been professors on the same university faculty. He shook hands with Trask, assuring him of
the gratitude of the Court and Royal Family.

"You know, Simon is next in succession, after myself
and my little daughter," he said. "That's too close to take
chances with him." He turned to Bentrik. "I'm afraid this
is your last space adventure, Simon. You'll have to be a
spaceport spaceman from now on."

"I shan't be sorry," Princess Bentrik said. "And if
anybody owes Prince Trask gratitude, I do." She pressed
his hand warmly. "Prince Trask, my son wants to meet
you, very badly. He's ten years old, and he thinks Space
Vikings are romantic heroes."

"He should be one, for a while."

He should just see a planet Space Vikings had raided.

Most of the people at the upper end of the table were diplomats—ambassadors from Odin and Baldur and Isis and Ishtar and Aton and the other civilized worlds. No doubt they hadn't actually expected horns and a spike tail, or even tattooing and a nose-ring, but after all, Space Vikings were just some sort of Neobarbarians, weren't they? On the other hand, they had all seen views and gotten descriptions of the *Nemesis*, and had heard about the ship-action on Audhumla, and this Prince Trask—a Space Viking prince; that sounded civilized enough—had saved a life with only three other lives, one almost at an end, between it and the throne. And they had heard about the screen conversation with King Mikhyl. So they were affably courteous through the meal, and tried to get as close as possible to him in the procession to the throne-room.

King Mikhyl wore a golden crown topped by the planetary emblem, which must have weighed twice as much as a combat helmet, and fur-edged robes that would weigh more than a suit of space-armor. They weren't nearly as ornate, though, as the regalia of King Angus I of Gram. He rose to clasp Prince Bentrik's hand, calling him "dear cousin," and congratulating him on his gallant fight and fortunate escape. That knocks any court-martial talk on the head, Trask thought. He remained standing to shake hands with Trask, calling him "valued friend to me and my house." First person singular; that must be causing some lifted eyebrows.

Then the King sat down, and the rest of the roomful filed up onto the dais to be received, and finally it was over and the king rose and proceeded, followed by his immediate suite, between the bowing and curtsying court and out the wide doors. After a decent interval, Crown Prince Edvard escorted him and Prince Bentrik down the same route, the others falling in behind, and across the hall to the ballroom, where there was soft music and refreshments. It wasn't too unlike a court reception on Excalibur, except that the drinks and canapes were being dispensed by human servants.

He was wondering what sort of court functions Angus the First of Gram was holding by now.

After half an hour, a posse of court functionaries approached and informed him that it had pleased his Majesty to command Prince Trask to attend him in his private chambers. There was an audible gasp at this; both Prince Bentrik and the Crown Prince were trying not to grin too broadly. Evidently this didn't happen too often. He followed the functionaries from the ballroom, and the eyes of everybody else followed him.

Old King Mikhyl received him alone, in a small, comfortably shabby room behind vast ones of incredible splendor. He wore fur-lined slippers and a loose robe with a fur collar, and his little black cap-of-maintenance. He was standing when Trask entered; when the guards closed the door and left them alone, he beckoned Trask to a couple of chairs, with a low table, on which were decanters and glasses and cigars, between.

"It's a presumption on royal authority to summon you from the ballroom," he began, after they had seated themselves and filled glasses. "You are quite the cynosure, you know."

"I'm grateful to your Majesty. It's both comfortable and quiet here, and I can sit down. Your Majesty was the center of attention in the throne-room, yet I seemed to detect a look of relief as you left it."

"I try to hide it, as much as possible." The old King took off the little gold-circled cap and hung it on the back of his chair. "Majesty can be rather wearying, you know."

So he could come here and put it off. Trask felt that some gesture should be made on his own part. He unfastened the dress-dagger from his belt and laid it on the table. The King nodded.

"Now, we can be a couple of honest tradesmen, our ships closed for the evening, relaxing over our wine and tobacco," he said. "Eh, Goodman Lucas?"

It seemed like an initiation into a secret society whose ritual he must guess at step by step.

"Right, Goodman Mikhyl."

They lifted their glasses to each other and drank; Goodman Mikhyl offered cigars, and Goodman Lucas held a light for him.

"I hear a few hard things about your trade, Goodman Lucas."

"All true, and mostly understated. We're professional murderers and robbers, as one of my fellow tradesmen says. The worst of it is that robbery and murder become just that: a trade, like servicing robots or selling groceries."

"Yet you fought two other Space Vikings to cover my cousin's crippled *Victrix*. Why?"

So he must tell his tale, so worn and smooth, again. King Mikhyl's cigar went out while he listened to it.

"And you have been hunting him ever since? And now, you can't be sure whether you killed him or not?"

"I'm afraid I didn't. The man in the screen is the only man Dunnan can really trust. One or the other would stay wherever he has his base all the time."

"And when you do kill him; what then?"

"I'll go on trying to make a civilized planet of Tanith. Sooner or later, I'll have one quarrel too many with King Angus, and then we will be our Majesty Lucas the First of Tanith, and we will sit on a throne and receive our subjects, and I'll be damned glad when I can get my crown off and talk to a few men who call me 'shipmate,' instead of 'your Majesty.' "

"Well, it would violate ethics for me to advise a subject to renounce his sovereign, of course, but that might be an excellent thing. You met the ambassador from Ithavoll at dinner, did you not? Three centuries ago, Ithavoll was a colony of Marduk—it seems we can't afford colonies, any more—and it seceded from us. Ithavoll was then a planet like your Tanith seems to be. Today, it is a civilized world, and one of Marduk's best friends. You know, sometimes I think a few lights are coming on again, here and there in the Old Federation. If so, you Space Vikings are helping to light them."

"You mean the planets we use as bases, and the things we teach the locals?"

"That, too, of course. Civilization needs civilized technologies. But they have to be used for civilized ends. Do you know anything about a Space Viking raid on Aton, about a century ago?"

"Six ships from Haulteclere; four destroyed, the other two returned damaged and without booty."

The King of Marduk nodded.

"That raid saved civilization on Aton. There were four

great nations; the two greatest were at the brink of war, and the others were waiting to pounce on the exhausted victor and them fight each other for the spoils. The Space Vikings forced them to unite. Out of that temporary alliance came the League of Common Defense, and from that the Planetary Republic. The Republic's a dictatorship, now, and just between Goodman Mikhyl and Goodman Lucas it's a damned nasty one and our Majesty's Government doesn't like it at all. It will be smashed, those kind of things usually are, sooner or later, but they'll never go back to divided sovereignty and nationalism again. The Space Vikings frightened them out of that when the dangers inherent in it couldn't. Maybe this man Dunnan will do the same for us on Marduk."

"You have troubles?"

"You've seen decivilized planets. How does it happen?"

"I know how it's happened on a good many: War. Destruction of cities and industries. Survivors among ruins, too busy keeping their own bodies alive to try to keep civilization alive. Then they lose all knowledge of how to be civilized."

"That's catastrophic decivilization. There is also decivilization by erosion, and while it's going on, nobody notices it. Everybody is proud of their civilization, their wealth and culture. But trade is falling off; fewer ships come in each year. So there is boastful talk about planetary self-sufficiency; who needs off-planet trade anyhow? Everybody seems to have money, but the government is always broke. Deficit spending—and always more vital social services for which the government has to spend money. The most vital one, of course, is buying votes to keep the government in power. And it gets harder for the government to get anything done.

"The soldiers are sloppier at drill, and their uniforms and weapons aren't taken care of. The non-coms are insolent. And more and more parts of the city are dangerous at night, and then even in the daytime. And it's been years since a new building went up, and the old ones aren't being repaired any more."

Trask closed his eyes. Again, he could feel the mellow sun of Gram on his back, and hear the laughing voices on the lower terrace, and he was talking to Lothar Ffayle and Rovard Grauffis and Alex Gorram and Cousin Nikkolay and Otto Harkaman. He said:

"And finally, nobody bothers fixing anything up. And the power-reactors stop, and nobody seems to be able to get them started again. It hasn't gotten that far on the Sword-Worlds yet."

"It hasn't here, either. Yet." Goodman Mikhyl slipped away; King Mikhyl VIII looked across the low table at his guest. "Prince Trask, have you heard of a man named Zaspar Makann?"

"Occasionally. Nothing good about him."

"He is the most dangerous man on this planet," the King said. "And I can make nobody believe it. Not even my son."

III

PRINCE BENTRIK'S ten-year-old son, Count Steven of Ravary, wore the uniform of an ensign of the Royal Navy; he was accompanied by his tutor, an elderly Navy captain. They both stopped in the doorway of Trask's suite, and the boy saluted smartly.

"Permission to come aboard, sir?" he asked.

"Welcome aboard, Count; Captain. Belay the ceremony and find seats; you're just in time for second breakfast."

As they sat down, he aimed his ultraviolet light-pencil at a serving robot. Unlike Mardukan robots which looked like surrealist conceptions of Pre-Atomic armored knights, it was a smooth ovoid floating a few inches from the floor on its own contragravity; as it approached, its top opened like a bursting beetle-shell and hinged trays of food swung out. The boy looked at it in fascination.

"Is that a Sword-World robot, sir, or did you capture it somewhere?"

"It's one of our own." He was pardonably proud; it had been built on Tanith a year before. "Has an ultrasonic dishwasher underneath, and it does some cooking on top, at the back."

The elderly captain was, if anything, even more impressed than his young charge. He knew what all went into it, and he had some conception of the society that would develop things like that.

"I take it you don't use many human servants, with robots like that," he said.

"Not many. We're all low-population planets, and nobody wants to be a servant."

"We have too many people on Marduk, and all of them want soft jobs as nobles' servants," the captain said. "Those that want any kind of jobs."

"You need all your people for fighting-men, don't you?" the boy count asked.

"Well, we need a good many. The smallest of our ships will carry five hundred men; most of them around eight hundred."

The captain lifted an eyebrow. The complement of the *Victrix* had been three hundred, and she'd been a big ship. Then he nodded.

"Of course. Most of them are ground-fighters."

That started Count Steven off. Questions, about battles and raids and booty and the planets Trask had seen.

"I wish I were a Space Viking!"

"Well, you can't be, Count Ravary. You're an officer of the Royal Navy. You're supposed to fight Space Vikings."

"I won't fight you."

"You'd have to, if the King commanded," the old captain told him.

"No. Prince Trask is my friend. He saved my father's life."

"And I won't fight you, either, Count. We'll make a lot of fireworks, and then we'll each go home and claim victory. How would that be?"

"I've heard of things like that," the captain said. "We had a war with Odin, seventy years ago, that was mostly that sort of battles."

"Beside, the King is Prince Trask's friend, too," the

boy insisted. "Father and Mummy heard him say so, right on the Throne. Kings don't lie when they're on the Throne, do they?"

"Good Kings don't," Trask told him.

"Ours is a good King," the young Count of Ravary declared proudly. "I would do anything my King commanded. Except fight Prince Trask. My house owes Prince Trask a debt."

Trask nodded approvingly. "That's the way a Sword-World noble would talk, Count Steven," he said.

The Board of Inquiry, that afternoon, was more like a small and very sedate cocktail party. An Admiral Shefter, who seemed to be very high high-brass, presided while carefully avoiding the appearance of doing so. Alvyn Karffard and Vann Larch and Paytrik Morland were there from the *Nemesis,* and Bentrik and several of the officers from the *Victrix,* and there were a couple of Naval Intelligence officers, and somebody from Operational Planning, and from Ship Construction and Research & Development. They chatted pleasantly and in a deceptively random manner for a while. Then Shefter said:

"Well, there's no blame or censure of any sort for the way Commodore Prince Bentrik was surprised. That couldn't have been avoided, at the time." He looked at the Research & Development officer. "It shouldn't be allowed to happen many more times, though."

"Not many more, sir. I'd say it'll take my people a month, and then the time it'll take to get all the ships equipped as they come in."

Ship Construction didn't think that would take too long.

"We'll see to it that you get full information on the new submarine detection system, Prince Trask," the Admiral said.

"You gentlemen understand you'll have to keep it under your helmets, though," one of the Intelligence men added. "If it got out that we were informing Space Vikings about our technical secrets . . ." He felt the back of his neck in a way that made Trask suspect that beheadment was the customary form of execution on Marduk.

"We'll have to find out where the fellow has his base," Operational Planning said. "I take it, Prince Trask, that you're not going to assume that he was on his flagship when you blew it, and just put paid to him and forget him?"

"Oh, no. I'm assuming that he wasn't. I don't believe he and Ormm went anywhere on the same ship, after he came out here and established a base. I think one of them would stay home all the time."

"Well, we'll give you everything we have on them," Shefter promised. "Most of that is classified and you'll have to keep quiet about it, too. I just skimmed over the summary of what you gave us; I daresay we'll both get a lot of new information. Have you any idea at all where he might be based, Prince Trask?"

"Only that we think it's a non-Terra-type planet." He told them about Dunnan's heavy purchases of air-and-water recycling equipment and carniculture and hydroponic material. "That, of course, helps a great deal."

"Yes, there are only about five million planets in the former Federation space-volume that are inhabitable in artificial environment. Including a few completely covered by seas, where you could put in underwater dome cities if you had the time and material."

One of the Intelligence officers had been nursing a glass with a tiny remnant of cocktail in it. He downed it suddenly, filled the glass again, and glowered at it in silence for a while. Then he drank it briskly and refilled it.

"What I should like to know," he said, "is how this double obscenity of a Dunnan knew we'd have a ship on Audhumla just when we did," he said. "Your talking about underwater dome-cities reminded me of it. I don't think he just pulled that planet out of a hat and then went there prepared to sit on the bottom of the ocean for a year to a year and a half waiting for something to turn up. I think he knew the *Victrix* was coming to Audhumla, and just about when."

"I don't like that, Commodore," Shefter said.

"You think I do, sir?" the Intelligence officer countered. "There it is, though. We all have to face it."

"We do," Shefter agreed. "Get on it, Commodore, and I don't need to caution you to screen everybody you put onto it very carefully." He looked at his own glass; it had a bare thimbleful in the bottom. He replenished it slowly and carefully. "It's been a long time since the Navy's had anything like this to worry about." He turned to Trask. "I suppose I can get in touch with you at the Palace whenever I must?"

"Well, Prince Trask and I have been invited as house-guests at Prince Edvard's, I mean Baron Cragdale's, hunting-lodge," Bentrik said. "We'll be going there directly from here."

"Ah," Admiral Shefter smiled slightly. Beside not

having three horns and a spiked tail, this Space Viking was definitely persona grata with the Royal Family. ''Well, we'll keep in contact, Prince Trask.''

The hunting-lodge where Crown Prince Edvard was simple Baron Cragdale lay at the head of a sharply-sloping mountain valley down which a river tumbled. Mountains rose on either side in high scarps, some topped with perpetual snow, glaciers curling down from them. The lower ranges were forested, as was the valley between, and there was a red-mauve alpenglow on the great peak that rose from the head of the valley. For the first time in over a year, Elaine was with him, silently clinging to him to see the beauty of it through his eyes. He had thought that she had gone from him forever.

The hunting-lodge itself was not quite what a Sword-Worlder would expect a hunting-lodge to be. At first sight, from the air, it looked like a sundial, a slender tower rising like a gnomen above a circle of low buildings and formal gardens. The boat landed at the foot of it, and he and Prince and Princess Bentrik and the young Count of Ravary and his tutor descended. Immediately, they were beset by a flurry of servants; the second boat, with the Bentrik servants and their luggage was circling in to land. Elaine, he discovered, wasn't with him any more, and then he was separated from the Bentriks and was being floated up an inside shaft on a lifter-car. More servants installed him in his rooms, unpacked his cases, drew his bath and even tried to help him take it, and fussed over him while he dressed.

There were over a score for dinner. Bentrik had warned him that he'd find some odd types; maybe he meant that they wouldn't all be nobles. Among the commoners there were some professors, mostly social sciences, a labor-leader, a couple of Representatives and a member of the Chamber of Delegates, and a couple of social workers, whatever that meant.

His own table companion was a Lady Valerie Alvarath. She was beautiful—black hair, and almost startling blue eyes, a combination unusual in the Sword-Worlds—and she was intelligent, or at least cleverly articulate. She was introduced as the lady-companion of the Crown Prince's daughter. When he asked where the daughter was, she laughed.

"She won't be helping entertain visiting Space Vikings for a long time, Prince Trask. She is precisely eight years old; I saw her getting ready for bed before I came down here. I'll look in on her after dinner."

Then the Crown Princess Melanie, on his other hand, asked him some question about Sword-World court etiquette. He stuck to generalities, and what he could remember from a presentation at the court of Excalibur during his student days. These people had a monarchy since before Gram had been colonized; he wasn't going to admit that Gram's had been established since he went off-planet. The table was small enough for everybody to hear what he was saying and to feed questions to him. It lasted all through the meal, and continued when they adjourned for coffee in the library.

"But what about your form of government, your social structure, that sort of thing?" somebody, impatient with the artificialities of the court, wanted to know.

"Well, we don't use the word government very much," he replied. "We talk a lot about authority and sovereignty, and I'm afraid we burn entirely too much powder over it, but government always seems to us like sovereignty interfering in matters that don't concern it. As long as sovereignty maintains a reasonable semblance of good public order and makes the more serious forms of crime fairly hazardous for the criminals, we're satisfied."

"But that's just negative. Doesn't the government do anything positive for the people?"

He tried to explain the Sword-World feudal system to them. It was hard, he found, to explain something you have taken for granted all your life to somebody who is quite unfamiliar with it.

"But the government—the sovereignty, since you don't like the other word—doesn't do anything for the people!" one of the professors objected. "It leaves all the social services to the whim of the individual lord or baron."

"And the people have no voice at all; why, that's tyranny," an Assemblyman added.

He tried to explain that the people had a very distinct and commanding voice, and that barons and lords who wanted to stay alive listened attentively to it. The Assemblyman changed his mind; that wasn't tyranny, it was anarchy. And the professor was still insistent about who performed the social services.

"If you mean schools and hospitals and keeping the city clean, the people do that for themselves. The government, if you want to think of it as that, just sees to it that nobody's shooting at them while they're doing it."

"That isn't what Professor Pullwell means, Lucas. He means old-age pensions," Prince Bentrik said. "Like this thing Zaspar Makann's whooping for."

He'd heard about that, on the voyage from Audhumla.

Every person on Marduk would be retired on an adequate pension after thirty years' regular employment or at the age of sixty. When he had wanted to know where the money would come from, he had been told that there would be a sales-tax, and that the pensions must all be spent within thirty days, which would stimulate business, and the increased business would provide tax-money to pay the pensions.

"We have a joke about three Gilgameshers space-wrecked on an uninhabited planet," he said. "Ten years later, when they were rescued, all three were immensely wealthy, from trading hats with each other. That's about the way this thing will work."

One of the lady social workers bristled; it wasn't right to make derogatory jokes about racial groups. One of the professors harrumphed; wasn't a parallel at all, the Self-Sustaining Rotary Pension Plan was perfectly feasible. With a shock, Trask recalled that he was a professor of economics.

Alvyn Karffard wouldn't need any twenty ships to loot Marduk. Just infiltrate it with about a hundred smart confidence-men and inside a year they'd own everything on it.

That started them all off on Zaspar Makann, though. Some of them thought he had a few good ideas, but was damaging his own case by extremism. One of the wealthier nobles said that he was a reproach to the ruling-class; it was their fault that people like Makann could gain a following. One old gentleman said that maybe the Gilgameshers were to blame, themselves, for some of the animosity toward them. He was immediately set upon by all the others and verbally torn to pieces on the spot.

Trask didn't feel it proper to quote Goodman Mikhyl to

this crowd. He took the responsibility upon himself for saying:

"From what I've heard of him, I think he's the most serious threat to civilized society on Marduk."

They didn't call him crazy, after all he was a guest, but they didn't ask him what he meant, either. They merely told him that Makann was a crackpot with a contemptible following of half-wits, and just wait till the election and see what happened.

"I'm inclined to agree with Prince Trask," Bentrik said soberly. "And I'm afraid the election results will be a shock to us, not to Makann."

He hadn't talked that way on the ship. Maybe he'd been looking around and doing some thinking, since he got back. He might have been talking to Goodman Mikhyl, too. There was a screen in the room. He nodded toward it.

"He's speaking at a rally on the Pelple's Welfare Party at Drepplin, now," he said. "May I put it on, to show you what I mean?"

When the Crown Prince assented, he snapped on the screen and twiddled at the selector.

A face looked out of it. The features weren't Andray Dunnan's—the mouth was wider, the cheekbones broader, the chin more rounded. But his eyes were Dunnan's, as Trask had seen them on the terrace of Karvall House. Mad eyes. His high-pitched voice screamed:

"Our beloved sovereign is a prisoner! He is surrounded by traitors! The Ministeries are full of them! They are all traitors! The bloodthirsty reactionaries of the falsely so-called Crown Loyalist Party! The grasping conspiracy of the interstellar bankers! The dirty Gilgameshers! They are all leagued together in an unholy conspiracy! And now this Space Viking, this bloody-handed monster from the Sword-Worlds . . ."

"Shut the horrible man off," somebody was yelling, in competition with the hypnotic scream of the speaker.

The trouble was, they couldn't. They could turn off the screen, but Zaspar Makann would go on screaming, and millions all over the planet would still hear him. Bentrik twiddled the selector. The voice stuttered briefly, and then came echoing out of the speaker, but this time the pickup was somewhere several hundred feet above a great open park. It was densely packed with people, most of them wearing clothes a farm-tramp on Gram wouldn't be found dead in, but here and there among them were blocks of men in what was almost but not quite military uniform, each with a short and thick swagger-stick with a knobbed head. Across the park, in the distance, the head and shoulders of Zaspar Makann loomed a hundred feet high in a huge screen. When ever he stopped for breath, a shout would go up, beginning with the blocks of uniformed men:

"Makann! Makann! Makann the Leader! Makann to Power!"

"You even let him have a private army?" he asked the Crown Prince.

"Oh, those silly buffoons and their musical-comedy uniforms," the Crown Prince shrugged. "They aren't armed."

"Not visibly," he granted. "Not yet."

"I don't know where they'd get arms."

"No, your Highness," Prince Bentrik said. "Neither do I. That's what I'm worried about."

IV

HE SUCCEEDED, the next morning, in convincing everybody that he wanted to be alone for a while, and was sitting
alone in a garden, watching the rainbows in the mist of a
big waterfall across the valley. Elaine would have liked
that, but she wasn't with him, now.

Then he realized that somebody was speaking to him, in
a small, bashful voice. He turned, and saw a little girl in
shorts and a sleeveless jacket, holding in her arms a
long-haired blond puppy with big ears and appealing eyes.

"Hello, both of you," he said.

The puppy wriggled and tried to lick the girl's face.

"Don't, Mopsy. We want to talk to this gentleman,"
she said. "Are you really and truly the Space Viking?"

"Really and truly. And who are you two?"

"I'm Myrna. And this is Mopsy."

"Hello, Myrna. Hello, Mopsy."

Hearing his name, the puppy wriggled again and dropped from the child's arms; after a brief hesitation, he came
over and jumped onto Trask's lap, licking his face. While
he petted the dog, the girl came over and sat on the bench
beside him.

"Mopsy likes you," she said. After a moment, she
added: "I like you, too."

"And I like you," he said. "Would you want to be my
girl? You know, a Space Viking has to have a girl on every
planet. How would you like to be my girl on Marduk?"

Myrna thought that over carefully. "I'd like to, but I

couldn't. You see, I'm going to have to be Queen, some day."

"Oh?"

"Yes. Grandpa is King now, and when he's through being King, Pappa will have to be King, and then when he's through being King, I can't be King because I'm a girl, so I'll have to be Queen. And I can't be anybody's girl, because I'm going to have to marry somebody I don't know, for reasons of state." She thought some more, and lowered her voice. "I'll tell you a secret. I am a Queen now."

"Oh, you are?"

She nodded. "We are Queen, in our own right, of our Royal Bedroom, our Royal Playroom, and our Royal Bathroom. And Mopsy is our faithful subject."

"Is your Majesty absolute ruler of these domains?"

"No," she said disgustedly. "We must at all times defer to our Royal Ministers, just like Grandpa has to. That means, I have to do just what they tell me to. That's Lady Valerie, and Margot, and Dame Eunice, and Sir Thomas. But Grandpa says they are good and wise ministers. Are you really a Prince. I didn't know Space Vikings were Princes."

"Well, my King says I am. And I am ruler of my planet, and I'll tell you a secret. I don't have to do what anybody tells me."

"Gee! Are you a tyrant? You're awfully big and strong. I'll bet you've slain just hundreds of cruel and wicked enemies."

"Thousands, your Majesty."

He wished that weren't literally true; he didn't know how many of them had been little girls like Myrna and little dogs like Mopsy. He found that he was holding both of them tightly. The girl was saying: "But you feel bad about it." These infernal children must be telepaths!

"A Space Viking who is also a Prince must do many things he doesn't want to do."

"I know. So does a Queen. I hope Grandpa and Pappa don't get through being King for just years and years." She looked over his shoulder. "Oh! And now I suppose I've got to do something else I don't want to. Lessons, I bet."

He followed her eyes. The girl who had been his dinner companion was approaching; she wore a wide sunshade hat, and a gown that trailed filmy gauze like sunset-colored mist. There was another woman, in the garb of an upper servant, with her.

"Lady Valerie and who else?" he whispered.

"Margot. She's my nurse. She's awful strict, but she's nice."

"Prince Trask, has her Highness been bothering you?" Lady Valerie asked.

"Oh, far from it." He rose, still holding the funny little dog. "But you should say, her Majesty. She has informed me that she is sovereign of three princely domains. And of one dear loving subject." He gave the subject back to the sovereign.

"You should not have told Prince Trask that," Lady Valerie chided. "When your Majesty is outside her domains, your Majesty must remain incognito. Now, your Majesty must go with the Minister of the Bedchamber; the Minister of Education awaits an audience."

"Arithmetic, I bet. Well, goodbye, Prince Trask. I hope I can see you again. Say goodbye, Mopsy."

She went away with her nurse, the little dog looking back over her shoulder.

"I came out to enjoy the gardens alone," he said, "and now I find I'd rather enjoy them in company. If your Ministerial duties do not forbid, could you be the company?"

"But gladly, Prince Trask. Her Majesty will be occupied with serious affairs of state. Square root. Have you seen the grottoes? They're down this way."

That afternoon, one of the gentlemen-attendants caught up with him; Baron Cragdale would be gratified if Prince Trask could find time to talk with him privately. Before they had talked more than a few minutes, however, Baron Cragdale abruptly became Crown Prince Edvard.

"Prince Trask, Admiral Shefter tells me that you and he are having informal discussions about cooperation against this mutual enemy of ours, Dunnan. This is fine; it has my approval, and the approval of Prince Vandarvant, the Prime Minister, and, I might add, that of Goodman Mikhyl. I think it ought to go further, though. A formal treaty between Tanith and Marduk would be greatly to the advantage of both."

"I'd be inclined to think so, Prince Edvard. But aren't you proposing marriage on rather short acquaintance? It's only been fifty hours since the *Nemesis* orbited in here."

"Well, we knew a bit about you and your planet beforehand. There's a large Gilgamesher colony here. You have a few on Tanith, haven't you? Well, anything one Gilgamesher knows, they all find out, and ours are cooperative with Naval intelligence."

That would be why Andray Dunnan was having no

dealings with Gilgameshers. It would also be what Zaspar Makann meant when he ranted about the Gilgamesh Interstellar Conspiracy.

"I can see where an arrangement like that would be mutually advantageous. I'd be quite in favor of it. Cooperation against Dunnan, of course, and reciprocal traderights on each other's trade planets, and direct trade between Marduk and Tanith, and Beowulf and Amaterasu would come into it, too. Does this also have the approval of the Prime Minister and the King?"

"Goodman Mikhyl's in favor of it; there's a distinction between him and the King, as you'll have noticed. The King can't be in favor of anything till the Assembly or the Chancellor express an opinion. Prince Vandarvant favors it personally; as Prime Minister, he is reserving his opinion. We'll have to get the support of the Crown Loyalist party before he can take an unequivocal position."

"Well, Baron Cragdale; speaking as Baron Trask of Traskon, suppose we just work out a rough outline of what this treaty ought to be, and then consult, unofficially, with a few people whom you can trust, and see what can be done about presenting it to the proper government officials . . ."

The Prime Minister came to Cragdale that evening, heavily incognito and accompanied by several leaders of the Crown Loyalist Party. In principle, they all favored a treaty with Tanith. Politically, they had doubts. Not before the election; too controversial a subject. "Controversial," it appeared, was the dirtiest dirty-name anything could be called on Marduk. It would alienate the labor vote; they'd think increased imports would threaten employment in Mardukan industries. Some of the interstellar trading companies would like a chance at the Tanith planets; others would resent Tanith ships being given access to theirs. And Zaspar Makann's party were already shrieking protests about the *Nemesis* being repaired by the Royal Navy.

And a couple of Assemblymen who inclined toward Makann had introduced a resolution calling for the court-martial of Prince Bentrik and an investigation of the loyalty of Admiral Shefter. And somebody else, probably a stooge of Makann's, was claiming that Bentrik had sold the *Victrix* to the Space Vikings and that the films of the battle of Audhumla were fakes, photographed in minia-ture at the Navy Moonbase.

Admiral Shefter, when Trask flew in to see him the next day, was contemptuous about this last.

"Ignore the whole bloody thing; we get something like that before every general election. On this planet, you can always kick the Gilgameshers and the Armed Forces with impunity, neither have votes and neither can kick back. The whole thing'll be forgotten the day after the election. It always is."

"That's if Makann doesn't win the election," Trask said.

"That's no matter who wins the election. They can't any of them get along without the Navy, and they bloody well know it."

Trask wanted to know if Intelligence had been getting anything.

"Not on how Dunnan found out the *Victrix* had been ordered to Audhumla, no," Shefter said. "There wasn't any secrecy about it; at least a thousand people, from myself down to the shoeshine boys, could have known about it as soon as the order was taped. We'll have to start screwing down some lids around here.

"As for the list of ships you gave me, yes. One of them puts in to this planet regularly; she spaced out from here only yesterday morning. The *Honest Horris*."

"Well, great Satan, haven't you done anything?"

"I don't know if there's anything we can do. Oh, we're investigating, but . . . You see, this ship first showed up here four years ago, commanded by some kind of a Neobarb, not a Gilgamesher, named Horris Sasstroff. He claimed to be from Skathi; the locals there have a few ships. The Space Vikings had a base on Skathi about a hundred or so years ago. Naturally, the ship had no papers. Tramp trading among the Neobarbs, it might be years before you'd put in on a planet where they'd ever heard of ship's papers.

"The ship seems to have been in bad shape, probably abandoned on Skathi as junk a century ago and tinkered up by the locals. She was in here twice, according to the commercial shipping records, and the second time she was in too bad shape to be moved out, and Sasstroff couldn't pay to have her rebuilt, so she was libelled for spaceport charges and sold. Some one-lung trading company bought her and fixed her up a little; they went bankrupt in a year or so, and she was bought by another small company, Star-traders, Ltd., and they've been using her on a milk-run to and from Gimli. They seem to be a legitimate outfit, but we're looking into them. We're looking for Sasstroff, too, but we haven't been able to find him."

"If you have a ship out Gimli way, you might find out if anybody there knows anything about her. You may discover that she hasn't been going there at all."

"We might, at that," Shefter agreed. "We'll just find out."

Everybody at Cragdale knew about the projected treaty with Tanith by the morning after Trask's first conversation with Prince Edvard on the subject. The Queen of the Royal Bedroom, the Royal Playroom and the Royal Bathroom was insisting that her domains should have a treaty with Tanith, too.

It was beginning to look to Trask as though that would be the only treaty he'd sign on Marduk, and he was having his doubts about that.

"Do you think it would be wise?" he asked Lady Valerie Alvarath. The Queen of three rooms and one four-footed subject had already decreed that Lady Valerie should be the Space Viking Prince's girl on the planet of Marduk. "If it got out, those People's Welfare lunatics would pick it up and twist it into evidence of some kind of a sinister plot."

"Oh, I believe her Majesty could sign a treaty with Prince Trask," her Majesty's Prime Minister decided. "But it would have to be kept very secret."

"Gee!" Myrna's eyes widened. "A real secret treaty; just like the wicked rulers of the old dictatorship!" She hugged her subject ecstatically. "I'll bet Grandpa doesn't even have any secret treaties!"

In a few days, everybody on Marduk knew that a treaty with Tanith was being discussed. If they didn't, it was no fault of Zaspar Makann's party, who seemed to command a disconcertingly large number of telecast stations, and who drenched the ether with horror-stories of Space Viking atrocities and denunciations of carefully unnamed traitors surrounding the King and the Crown Prince who were about to betray Marduk to rapine and plunder. The leak evidently did not come from Cragdale, for it was generally believed that Trask was still at the Royal Palace in Malverton. At least, that was where the Makannists were demonstrating against him.

He watched such a demonstration by screen; the pickup was evidently on one of the landing-stages of the palace, overlooking the wide parks surrounding it. They were packed almost solid with people, surging forward toward the thin cordon of police. The front of the mob looked like a checkerboard—a block in civilian dress, than a block in the curiously effeminate-looking uniforms of Zaspar Makann's People's Watchmen, then more in ordinary garb, and more People's Watchmen. Over the heads of the crowds, at intervals, floated small contragravity lifters on which were mounted the amplifiers that were bellowing:

"SPACE VI-KING—GO HOME! SPACE VI-KING—GO HOME!"

The police stood motionless, at parade rest; the mob surged closer. When they were fifty yards away, the blocks of People's Watchmen ran forward, then spread out until they formed a line six deep across the entire front; other blocks, from the rear, pushed the ordinary demonstrators aside and took their place. Hating them more every second, Trask grudged approval of a smart and disciplined maneuver. How long, he wondered, had they been drilling in that sort of tactics? Without stopping, they continued their advance on the police, who had now shifted their stance.

"SPACE VI-KING—GO HOME! SPACE VI-KING—GO HOME!"

"Fire!" he heard himself yelling. "Don't let them get any closer; fire now!"

They had nothing to fire with; they had only truncheons, no better weapons than the knobbed swagger-sticks of the People's Watchmen. They simply disappeared, after a brief flurry of blows, and the Makann storm-troopers continued their advance.

And that was that. The gates of the Palace were shut; the mob, behind a front of Makann People's Watchmen, surged up to them and stopped. The loudspeakers bellowed on, reiterating their four-word chant.

"Those police were murdered," he said. "They were murdered by the man who ordered them out there unarmed."

"That would be Count Naydnayr, the Minister of Security," somebody said, as though to rebuke him.

"Then he's the one you want to hang for it."

"What else would you have done?" Crown Prince Edvard challenged.

"Put up about fifty combat-cars. Drawn a deadline, and opened a machine-gun fire as soon as the mob crossed it, and kept on firing till the survivors turned tail and ran. Then sent out more cars, and shot everybody wearing a People's Watchmen uniform, all over town. Inside forty-eight hours, there'd be no People's Welfare party, and no Zaspar Makann either."

The Crown Prince's face stiffened. "That may be the way you do things in the Sword-Worlds, Prince Trask. It's not the way we do things here on Marduk. Our government does not propose to be guilty of shedding the blood of its people.''

He had it on the tip of his tongue to retort that if they didn't, the people would end by shedding theirs. Instead, he said softly:

"I'm sorry, Prince Edvard. You had a wonderful civilization here on Marduk. You could have made almost anything of it. But it's too late now. You've torn down the gates; the barbarians are in.''

V

THE COLORED turbulence faded into the gray of hyperspace; five hundred hours to Tanith. Guatt Kirbey was securing his control-panel, happy to return to his music. And Vann Larch would go back to his paints and brushes, and Alvyn Karffard to the working model of whatever it was he had left unfinished when the *Nemesis* had emerged at the end of the jump from Audhumla.

Trask went to the index of the ship's library and punched for *History, Old Terran*. There was plenty of that, thanks to Otto Harkaman. Then he punched for *Hitler, Adolf*. Harkaman was right; anything that could happen in a human society had already happened, in one form or another, somewhere and at some time. Hitler could help him understand Zaspar Makann.

By the time the ship came out, with the yellow sun of Tanith in the middle of the screen, he knew a great deal about Hitler, occasionally referred to as Schicklegruber, and he understood, with sorrow, how the lights of civilization on Marduk were going out.

Beside the *Lamia*, stripped of her Dillinghams and crammed with heavy armament and detection instruments, the *Space-Scourge* and the *Queen Flavia* were on off-planet watch. There were half a dozen other ships on orbit just above atmosphere; a Gilgamesher, one of the Gram-Marduk freighters, a couple of freelance Space Vikings, and a new and unfamiliar ship. When he asked the moonbase who she was, he was told that she was the *Sun-Goddess*, Amaterasu. That was, by almost a year, better than he had expected of them. Otto Harkaman was out in the *Corisande*, raiding, trading, and visiting the trade-planets.

He found his cousin, Nikkolay Trask, at Rivington; when he inquired about Traskon, Nikkolay cursed.

"I don't know anything about Traskon; I haven't anything to do with Traskon, any more. Traskon is now the personal property of our well-loved—very well-loved—Queen Evita. The Trasks don't own enough land on Gram now for a family cemetery. You see what you did?" he added bitterly.

"You needn't rub it in, Nikkolay. If I'd stayed on Gram, I'd have helped put Angus on the throne, and it would have been about the same in the end."

"It could be a lot different," Nikkolay said. "You could bring your ships and men back to Gram and put yourself on the throne."

"No; I'll never go back to Gram. Tanith's my planet, now. But I will renounce my allegiance to Angus. I can trade on Morglay or Joyeuse or Flamberge just as easily."

"You won't have to; you can trade with Newhaven and

Bigglersport. Count Lionel and Duke Joris are both defying Angus; they've refused to furnish him men, they've driven out his tax collectors, those they haven't hanged, and they're building ships of their own. Angus is building ships, too. I don't know whether he's going to use them to fight Bigglersport and Newhaven, or attack you, but there's going to be a war before another year's out.''

The *Goodhope* and the *Speedwell,* he found, had gone back to Gram. They were commanded by men who had come into favor at the court of King Angus recently. The *Black Star* and the *Queen Flavia*—whose captain had contemptuously ignored an order from Gram to rechristen her *Queen Evita*—had remained. They were his ships, not King Angus'. The captain of the merchantman from Wardshaven now on orbit refused to take a cargo to Newhaven; he had been chartered by King Angus, and he was taking orders from nobody else.

"All right," Trask told him. "This is your last voyage here. You bring that ship back under Angus of Wardshaven's charter and we'll fire on her."

Then he had the regalia he had worn in his last audiovisual to Angus dusted off. At first, he had decided to proclaim himself King of Tanish. Lord Valpry, Baron Rathmore and his cousin all advised against it.

"Just call yourself Prince of Tanith," Valpry said. "The title won't make any difference in your authority here, and if you do lay claim to the throne of Gram, nobody can say you're a foreign king trying to annex the planet."

He had no intention of doing anything of the kind, but Valpry was quite in earnest. He shrugged. The title meant nothing.

So he sat on his throne, as sovereign Prince of Tanith, and renounced his allegiance to "Angus, Duke of Wardshaven, self-styled King of Gram." They sent it back on the otherwise empty freighter. Another copy went to the Count of Newhaven, along with a cargo in the *Sun-Goddess*, the first non-Space-Viking ship into Gram from the Old Federation.

Seven hundred and fifty hours after the return of the *Nemesis*, the *Corisande II* emerged from her last micro-jump and immediately Harkaman began hearing of the Battle of Audhumla and the destruction of the *Yo-Yo* and the *Enterprise*. At first, he merely reported a successful raiding voyage, from which he was bringing rich booty. Oddly variegated booty, it was remarked, when he began itemizing it.

"Why, yes," he replied. "Second-hand booty. I raided Dagon for it."

Dagon was a Space Viking base planet, occupied by a character named Fedrig Barragon. A number of ships operated from it, including a couple commanded by Barragon's half-breed sons.

"Barragon's ships were raiding one of our planets," Harkaman said. "Ganpat. They looted a couple of cities, destroyed one, killed a lot of the locals. I found out about it from Captain Ravallo of the *Black Star*, on Indra; he'd just been from Ganpat. Beowulf wasn't too far out of the way, so we put in there, and found the *Grendelsbane* just ready to space out." The *Grendelsbane* was the second of Beowulf's ships, sister to the *Viking's Gift*. "So she joined us, and the three of us went to Dagon. We blew up one of Barragon's ships, and put the other one down out of commission, and then we sacked his base. There was a Gilgamesher colony there; we didn't bother them. They'll spread the news of what we did, and why.''

"That should furnish Prince Viktor of Xochitl something to ponder," Trask said. "Where are the other ships, now?"

"The *Grendelsbane* went back to Beowulf; she'll stop at Amaterasu to do a little trading on the way. The *Black Star* went to Xochitl. Just a friendly visit, to say hello to Prince Viktor for you. Ravallo has a lot of audiovisuals we made during the Dagon Operation. Then she's going to Jagannath to visit Nikky Gratham.''

Harkaman approved his attitude and actions with regard to King Angus.

"We don't need to do business with the Sword-Worlds at all. We have our own industries, we can produce what we need, and we can trade with Beowulf and Amaterasu, and with Xochitl and Jagannath and Hoth, if we can make any sort of agreement with them; everybody agree to let everybody's else's trade-planets alone. It's too bad you couldn't get some kind of an agreement with Marduk.'' Harkaman regretted that for a few seconds, and then shrugged. ''Our grandchildren, if any, will probably be raiding Marduk.''

"You think it'll be like that?"

"Don't you? You were there; you saw what's happening. The barbarians are rising; they have a leader, and they're uniting. Every society rests on a barbarian base. The people who don't understand civilization, and wouldn't like it if they did. The hitchhikers. The people who create nothing, and who don't appreciate what others have created for them, and who think civilization is something that just exists and that all they need to do is enjoy what they can understand of it—luxuries, a high living standard, and easy work for high pay. Responsibilities? Phooey! What do they have a government for?''

Trask nodded.

''And now, the hitchhikers think they know more about the car than the people who designed it, so they're going to grab the controls. Zaspar Makann says they can, and he's the Leader.'' He poured a drink from a decanter that had been looted on Pushan; there was a planet where a republic had been overthrown in favor of a dictatorship four centuries ago, and the planetary dictatorship had fissioned into a dozen regional dictatorships, and now they were down to the peasant-village and handcraft-industry level. ''I don't understand it, though. I was reading about Hitler, on the way home. I wouldn't be surprised if Zaspar Makann had been reading about Hitler, too. He's using all Hitler's tricks. But Hitler came to power in a country which had been impoverished by a military defeat. Marduk hasn't fought a war in almost two generations, and that one was a farce.''

''It wasn't the war that put Hitler into power. It was the fact that the ruling class of his nation, the people who kept things running, were discredited. The masses, the homemade barbarians, didn't have anybody to take their responsibilities for them. What they have on Marduk is a ruling class that has been discrediting itself. A ruling class that's ashamed of its privileges and shirks its duties. A ruling class that has begun to believe that the masses are just as good as they are, which they manifestly are not. And a ruling class that won't use force to maintain its

191

position. And they have a democracy, and they are letting the enemies of democracy shelter themselves behind democratic safeguards.''

''We don't have any of this democracy in the Sword-Worlds, if that's the word for it,'' he said. And our ruling class aren't ashamed of their power, and our people aren't hitchhikers, and as long as they get decent treatment they don't try to run things. And we're not doing so well.''

The Morglay dynastic war of a couple of centuries ago, still sputtering and smoking. The Oaskarsan-Elmersan War on Durendal, into which Flamberge and now Joyeuse had intruded. And the situation on Gram, fast approaching critical mass. Harkaman nodded agreement.

''You know why? Our rulers are the barbarians among us. There isn't one of them—Napolyon of Flamberge, Rodolf of Excalibur, or Angus of about half of Gram —who is devoted to civilization or anything else outside himself, and that's the mark of the barbarian.''

''What are you devoted to, Otto?''

''You. You are my chieftain. That's another mark of the barbarian.''

Before he had left Marduk, Admiral Shefter had ordered a ship to Gimli to check on the *Honest Horris;* a few men and a pinnace would be left behind to contact any ship from Tanith. He sent Boake Valkanhayn off in the *Space-Scourge*.

Lionel of Newhaven's *Blue Comet* came in from Gram with a cargo of general merchandise. Her captain wanted fissionables and gadolinium; Count Lionel was building more ships. There was a rumor that Omfray of Glaspyth was laying claim to the throne of Gram, in the right of his great-grandmother's sister, who had been married to the great-grandfather of Duke Angus. It was a completely trivial and irrelevant claim, but the story was that it would be supported by men and ships furnished by King Konrad of Haulteclere.

Immediately, Baron Rathmore, Lord Valpry, Lothar Ffayle and the other Gram people began clamoring that he should go back with a fleet and seize the throne for himself. Harkaman, Valkanhayn, Karffard and the other Space Vikings were as vehement against it. Harkaman had the loss of the other *Corisande* on Durendal to remember, and the others wanted no part in Sword-World squabbles, and there was renewed agitation that he should start calling himself King of Tanith.

He refused to do either, which left both parties dissatisfied. So partisan politics had finally come to Tanith. Maybe that was another milestone of progress.

And there was the Treaty of Khepera, between the Princely State of Tanith, the Commonwealth of Beowulf, and the Planetary League of Amaterasu. The Kheperans agreed to allow bases on their planet, to furnish workers, and to send students to school on all three planets. Tanith, Beowulf and Amaterasu obligated themselves to joint defense of Khepera, to free trade among themselves, and to render one another armed assistance.

That *was* a milestone of progress, and no argument about it.

The *Space-Scourge* returned from Gimli, and Valkanhayn reported that nobody on the planet had ever seen or heard of the *Honest Horris*. They had found a Mardukan Navy ship's pinnace there, manned entirely by officers, some of them Navy Intelligence. According to them, the investigation into the activities of that ship had come to an impasse. The trading ostensible owners claimed, and had papers to prove it, that they had chartered her to a private trader, and he claimed, and had papers to prove it, that he was a citizen of the Planetary Republic of Aton, and as soon as they began questioning him, he was rescued by the Atonian ambassador, who lodged a vehement protest with the Mardukan Foreign Ministry. Immediately, the People's Welfare Party had leaped into the incident and branded the investigation as an unwarranted persecution of a national of a friendly power at the instigation of corrupt tools of the Gilgamesh Interstellar Conspiracy.

"So that's it," Valkanhayn finished. "It means they're having an election and they're afraid to antagonize anybody who might have a vote. So the Navy had to drop the investigation. Everybody on Marduk's scared of this Makann. You think there might be some tie-up between him and Dunnan?"

"The idea's occurred to me. Have there been any more raids on Marduk trade-planets since the Battle of Audhumla?"

"A couple. The *Bolide* was on Audhumla a while ago. There were a couple of Mardukan ships there, and they had the *Victrix* fixed up enough to do some fighting. They ran the *Bolide* out."

A study of the time between the destruction of the *Enterprise* and *Yo-Yo* and the appearance of the *Bolide* could give them a limiting radius around Audhumla. It did; seven hundred light-years, which also included Tanith.

So he sent Harkaman in the *Corisande* and Ravallo in the *Black Star* to visit the planets Marduk traded with, looking for Dunnan ships and exchanging information and assistance with the Royal Mardukan Navy. Almost at once, he regretted it; the next Gilgamesher into orbit on Tanith brought a story that Prince Viktor was collecting a fleet on Xochitl. He sent warnings off to Amaterasu and Beowulf and Khepera.

A ship came in from Bigglersport, a heavily armed chartered freighter. There was sporadic fighting in a dozen places on Gram, now—resistance to efforts on the part of King Angus to collect taxes, and raids by unidentified persons on estates confiscated from alleged traitors and given to Garvan Spasso, who had now been promoted from Baron to Count. And Rovard Grauffis was dead; poisoned, everybody said, either by Spasso or Queen Evita or both. Even with the threat from Xochitl, some of the former Wardshaven nobles began talking about sending ships to Gram.

Less than a thousand hours after he had left, Ravallo was back in the *Black Star*.

"I went to Gimli, and I wasn't there fifty hours before a Mardukan Navy ship came in. They were glad to see me; it saved them sending off a pinnace for Tanith. They had news for you, and a couple of passengers."

"Passengers?"

"Yes. You'll see who it is when they come down. And don't let anybody with side-whiskers and buttoned-up coats see them," Ravallo said. "What any of those people know gets all over the place before long."

The visitors were Lucile, Princess Bentrik, and her son, the young Count of Ravary. They dined with Trask; only Captain Ravallo was also present.

"I didn't want to leave my husband, and I didn't want to

come here and impose myself and Steven on you, Prince Trask," she began, "but he insisted. We spent the whole voyage to Gimli concealed in the captain's quarters; only a few of the officers knew we were aboard."

"Makann won the election. Is that it?" he asked. "And Prince Bentrik doesn't want to risk you and Steven being used as hostages?"

"That's it," she said. "He didn't really win the election, but he might as well have. Nobody has a majority of seats in the Chamber of Representatives but he's formed a coalition with several of the splinter parties, and I'm ashamed to say that a number of Crown Loyalist members—Crowd of Disloyalists, I call them—are voting with him, now. They've coined some ridiculous phrase about the 'wave of the future,' whatever that means."

"If you can't lick them, join them," Trask said.

"If you can't lick them, lick their boots," the Count of Ravary put in.

"My son is a trifle bitter," Princess Bentrik said. "I must confess to a trace of bitterness, too."

"Well, that's the Representatives," Trask said. "What about the rest of the government?"

"With the splinter-party and Disloyalist support, they got a majority of seats in the Delegates. Most of them would have indignantly denied, a month before, having any connection with Makann, but a hundred out of a hundred and twenty are his supporters. Makann, of course, is Chancellor."

"And who is Prime Minister?" he asked. "Andray Dunnan?"

She looked slightly baffled for an instant then said, "Oh. No. The Prime Minister is Crown Prince Edvard.

No; Baron Cragdale. That isn't a royal title, so by some kind of a fiction I can't pretend to understand he is not Prime Minister as a member of the Royal Family.''

"If you can't . . ." the boy started.

"Steven! I forbid you to say that about . . . Baron Cragdale. He believes, very sincerely, that the election was an expression of the will of the people, and that it is his duty to bow to it.''

He wished Otto Harkaman were there. He could probably name, without stopping for breath, a hundred great nations that went down into rubble because their rulers believed that they should bow instead of rule, and couldn't bring themselves to shed the blood of their people. Edvard would have been a fine and admirable man, as a little country baron. Where he was, he was a disaster.

He asked if the People's Watchmen had dragged their guns out from under the bed and started carrying them in public yet.

"Oh, yes. You were quite right; they were armed, all the time. Not just smallarms; combat vehicles and heavy weapons. As soon as the new government was formed, they were given status as a part of the Planetary Armed Forces. They have taken over every police station on the planet.''

"And the King?''

"Oh, he carries on, and shrugs and says, 'I just reign here.' What else can he do? We've been whittling down and filching away the powers of the Throne for the last three centuries.''

"What is Prince Bentrik doing, and why did he think there was danger that you two would be used as hostages?''

"He's going to fight," she said. "Don't ask me how, or what with. Maybe as a guerrilla in the mountains, I don't know. But even if he can't lick them, he won't join them. I wanted to stay with him and help him; he told me I could help him best by placing myself and Steven where he wouldn't be continually afraid for us."

"I wanted to stay," the boy said. "I could have fought with him. But he said that I must take care of Mother. And if he were killed, I must be able to avenge him."

"You talk like a Sword-Worlder; I told you that once before." He hesitated, then turned again to Princess Bentrik. "How is little Princess Myrna?" he asked, and then, trying to be casual, added, "and Lady Valerie?"

She seemed so clearly real and present to him, blue eyes and space-black hair, more real than Elaine had been to him for years.

"They're at Cragdale; they'll be safe there. I hope."

VI

ATTEMPTING TO conceal the presence on Tanith of Prince Bentrik's wife and son was pushing caution beyond necessity. Admitted that the news would leak back to Marduk via Gilgamesh, it was over seven hundred light-years to the latter and almost a thousand from there to the former. Better that Princess Lucile should enjoy Rivington society, such as it was, and escape, for a moment now and then, from anxiety about her husband. At ten—no, almost twelve; it had been a year and a half since Trask had left

Marduk—the boy Count of Ravary was more easily diverted. At last, he was among real Space Vikings, on a Space Viking planet, and he was trying to be everywhere and see everything at once. No doubt he would be imagining himself a Space Viking, returning to Marduk with a vast armada to rescue his father and the King from Zaspar Makann.

Trask was satisfied with that; as a host he left much to be desired. He had his worries, too, and all of them bore the same name: Prince Viktor of Xochitl. He went over with Manfred Ravallo everything the captain of the *Black Star* could tell him. He had talked once with Viktor; the lord of Xochitl had been coldly polite and non-committal. His subordinates had been frankly hostile. There had been five ships on orbit or landed at Viktor's spaceport beside the usual Gilgameshers and itinerant traders, two of them Viktor's own, and a big armed freighter had come in from Haulteclere as the *Black Star* was leaving. There was considerable activity at the shipyards and around the spaceport, as though in preparation for something on a large scale.

Xochitl was a thousand light-years from Tanith. He rejected immediately the idea of launching a preventative attack; his ships might reach Xochitl to find it undefended, and then return to find Tanith devastated. Things like that had happened in space-war. The only thing to do was sit tight, defend Tanith when Viktor attacked, and then counter attack if he had any ships left by that time. Prince Viktor was probably reasoning in the same way.

He had no time to think about Andray Dunnan, except, now and then, to wish that Otto Harkaman would stop thinking about him and bring the *Corisande* home. He needed that ship on Tanith, and the wits and courage of her commander.

More news—Gilgamesh sources—came in from Xochitl. There were only two ships, both armed merchantmen, on the planet. Prince Viktor had spaced out with the rest an estimated two thousand hours before the story reached him. That was twice as long as it would take the Xochitl armada to reach Tanith. He hadn't gone to Beowulf; that was only sixty-five hours from Tanith and they would have heard about it long ago. Or Amaterasu, or Khepera. How many ships he had was a question; not fewer than five, and possibly more. He could have slipped into the Tanith system and hidden his ships on one of the outer uninhabitable planets. He sent Valkanhayn and Ravallo microjumping their ships from one to another to check. They returned to report in the negative. At least, Viktor of Xochitl wasn't camped inside their own system, waiting for them to leave Tanith open to attack.

But he was somewhere, and up to nothing even resembling good, and there was no possible way of guessing when his ships would be emerging on Tanith. The only thing to do was wait for him. When he did, Trask was confident that he would emerge from hyperspace into serious trouble. He had the *Nemesis*, the *Space-Scourge*, the *Black Star* and *Queen Flavia*, the strongly rebuilt *Lamia*, and several independent Space Viking ships, among them the *Damnthing* of his friend Roger-fan-Morvill Esthersan, who had volunteered to stay and help in the defense. This, of course, was not pure altruism. If Viktor attacked and had his fleet blown to Em-See-Square, Xochitl would lie open and unprotected, and there was enough loot on Xochitl to cram everybody's ships. Everybody's ships who had ships when the Battle of Tanith was over, of course.

He was apologetic to Princess Bentrik:

"I'm very sorry you jumped out of Zaspar Makann's frying pan into Prince Viktor's fire," he began.

She laughed at that. "I'll take my chances on the fire. I seem to see a lot of good firemen around. If there is a battle you will see that Steven's in a safe place, won't you?"

"In a space attack, there are no safe places. I'll keep him with me."

The young Count of Ravery wanted to know which ship he would serve on when the attack came.

"Well, you won't be on any ship, Count. You'll be on my staff."

Two days later, the *Corisande* came out of hyperspace. Harkaman was guardedly non-committal by screen. Trask took a landing-craft and went out to meet the ship.

"Marduk doesn't like us, any more," Harkaman told him. "They have ships on all their trade planets, and they all have orders to fire on any, repeat any, Space Vikings, including the ships of the self-styled Prince of Tanith. I got this from Captain Garravay of the *Vindex*. After we were through talking, we fought a nice little ship-to-ship action for him to make films of. I don't think anybody could see anything wrong with it."

"This order came from Makann?"

"From the Admiral Commanding. He isn't your friend Shefter; Shefter retired on account of quote ill-health unquote. He is now in a quote hospital unquote."

"Where is Prince Bentrik?"

"Nobody knows. Charges of high treason were brought against him, and he just vanished. Gone underground, or secretly arrested and executed; take your choice."

He wondered just what he'd tell Princess Lucile and Count Steven.

"They have ships on all the planets they trade with. Fourteen of them. That isn't to catch Dunnan. That's to disperse the Navy away from Marduk. They don't trust the Navy. Is Prince Edvard still Prime Minister?"

"Yes, as of Garravay's last information. It seems Makann is behaving in a scrupulously legal manner, outside of making his People's Watchmen part of the armed forces. Protesting his devotion to the King every time he opens his mouth."

"When will the fire be, I wonder?"

"Huh? Oh yes, you were reading up on Hitler. That I don't know. Probably happened by now."

He just told Princess Lucile that her husband had gone into hiding; he couldn't be sure whether she was relieved or more worried. The boy was sure that he was doing something highly romantic and heroic.

Some of the volunteers tired of waiting, after another thousand hours, and spaced out. The *Viking's Gift* of Beowulf came in with a cargo, and went on orbit after discharging it to join the watch. A Gilgamesher came in from Amaterasu and reported everything quiet there; as soon as her captain had sold his cargo, with a minimum of haggling, he spaced out again. His behavior convinced everybody that the attack would come in a matter of hours.

It didn't.

Three thousand hours had passed since the first warning

had reached Tanith; that made five thousand since Viktor's ships were supposed to have left Xochitl. There were those, Boake Valkanhayn among them, who doubted, now, if he ever had.

"The whole thing's just a big Gilgamesher lie," he was declaring. "Somebody—Nikky Gratham, or the Everrards, or maybe Viktor himself,—paid them to tell us that, to pin our ships down here. Or they made it up themselves, so they could make hay on our trade-planets."

"Let's go down to the Ghetto and clean out the whole gang," somebody else took up. "Anything one of them's in, they're all in together."

"Nifflheim with that; let's all space out for Xochitl," Manfred Ravallo proposed. "We have enough ships to lick them on Tanith, we have enough to lick them on their own planet."

He managed to talk them out of both courses of action—what was he, anyhow; sovereign Prince of Tanith; or the non-ruling King of Marduk; or just the chieftain of a disciplineless gang of barbarians? One of the independents spaced out in disgust. The next day, two others came in, loaded with booty from a raid on Braggi, and decided to stay around for a while and see what happened.

And four days after that, a five hundred foot hyperspace yacht, bearing the daggers and chevrons of Bigglersport, came in. As soon as she was out of the last microjump, she began calling by screen.

Trask didn't know the man who was screening, but Hugh Rathmore did; Duke Joris' confidential secretary.

"Prince Trask; I must speak to you as soon as possible," he began, almost stuttering. Whatever the urgency of his mission, one would have thought that a three thousand hour voyage would have taken some of the edge from it. "It is of the first importance."

"You are speaking to me. This screen is reasonably secure. And if it's of the first importance, the sooner you tell me about it . . ."

"Prince Trask, you must come to Gram, with every man and every ship you can command. Satan only knows what's happening there now, but three thousand hours ago, when the Duke sent me off, Omfray of Glaspyth was landing on Wardshaven. He has a fleet of eight ships, furnished to him by his wife's kinsman, the King of Haulteclere. They are commanded by King Konrad's Space Viking cousin, the Prince of Xochitl."

Then a look of shocked surprise came into the face of the man in the screen, and Trask wondered why, until he realized that he had leaned back in his chair and was laughing uproariously. Before he could apologize, the man in the screen had found his voice.

"I know, Prince Trask; you have no reason to think kindly of King Angus—the former King Angus, or maybe even the late King Angus, I suppose he is now—but a bloody-handed murderer like Omfray of Glaspyth . . ."

It took a little time to explain to the confidential secretary of the Duke of Bigglersport the humor of the situation.

There were others at Rivington to whom it was not immediately evident. The professional Space Vikings, men like Valkanhayn and Ravallo and Alvyn Karffard, were disgusted. Here they'd been sitting, on combat alert, all these months, and, if they'd only known, they would have gone to Xochitl and looted it clean long ago. The Gram party were outraged. Angus of Wardshaven had

SPACE VIKING

been bad enough, with the hereditary taint of the Mad Baron of Blackcliffe, and Queen Evita and her rapacious family, but even he was preferable to a murderous villain—some even called him a fiend in human shape—like Omfray of Glaspyth.

Both parties, of course, were positive as to where their Prince's duty lay. The former insisted that everything on Tanith that could be put into hyperspace should be dispatched at once to Xochitl, to haul back from it everything except a few absolutely immovable natural features of the planet. The latter clamored, just as loudly and passionately, that everybody on Tanith who could pull a trigger should be embarked at once on a crusade for the deliverance of Gram.

"You don't want to do either, do you?" Harkaman asked him, when they were alone after the second day of acrimony.

"Nifflheim, no! This crowd that wants an attack on Xochitl; you know what would happen if we did that?" Harkaman was silent, waiting for him to continue. "Inside a year, four or five of these small planetholders like Gratham and the Everrards would combine against us and make a slag-pile of Tanith."

Harkaman nodded agreement. "Since we warned him the first time, Viktor's kept his ships away from our planets. If we attacked Xochitl now, without provocation, nobody'd know what to expect from us. People like Nikky Gratham and Tobbin of Nergal and the Everrards of Hoth get nervous around unpredictable dangers, and when they get nervous they get trigger-happy." He puffed slowly on his pipe and then said: "Then you'll be going back to Gram."

"That doesn't follow; just because Valkanhayn and

Ravallo and that crowd are wrong doesn't make Valpry and Rathmore and Ffayle right. You heard what I was telling those very people at Karvall House, the day I met you. And you've seen what's been happening on Gram since we came out here. Otto, the Sword-Worlds are finished; they're half decivilized now. Civilization is alive and growing here on Tanith. I want to stay here and help it grow."

"Look, Lucas," Harkaman said. "You're Prince of Tanith, and I'm only the Admiral. But I'm telling you; you'll have to do something, or this whole setup of yours will fall apart. As it stands, you can attack Xochitl and the Back-To-Gram party would go along, or you can decide on this crusade against Omfray of Glaspyth and the Raid-Xochitl-Now party would go along. But if you let this go on much longer, you won't have any influence over either party."

"And then I will be finished. And in a few years, Tanith will be finished." He rose and paced across the room and back. "Well, I won't raid Xochitl; I told you why, and you agreed. And I won't send the men and ships and wealth of Tanith in any Sword-World dynastic squabble. Great Satan, Otto; you were in the Durendal War. This is the same thing, and it'll go on for another half a century."

"Then what will you do?"

"I came out here after Andray Dunnan, didn't I?" he asked.

"I'm afraid Ravallo and Valpry, or even Valkanhayn and Morland, won't be as interested in Dunnan as you are."

"Then I will interest them in him. Remember, I was reading up on Hitler, coming in from Marduk? I will tell them all a big lie. Such a big lie that nobody will dare to disbelieve it.''

VII

"DO YOU THINK I was afraid of Viktor of Xochitl?" he demanded. "Half a dozen ships; we could make a new Van Allen belt around Tanith of them, with what we have here. Our real enemy is on Marduk, not Xochitl; his name's Zaspar Makann. Zaspar Makann, and Andray Dunnan, the man I came out from Gram to hunt; they're in alliance, and I believe Dunnan is on Marduk, himself, now.''

The delegation who had come out from Gram in the yacht of the Duke of Bigglersport were unimpressed. Marduk was only a name to them, one of the fabulous civilized Old Federation planets no Sword-Worlder had ever seen. Zaspar Makann wasn't even that. And so much had happened on Gram since the murder of Elaine Karvall and the piracy of the *Enterprise* that they had completely forgotten Andray Dunnan. That put them at a disadvantage. All the people whom they were trying to convince, the half-hundred members of the new nobility of Tanith, spoke a language they didn't understand. They didn't even understand the proposition, and couldn't argue against it.

Paytrik Morland, who was Gram-born and had been speaking for a return in force to fight against Omfray of Glaspyth and his supporters, defected from them at once. He had been on Marduk and knew who Zaspar Makann was; he had made friends with the Royal Navy officers, and had been shocked to hear that they were now enemies. Manfred Ravallo and Boake Valkanhayn, among the more articulate of the Raid-Xochitl-Now party, snatched up the idea and seemed convinced that they'd thought of it themselves all along. Valkanhayn had been on Gimli and talked to Mardukan naval officers; Ravallo had brought Princess Bentrik to Tanith and heard her stories on the voyage. They began adducing arguments in support of Trask's thesis. Of course Dunnan and Makann were in collusion. Who tipped Dunnan off that the *Victrix* would be on Audhumla? Makann; his spies in the Navy tipped him. What about the *Honest Horris;* wasn't Makann blocking any investigation about her? Why was Admiral Shefter retired as soon as Makann got into power?

"Well, here; we don't know anything about this Zaspar Makann," the confidential secretary and spokesman of the Duke of Bigglersport began.

"No, you don't," Otto Harkaman told him. "I suggest you keep quiet and listen, till you find out a little about him."

"Why, I wouldn't be surprised if Dunnan was on Marduk all the time we were hunting for him," Valkanhayn said.

Trask began to wonder. What would Hitler have done if he'd told one of his big lies, and then found it turning into the truth? Maybe Dunnan had been on Marduk . . . No; he couldn't have hidden half a dozen ships on a civilized planet. Not even at the bottom of an ocean.

"I wouldn't be surprised," Alvyn Karffard was shouting, "if Andray Dunnan *was* Zaspar Makann. I know he doesn't look like Dunnan, we all saw him on screen, but there's such a thing as plastic surgery."

That was making the big lie just a trifle too big. Zaspar Makann was six inches shorter than Dunnan; there are some things no plastic surgery could do. Paytrik Morland, who had known Dunnan and had seen Makann on screen, ought to have known that too, but he either didn't think of that or didn't want to weaken a case he had completely accepted.

"As far as I can find out, nobody even heard of Makann till about five years ago. That would be about the same time Dunnan would have arrived on Marduk," he said.

By this time, the big room in which they were meeting had become a babel of voices, everybody trying to convince everybody else that they'd known it all along. Then the Back-To-Gram party received its *coup-de-grace*; Lothar Ffayle, to whom the emissaries of Duke Joris had looked for their strongest support, went over.

"You people want us to abandon a planet we've built up from nothing, and all the time and money we've invested in it, to go back to Gram and pull your chestnuts out of the fire? Gehenna with you! We're staying here and defending our own planet. If you're smart, you'll stay here with us."

The Bigglersport delegation was still on Tanith, trying to recruit mercenaries from the King of Tradetown and dickering with a Gilgamesher to transport them to Gram, when the big lie turned into something like the truth.

The observation post on the Moon of Tanith picked up an emergence at twenty light-minutes due north of the planet. Half an hour later, there was another one at five light-minutes; a very small one, and then a third at two light-seconds, and this was detectable by radar and microray as a ship's pinnace. He wondered if something had happened on Amaterasu or Beowulf; somebody like

Gratham or the Everrards might have decided to take advantage of the defensive mobilization on Tanith. Then they switched the call from the pinnace over to his screen, and Prince Simon Bentrik was looking out of it.

"I'm glad to see you! Your wife and son are here, worried about you, but safe and well." He turned to shout to somebody to find young Count Steven of Ravary and tell him to tell his mother. "How are you?"

"I had a broken leg when I left Moonbase, but that's mended on the way," Bentrik said. "I have little Princess Myrna aboard with me. For all I know, she's Queen of Marduk, now." He gulped slightly. "Prince Trask, we've come as beggars. We're begging help for our planet."

"You've come as honored guests, and you'll get all the help we can give you." He blessed the Xochitl invasion scare, and the big lie which was rapidly ceasing to be a lie; Tanith had the ships and men and the will to act. "What happened? Makann deposed the King and took over?"

It came to that, Bentrik told him. It had started even before the election. The People's Watchmen had possessed weapons that had been made openly and legally on Marduk for trade to the Neobarbarian planets and then clandestinely diverted to secret People's Welfare arsenals. Some of the police had gone over to Makann; the rest had been terrorized into inaction. There had been riots fomented in working-class districts of all the cities as pretexts for further terrorization. The election had been a farce of bribery and intimidation. Even so, Makann's party had failed of a complete majority in the Chamber of Representatives, and had been compelled to patch up a shaky coalition in order to elect a favorable Chamber of Delegates.

"And, of course, they elected Makann Chancellor; that did it," Bentrik said. "All the opposition leaders in the Chamber of Representatives have been arrested, on all kinds of ridiculous charges—sex-crimes, receiving bribes, being in the pay of foreign powers, nothing too absurd. Then they rammed through a law empowering the Chancellor to fill vacancies in the Chamber of Representatives by appointment."

"Why did the Crown Prince lend himself to a thing like that?"

"He hoped that he could exercise some control. The Royal Family is an almost holy symbol to the people. Even Makann was forced to pretend loyalty to the King and the Crown Prince . . ."

"It didn't work; he played right into Makann's hands. What happened?"

The Crown Prince had been assassinated. The assassin, an unknown man believed to be a Gilgamesher, had been shot to death by People's Watchmen guarding Prince Edvard at once. Immediately Makann had seized the Royal Palace to protect the King, and immediately there had been massacres by People's Watchmen everywhere. The Mardukan Planetary Army had ceased to exist; Makann's story was that there had been a military plot against the King and the government. Scattered over the planet in small garrisons, the army had been wiped out in two nights and a day. Now Makann was recruiting it up again, exclusively from the People's Welfare Party.

"You weren't just sitting on your hands, were you?"

"Oh, no," Bentrik replied. "I was doing something I wouldn't have thought myself capable of, a few years ago. Organizing a mutineering conspiracy in the Royal Mardukan Navy. After Admiral Shefter was forcibly retired and shut up in an insane asylum, I disappeared and turned into a civilian contragravity-lifter operator at the Malverton Navy Yard. Finally, when I was suspected, one of the officers—he was arrested and tortured to death later —managed to smuggle me onto a lighter for the Moonbase. I was an orderly in the hospital there. The day the Crown Prince was murdered, we had a mutiny of our own. We killed everybody we even suspected of being a Makannist. The Moonbase has been under attack from the planet ever since.''

There was a stir behind him; turning, he saw Princess Bentrik and the boy enter the room. He rose.

"We'll talk about this later. There are some people here . . .''

He motioned them forward and turned away, shoo-ing everybody else out of the room.

The news was all over Rivington, and then all over Tanith, while the pinnace was still coming down. There was a crowd at the spaceport, staring as the little craft, with its blazon of the crowned and planet-throned dragon, settled onto its landing legs, and reporters of the Tanith News Service with their screen pickups. He met Prince Bentrik, a little in advance of the others, and managed to whisper to him hastily:

"While you're talking to anybody here, always remember that Andray Dunnan is working with Zaspar Makann, and as soon as Makann consolidates his position he's sending an expedition against Tanith.''

"How in blazes did you find that out, here?'' Bentrik demanded. "From the Gilgameshers?''

Then Harkaman and Rathmore and Valkanhayn and

Lothar Ffayle and the others were crowding up behind, and more people were coming off the pinnace, and Prince Bentrik was trying to embrace both his wife and his son at the same time.

"Prince Trask." He started at the voice, and was looking into deep blue eyes under coal-black hair. His pulse gave a sudden jump, and he said, "Valerie!" and then, "Lady Alvarath; I'm most happy to see you here." Then he saw who was beside her, and squatted on his heels to bring himself down to a convenient size. "And Princess Myrna. Welcome to Tanith, your Highness!"

The child flung her arms around his neck. "Oh, Prince Lucas! I'm so glad to see you. There's been such awful things happened!"

"There won't be anything awful happen here, Princess Myrna. You are among friends; friends with whom you have a treaty. Remember?"

The child began to cry, bitterly. "That was when I was just a play-Queen. And now I know what they meant when they talked about when Grandpa and Pappa would be through being King. Pappa didn't even get to be King!"

Something big and warm and soft was trying to push between them; a dog with long blond hair and floppy ears. In a year and a half, puppies can grow surprisingly. Mopsy was trying to lick his face. He took the dog by the collar and straightened.

"Lady Valerie, will you come with us?" he asked. "I'm going to find quarters for Princess Myrna."

"Is it Princess Myrna, or is it Queen Myrna?" he asked.

Prince Bentrik shook his head. "We don't know. The

King was alive when we left Moonbase, but that was five hundred hours ago. We don't know anything about her mother, either. She was at the Palace when Prince Edvard was murdered; we've heard absolutely nothing about her. The King made a few screen appearances, parroting things Makann wanted him to say. Under hypnosis. That was probably the very least of what they did to him. They've turned him into a zombi."

"Well, how did Myrna get to Moonbase?"

"That was Lady Valerie, as much as anybody else. She and Sir Thomas Kobbly, and Captain Rainer. They armed the servants at Cragdale with hunting rifles and everything else they could scrape up, captured Prince Edvard's spaceyacht, and took off in her. Took a couple of hits from ground batteries getting off, and from ships around Moonbase getting in. Ships of the Royal Mardukan Navy!" he added furiously.

The pinnace in which they had made the trip to Tanith had taken a few hits, too, running the blockade. Not many; her captain had thrown her into hyperspace almost at once.

"They're sending the yacht off to Gimli," Bentrik said. "From there, they'll try to rally as many of the Royal Navy units as haven't gone over to Makann. They're to assemble on Gimli and await my return. If I don't return in fifteen hundred hours from the time I left Moonbase, they're to use their own judgment. I'd expect that they'd move in on Marduk and attack."

"That's sixty-odd days," Otto Harkaman said. "That's an awfully long time to expect that lunar base to hold out, against a whole planet."

"It's a strong base. It was built four hundred years ago, when Marduk was fighting a combination of six other planets. It held out against continuous attack, once, for almost a year. It's been constantly strengthened ever since.''

"And what have they to throw at it?'' Harkaman persisted.

"When I left, six ships of the former Royal Navy, that had gone over to Makann. Four fifteen-hundred-footers, same class as the *Victrix*, and two thousand-footers. Then, there were four of Andray Dunnan's ships—''

"You mean, he really is on Marduk?''

"I thought you knew that, and I was wondering how you'd found out. Yes; *Fortuna*, *Bolide*, and two armed merchantmen, a Baldur-built ship called the *Reliable*, and your friend *Honest Horris*.''

"You didn't really believe Dunnan was on Marduk?'' Boake Valkanhayn asked.

"Actually, I didn't. I had to have some kind of a story, to talk those people out of that crusade against Omfray of Glaspyth.'' He left unmentioned Valkanhayn's own insistence on a plundering expedition against Xochitl. "Now that it turns out to be true, I'm not surprised. We decided, long ago, that Dunnan was planning to raid Marduk. It appears that we underestimated him. Maybe he was reading about Hitler, too. He wasn't planning any raid; he was planning conquest, in the only way a great civilization can be conquered—by subversion.''

"Yes,'' Harkaman put in. "Five years ago, when Dunnan started this program, who was this Makann, anyhow?''

"Nobody,'' Bentrik said. "A crackpot agitator in Drepplin; he had a coven of fellow-crackpots, who met in the back room of a saloon and had their office in a cigar-box. The next year, he had a suite of offices and was buying time on a couple of telecasts. The year after that, he had three telecast stations of his own, and was holding rallies and meetings of thousands of people. And so on, upward.''

"Yes. Dunnan financed him, and moved in behind him, the same way Makann moved in behind the King. And Dunnan will have him shot the way he had Prince Edvard shot, and use the murder as a pretext to liquidate his personal followers.''

"And then he'll own Marduk. And we'll have the Mardukan navy coming out of hyperspace on Tanith,'' Valkanhayn added. "So we go to Marduk and smash him now, while he's still little enough to smash.''

There had been a few who had wanted to do that about Hitler, and a great many, later, who had regretted that it hadn't been done.

"The *Nemesis*, the *Corisande*, and the *Space-Scourge* for sure?'' he asked.

Harkaman and Valkanhayn agreed; Valkanhayn thought the *Viking's Gift* of Beowulf would go along, and Harkaman was almost sure of the *Black Star* and *Queen Flavia*. He turned to Bentrik.

"Start that pinnace off for Gimli at once; within the hour if possible. We don't know how many ships will be gathered there, but we don't want them wasted in detail-attacks. Tell whoever's in command there that ships from Tanith are on the way, and to wait for them.''

Fifteen hundred hours, less the five hundred Bentrik was in space from Marduk. He hadn't time to estimate voyage-time to Gimli from the other Mardukan trade-planets, and nobody could estimate how many ships would respond.

"It may take us a little time to get an effective fleet together. Even after we get through arguing about it. Argument," he told Bentrik, "is not exclusively a feature of democracies."

Actually, there was very little argument, and most of that among the Mardukans. Prince Bentrik insisted that Crown Princess Myrna would have to be taken along; King Mikhyl would be either dead or brainwashed into imbecility by now, and they would have to have somebody to take the throne. Lady Valerie Alvarath, Sir Thomas Kobbly, the tutor, and the nurse Margot refused to be separated from her. Prince Bentrik was equally firm, with less success, on leaving his wife and son on Tanith. In the end, it was agreed that the entire Mardukan party would space out on the *Nemesis*.

The leader of the Bigglersport delegation attempted an impassioned tirade about going to the aid of strangers while their own planet was being enslaved. He was booed down by everybody else and informed that Tanith was being defended where a planet ought to be, on somebody else's real estate. When the Bigglersporters emerged from the meeting, they found that their own space-yacht had been commandeered and sent off to Amaterasu and Beowulf for assistance, that the regiment of local infantry they had enlisted from the King of Tradetown had been taken over by the Rivington authorities, and that the Gilgamesh freighter they had chartered to transport them to Gram would now take them to Marduk.

The problem broke into two halves; the purely naval action that would be fought to relieve the Moon of Marduk, if it still held out, and to destroy the Dunnan and Makann ships, and the ground-fighting problem of wiping out Makann's supporters and restoring the Mardukan monarchy. A great many of the people of Marduk would be glad of a chance to turn on Makann, once they had arms and were properly supported. Combat weapons were almost unknown among the people, however, and even sporting arms uncommon. All the smallarms and light artillery and auto-weapons available were gathered up.

The *Grendelsbane* came in from Beowulf, and the *Sun-Goddess* from Amaterasu. Three independent Space Viking ships were still in orbit on Tanith; they joined the expedition. There would be trouble with them on Marduk; they'd want to loot. Let the Mardukans worry about that. They could charge it off as part of the price for letting Zaspar Makann get into power in the first place.

There were twelve spacecraft in line outside the Moon of Tanith, counting the three independents and the forcibly chartered Gilgamesher troop-transport; that was the biggest fleet Space Vikings had ever assembled in their history. Alvyn Karffard said as much while they were checking the formation by screen.

"It isn't a Space Viking fleet," Prince Bentrik differed. "There are only three Space Vikings in it. The rest are the ships of three civilized planets, Tanith, Beowulf and Amaterasu."

Karffard was surprised. "You mean *we're* civilized planets? Like Marduk, or Baldur, or Odin, or . . .?"

"Well, aren't you?"

Trask smiled. He'd begun to suspect something of the sort a couple of years ago. He hadn't really been sure until now. His most junior staff officer, Count Steven of Ravary, didn't seem to appreciate the compliment.

"We *are* Space Vikings!" he insisted. "And we are going to battle with the Neobarbarians of Zaspar Makann."

"Well, I won't argue the last half of it, Steven," his father told him.

"Are you people done yacking about who's civilized and who isn't?" Guatt Kirbey asked. "Then give the signal. All the other ships are ready to jump."

Trask pressed the button on the desk in front of him. A light went on over Kirbey's control panel, as one would on each of the other ships. He said, "Jumping," around the stem of his pipe, and twisted the red handle and shoved it in.

Four hundred and fifty hours, in the private universe that was the *Nemesis;* outside, nothing else existed, and inside there was nothing to do but wait, as each hour carried them six trillion miles nearer to Gimli. At first, the ruthless and terrible Space Viking, Steven, Count of Ravary, was wildly excited, but before long he found that there was nothing exciting going on; it was just a spaceship, and he'd been on ships before. Her Highness the Crown Princess, or maybe her Majesty the Queen of Marduk, stopped being excited about the same time, and she and Steven and Mopsy played together. Of course, Myrna was only a girl, and two years younger than Steven, but she was, or at least might be, his sovereign, and beside, she had been in a space action, if you call what lies between a planet and its satellite space and if you call being shot at without being able to shoot back an action, and Relentless Ravary, the Interstellar Terror, had not. This rather made up for being a girl and a mere baby of going-on-ten.

One thing, there were no lessons. Sir Thomas Kobbly fancied himself as a landscape-painter and spent most of his time arguing techniques with Vann Larch, and

Steven's tutor, Captain Rainer, was a normal-space astrogator and found a kindred spirit in Sharll Renner. This
left Lady Valerie Alvarath at a loose end. There were
plenty of volunteers to help her fill in the time, but Rank
Hath Its Privileges; Trask undertook to see to it that she did
not suffer excessively from shipboard ennui.

Sharll Renner and Captain Rainer approached him,
during the cocktail-hour before dinner, some hundred
hours short of emergence.

"We think we've figured out where Dunnan's base is,"
Renner said.

"Oh, good!" Everybody else had, on a different
planet. "Where's yours?"

"Abaddon," the Count of Ravary's tutor said. When
he saw that the name meant nothing to Trask, he added,
"The ninth, outer, planet of the Marduk system." He said
it disgustedly.

"Yes; remember how you had Boake and Manfred out
with their ships, checking our outside planets to see if
Prince Viktor might be hiding on one of them? Well, what
with the time element, and the way the *Honest Horris* was
shuttling back and forth from Marduk to someplace that
wasn't Gimli, and the way Dunnan was able to bring his
ships in as soon as the shooting started on Marduk, we
thought he must be on an uninhabited outer planet of the
Marduk system."

"I don't know why we never thought of that, ourselves," Rainer put in. "I suppose because nobody ever
thinks of Abaddon for any reason. It's only a small planet,
about four thousand miles in diameter, and it's three and a
half billion miles from primary, only ninety-five million
less from Marduk. It's frozen solid. It would take almost a

year to get to it on Abbot drive, and if your ship has Dillinghams, why not take a little longer and go to a good planet? So nobody bothered with Abaddon.''

But for Dunnan's purpose, it would be perfect. He called Prince Bentrik and Alvyn Karffard to him; they found the idea instantly convincing. They talked about it through dinner, and held a general discussion afterward. Even Guatt Kirbey, the ship's pessimist, could find no objection to it. Trask and Bentrik began at once making battle plans. Karffard wondered if they hadn't better wait till they got to Gimli and discuss it with the others.

"No," Trask told him. "This is the flagship; here's where the strategy is decided."

"Well, how about the Mardukan Navy?" Captain Rainer asked. "I think Fleet-Admiral Bargham's in command at Gimli."

Prince Simon Bentrik was silent for a moment, as though he realized, with reluctance, that the big decision was no longer avoidable.

"He may be, at present, but he won't be when I get there. I will be."

"But . . . Your Highness, he's a fleet-admiral; you're just a commodore."

"I am not just a commodore. The King is a prisoner, and for all we know dead. The Crown Prince is dead. The Princess Myrna is a child. I am assuming the position of Regent and Prince-Protector of the Realm."

VIII

THERE WAS A little difficulty on Gimli with Fleet-Admiral Bargham. Commodores didn't give orders to fleet-admirals. Well, maybe regents did, but who gave Prince Bentrik authority to call himself regent? Regents were elected by the Chamber of Delegates, on nomination of the Chancellor.

"That's Zaspar Makann and his stooges you're talking about?" Bentrik laughed.

"Well, the Constitution . . ." He thought better of that, before somebody asked him what Constitution. "Well, a Regent has to be chosen by election. Even members of the Royal Family can't just make themselves Regent by saying they are."

"I can. I just have. And I don't think there are going to be many more elections, at least for the present. Not till we make sure the people of Marduk can be trusted with the control of the government."

"Well, the pinnace from Moonbase reported that there were six Royal navy battleships and four other craft attacking them." Bargham objected. "I only have four ships here; I sent for the ones on the other trade-planets, but I haven't heard from any of them. We can't go there with only four ships."

"Sixteen ships," Bentrik corrected. "No, fifteen and one Gilgamesher we're using for a troopship. I think that's enough. You'll remain here on Gimli, in any case, Admiral; as soon as the other ships come in, you'll follow to

Marduk with them. I am now holding a meeting aboard the Tanith flagship *Nemesis*. I want your four ship commanders aboard immediately. I am not including you because you're remaining here to bring up the latecomers and as soon as this meeting is over we are spacing out.''

Actually, they spaced out sooner; the meeting lasted the whole three hundred and fifty hours to Abaddon. A ship's captain, if he has a good exec., as all of them had, needs only sit at his command-desk and look important while the ship is going into and emerging from a long jump; the rest of the time he can study ancient history or whatever his shipboard hobby is. Rather than waste three hundred and fifty hours of precious time, each captain turned his ship over to his exec. and remained aboard the *Nemesis;* even on so spacious a craft the officers' country north of the engine-rooms was crowded like a tourist hotel in mid-season. One of the four Mardukans was the Captain Garravay who had smuggled Bentrik's wife and son off Marduk, and the other three were just as pro-Bentrik, pro-Tanith, and anti-Makann. They were, on general principles, also anti-Bargham. There must be something wrong with any fleet-admiral who remained in his command after Zaspar Makann came to power.

So, as soon as they spaced out, there was a party. After that, they settled down to planning the Battle of Abaddon.

There was no Battle of Abaddon.

It was a dead planet, one side in night and the other in dim twilight from the little speck of a sun three and a half billion miles away, jagged mountains rising out of the snow that covered it from pole to pole. The snow on top would be frozen CO_2; according to the thermocouples, the surface temperature was well below minus-100 Centigrade. No ships on orbit circled it; there was a little faint radiation, which could have been from naturally radioactive minerals; there was no electrical discharge detectable.

There was considerable bad language in the command-room of the *Nemesis*. The captains of the other ships were screening in, wanting to know what to do.

"Go on in," Trask told them. "Englobe the planet, and go down to within a mile if necessary. They could be hiding somewhere on it."

"Well, they're not hiding at the bottom of any ocean, that's for sure," somebody said. It was one of those feeble jokes at which everybody laughs because nothing else is laughable about the situation.

Finally, they found it, at the north pole, which was no colder than anywhere else on the planet. First radiation leakage, the sort that would come from a closed-down nuclear power plant. Then a modicum of electrical discharge. Finally the telescopic screens picked up the spaceport, a huge oval amphitheater excavated out of a valley between two jagged mountain ranges.

The language in the command-room was just as bad, but the tone had changed. It was surprising what a wide range of emotions could be expressed by a few simple blasphemies and obscenities. Everybody who had been deriding Sharll Renner was now acclaiming him.

But it was lifeless. The ships came crowding in; air-locked landing-craft full of space-armored ground-fighters went down. Screens in the command-room lit as they transmitted in views. Depressions in the carbon-dioxide snow where the hundred-foot pad-feet of ships' landings-legs had pressed down. Ranks of cargo-lighters that had plied to and from other ships on orbit. And, all around the cliff-walled perimeter, airlocked doors to caverns and tunnels. A great many men, with a great deal of equipment, had been working there in the estimated five or six years since Andray Dunnan—or somebody —had constructed this base.

Andray Dunnan. They found his badge, the crescent, blue on black, on things. They found equipment that Harkaman recognized as having been part of the original cargo stolen with the *Enterprise*. They even found, in his living quarters, a blown-up photoprint picture of Nevil Ormm, draped in black. But what they did not find was a single vehicle small enough to be taken aboard a ship, or a single scrap of combat equipment, not even a pistol or a hand-grenade.

Dunnan had gone, but they knew whither, and where to find him. The conquest of Marduk had moved into its final phase.

Marduk was on the other side of the sun from Abaddon with ninety-five million miles—close, but not inconveniently so, Trask thought—to spare. Guatt Kirbey and the Mardukan astrogator who was helping him made it within a light-minute. The Mardukan thought that was fine; Kirbey didn't. The last microjump was aimed at the Moon of Marduk, which was plainly visible in the telescopic screen. They came out within a light-second and a half, which Kirbey admitted was reasonably close. As soon as the screens cleared, they saw that they weren't too late. The Moon of Marduk was under fire and firing back.

They'd have detection, and he knew what they were detecting—a clump of sixteen rending distortions of the fabric of space-time, as sixteen ships came into sudden existence in the normal continuum. Beside him, Bentrik had a screen on; it was still milky-white, and he was speaking into a radio handphone.

"Simon Bentrik, Prince-Protector of Marduk, calling Moonbase." Then, slowly, he repeated his screen-combination twice. "Come in, Moonbase; this is Simon Bentrik, Prince-Protector, speaking."

He waited ten seconds, and was about to start again, when the screen flickered. The man who appeared in it wore the insignia of a Mardukan navy officer. He needed a shave, but he was grinning happily. Bentrik greeted him by name.

"Hello, Simon; glad to see you. Your Highness, I mean; what is this Prince-Protector thing?"

"Somebody had to do it. Is the King still alive?"

The grin slid off the Commodore's face, starting with his eyes.

"We don't know. At first, Makann had him speaking by screen—you know what it was like—urging everybody to obey and cooperate with 'our trusted Chancellor.' Makann always appeared on the screen with him."

Bentrik nodded. "I remember."

"Before you left, Makann kept quiet, and let the King make the speech. After a while, the King wasn't able to speak coherently; he'd stammer, and repeat. So then Makann did all the talking; they couldn't even depend on him to parrot what they were giving him with an earplug phone. Then he stopped appearing entirely. I suppose there were physical symptoms they couldn't allow to be seen." Bentrik was cursing horribly under his breath; the officer at Moonbase nodded. "I hope for his sake that he is dead."

Poor Goodman Mikhyl. Bentrik was saying, "So do I." The Commodore at Moonbase was still talking:

"We got two more renegade RMN ships, within a hundred hours after you left." He named them. "And we got one of the Dunnan ships, the *Fortuna*. We blew out the Malverton Navy Yard. They're still using the Antarctic Naval Base, but we've knocked out a good deal of that. We got the *Honest Horris*. They made two attempts to land on us and lost a couple of ships. Eight hundred hours ago, they were joined by the rest of Dunnan's fleet, five ships. They made a landing on Malverton while it was turned away from us. Makann announced that they were RMN units from the trade-planets that had joined him. I suppose the planetside public swallowed that. He also announced that their commander, Admiral Dunnan, was in command of the People's Armed Forces."

Dunnan's ground-fighters would be in control of Malverton. By now, the odds were that Makann was as much his prisoner as King Mikhyl VIII had been Makann's.

"So Dunnan has conquered Marduk. All he has to do, now, is make it stick," he said. "I see four ships off Moonbase; how many more have they?"

"These are *Bolide* and *Eclipse*, Dunnan's ships, and former Royal Mardukan Navy ships *Champion* and *Guardian*. There are five orbiting off the planet: Ex-RMNS *Paladin*, and Dunnan ships *Starhopper*, *Banshee*, *Reliable* and *Exporter*. The last two are listed as merchantmen, but they're performing like regulation battle-craft."

The four that had been circling Moonbase broke orbit and started toward the relieving fleet; one took a hit from a Moonbase missile, which staggered her but did no evident damage. Two ships which had been orbiting the planet also changed course and started out. The command-room was silent except for a subdued chuckling from a computer which was estimating enemy intentions by observed data and Games Theory. Three more came hurrying out from the planet, and the two in the lead slowed to let them catch up. He wanted to be able to engage the four from off the satellite before the five from the planet joined them, but Karffard's computers said it couldn't be done.

"All right, we have to take all our bad eggs in one basket," he said. "Try to hit them as soon after they join as possible."

The computers began chuckling again. The serving-robots were doing a rush business in hot coffee. Prince Bentrik's son, sitting beside his father, had stopped being Ruthless Ravary the Demon of the Spaceways and was a very young officer going into his first space-battle, more scared and at the same time happier than he had ever been in his short life. Captain Garravay of the *Vindex* was making signal to the other ships from Gimli: "*Royal Navy; smash the traitors first!*" He could understand and sympathize, even if he couldn't approve of putting personal ahead of tactical considerations, and made a quick sealed-beam call to Harkaman to be prepared to plug any holes they left in formation if they broke away in search of vengeance. He also ordered the *Black Star* and the *Sun Goddess* to shepherd the lightly armed and troop-crammed Gilgamesh freighter out of danger. The two clumps of Dunnan Makann ships were converging rapidly, and Alvyn Karffard was screaming into a phone to somebody to get more speed.

At a thousand miles, the missiles started going out, and

the two groups of ships, four and five, were equidistant from each other and from the allied fleet, at the points of a triangle that was growing smaller by the second. The first fire-globes of intercepted missiles spread from their seeds of brief white light. A red light flashed on the damage-board. An enemy ship took a hit. The captain of the *Queen Flavia* was on a screen, saying that his ship was heavily damaged. Three ships bearing the Mardukan dragon-and-planet circled madly around each other at what looked, in the screen, like just over pistol-range, two of them firing into the third, which was replying desperately. The third one blew up, and somebody was yelling out a screen-speaker, "Scratch one traitor!"

Another ship blew up somewhere, and then another. He heard somebody say, "There went one of ours," and wondered which one it was. Not the *Corisande*, he hoped; no, it wasn't, he could see her rushing after two other ships which were, in turn, speeding toward the *Black Star*, the *Sun-Goddess* and the Gilgamesh freighter. Then the *Nemesis* and the *Starhopper* were within gun-range, pounding each other savagely.

The battle had tied itself into a ball of gyrating, fire-spitting ships that went rolling toward the planet, which was swinging in and out of the main viewscreen and growing rapidly larger. By the time they were down to the inner edge of the exosphere, the ball had started to un-wind, ship after ship dropping out of it and going into orbit, some badly damaged and some going to attack damaged enemies. Some of them were completely around the planet, hidden by it. He saw three ships approaching it—*Corisande*, *Sun-Goddess*, and the Gilgamesher. He got Harkaman on the screen.

"Where's the *Black Star?*" he asked.

"Gone to Em-See-Square," Harkaman replied. "We got the two Dunnan-Makanns, *Bolide* and *Reliable.*"

Then young Steven of Ravary, who had been monitoring one of the intership screens, had a call from Captain Gompertz of the *Grendelsbane*, and at the same moment somebody else was yelling, "Here comes the blank-dashed *Starhopper* again!"

"Tell him to wait a moment; we have troubles," he said.

Nemesis and *Starhopper* sledgehammered each other and parried with counter-missiles, and then, quite unexpectedly, the *Starhopper* went to Em-See-Square.

There was an awful lot of Em being converted to Ee off Marduk, today. Including Manfred Ravallo; that grieved him. Manfred was a good man, and a good friend. He had a girl in Rivington . . . Nifflheim, there were eight hundred good men aboard the *Black Star*, and most of them had girls who'd wait in vain for them on Tanith. Well, what had Otto Harkaman said, so long ago, on Gram? Something about old age not being a usual cause of death among Space Vikings, wasn't it?

Then he remembered that Gompertz of the *Grendelsbane* was trying to get him. He told young Count Steven to switch him over.

"We just lost one of our Mardukans," Gompertz told him, in his staccato Beowulf accent. "I think she was the *Challenger*. The ship that got her looks like the *Banshee;* I'm turning to engage her."

"Which way; west around the planet? Be right wih you, Captain."

It was like finishing a word-puzzle. You sit staring at it,

looking for more spaces to print letters into, and suddenly you realize that there are no more, the puzzle is done. That was how the space-battle of Marduk, the Battle *off* Marduk, ended. Suddenly there were no more colored fireglobes opening and fading, no more missiles coming, no more enemy ships to throw missiles at. Now it was time to take a count of his own ships, and then begin thinking about the Battle *on* Marduk.

The *Black Star* was gone. So was RMNS *Challenger*, and RMNS *Conquistador*. *Space-Scourge* was badly hammered; worse than after the Beowulf raid, Boake Valkanhayn said. The *Viking's Gift* was heavily damaged, too, and so was the *Corisande*, and so, from the looks of the damage-board, was the *Nemesis*. And three ships were missing—the three independent Space Vikings, *Harpy*, *Curse of Cagn*, and Roger-fan-Morvill Esthersan's *Damnthing*.

Prince Bentrik frowned over that. "I can't think that all three of those ships would have been destroyed, without anybody seeing it happen."

"Neither can I. But I can think that all those ships broke out of the battle together and headed in for the planet. They didn't come here to help liberate Marduk, they came here to fill their cargo-holds. I only hope the people they're robbing all voted the Makann ticket in the last election." A crumb of comfort occurred to him, and he passed it on. "The only people who are armed to resist them will be Makann's storm-troops and Dunnan's pirates; they'll be the ones to get killed."

"We don't want any more killing than . . ." Prince Simon broke off suddenly. "I'm beginning to talk like his late Highness Crown Prince Edvard," he said. "He didn't want bloodshed, either, and look whose blood was shed. If they're doing what you think they are, I'm afraid we'll have to kill a few of your Space Vikings, too.''

"They aren't my Space Vikings.'' He was a little surprised to find that, after almost eight years of bearing the name himself, he was using it as an other-people label. Well, why not? He was the ruler of the civilized planet of Tanith, wasn't he? "But let's not start fighting them till the main war's over. Those three shiploads are no worse than a bad cold; Makann and Dunnan are the plague.''

It would still take four hours to get down, in a spiral of deceleration. They started the telecasts which had been filmed and taped on the voyage from Gimli. The Prince-Protector Simon Bentrik spoke: The illegal rule of the traitor Makann was ended. His deluded followers were advised to return to their allegiance to the Crown. The People's Watchmen were ordered to surrender their arms and disband; in localities where they refused, the loyal people were called upon to cooperate with the legitimate armed forces of the Crown in exterminating them, and would be furnished arms as soon as possible.

Little Princess Myrna spoke: "If my grandfather is still alive, he is your King; if he is not, I am your Queen, and until I am old enough to rule in my own right, I accept Prince Simon as Regent and Protector of the Realm, and I call on all of you to obey him as I will.''

"You didn't say anything about representative government, or democracy, or the constitution,'' Trask mentioned. "And I noticed the use of the word 'rule,' instead of 'reign'.''

"That's right,'' the self-proclaimed Prince-Protector said. "There's something wrong with democracy. If there weren't, it couldn't be overthrown by people like

Makann, attacking it from within by democratic procedures. I don't think it's fundamentally unworkable. I think it just has a few of what engineers call bugs. It's not safe to run a defective machine till you learn the defects and remedy them."

"Well, I hope you don't think our Sword-World feudalism doesn't have bugs." He gave examples and then quoted Otto Harkaman about barbarism spreading downward from the top instead of upward from the bottom.

"It may just be," he added, "that there is something fundamentally unworkable about government itself. As long as *Homo sapiens terra* is a wild animal, which he has always been and always will be until he evolves into something different in a million or so years, maybe a workable system of government is a political-science impossibility, just as transmutation of elements was a physical-science impossibility as long as they tried to do it by chemical means."

"Then we'll just have to make it work the best way we can, and when it breaks down, hope the next try will work a little better, for a little longer," Bentrik said.

Malverton grew in the telescopic screens as they came down. The Navy Spaceport, where Trask had landed almost two years before, was in wreckage, sprinkled with damaged ships that had been blasted on the ground, and slagged by thermonuclear fires. There was fighting in the air all over the city proper, on building-tops, on the ground, and in the air. That would be the *Damn-thing-Harpy-Curse of Cagn* Space Vikings. The Royal Palace was the center of one of half a dozen swirls of battle that had condensed out of the general skirmishing. It had not yet been taken.

Paytrik Morland started for it with the first wave of

ground-fighters from the *Nemesis*. The Gilgamesh freighter, like most of her ilk, had huge cargo-ports all around; these began opening and disgorging a swarm of everything from landing-craft and hundred-foot airboats to one man aircavalry single-mounts. The top landing-stages and terraces of the palace were almost obscured by the flashes of auto-cannon shells and the smoke and dust of projectiles. Then the first vehicles landed, the firing from the air stopped, and men fanned out as skirmishers, occasionally firing with smallarms.

Trask and Bentrik were in the armory off the vehicle-bay, putting on combat equipment, when the twelve-year-old Count of Ravary joined them and began rummaging for weapons and a helmet.

"You're not going," his father told him. "I'll have enough to worry about taking care of myself . . ."

That was the wrong approach. Trask interrupted:

"You're to stay aboard, Count," he said. "As soon as things stabilize, Princess Myrna will have to come down. You'll act as her personal escort. And don't think you're being shoved into the background. She's Crown Princess, and if she isn't Queen now, she will be in a few years. Escorting her now will be the foundation of your naval career. There isn't a young officer in the Royal Navy who wouldn't trade places with you."

"That was the right way to handle him, Lucas," Bentrik approved, after the boy had gone away, proud of his opportunity and his responsibility.

"It'll do just what I said for him." He stopped for a moment, to play with an idea that had just struck him. "You know, the girl will be Queen in a few years, if she isn't now. Queens need Prince Consorts. Your son's a good boy; I liked him the first moment I saw him, and I've liked him better ever since. He'd be a good man on the Throne beside Queen Myrna.''

''Oh, that's out of the question. Not the matter of consanguinity, they're about sixteenth cousins. But people would say I was abusing the Protectorship to marry my son onto the Throne.''

''Simon, speaking as one sovereign prince to another, you have a lot to learn. You've learned one important lesson already, that a ruler must be willing to use force and shed blood to enforce his rule. You have to learn, too, that a ruler cannot afford to be guided by his fears of what people will say about him. Not even what history will say about him. A ruler's only judge is himself.''

Bentrik slid the transpex visor of his helmet up and down experimentally, checked the chambers of his pistol and carbine.

''All that matters to me is the peace and well-being of Marduk. I'll have to talk it over with—with my only judge. Well, let's go.''

The top terraces were secure when their car landed. More vehicles were coming down and discharging men; a swarm of landing-craft were sinking past the building toward the ground two thousand feet below. Auto-weapons and smallarms and light cannon banged, and bombs and recoilless-rifle shells crashed, on the lower terraces. They put the car down one of the shaftways until they ran into heavy fire from below, at the limit of the advance, and then turned into a broad hallway, floating high enough to clear the heads of the men on foot. It looked like the part of the Palace where he had lodged when he had been a guest there but it probably wasn't.

They came to hastily constructed barricades of furniture and statuary and furnishings, behind which Makann's People's Watchmen and Andray Dunnan's Space Vikings were making resistance. They entered rooms dusty with powdered plaster and acrid with powder fumes, littered with corpses. They passed lifter-skids being towed out with wounded. They went through rooms crowded with their own men—*"Keep your fingers off things; this isn't a looting expedition!" "You stupid cretin, how did you know there wasn't a man hiding behind that?"* In one huge room, ballroom or concertroom or something, there were prisoners herded, and men from the *Nemesis* were setting up polyencephalographic veridicators, sturdy chairs with wires and adjustable helmets and translucent globes mounted over them. A couple of Morland's men were hustling a People's Watchman to one and strapping him into a chair.

"You know what this is, don't you?" one of them was saying. "This is a veridicator. That globe'll light blue; the moment you try to lie to us, it'll turn red. And the moment it turns red, I'm going to hammer your teeth down your throat with the butt of this pistol."

"Have you found anything out about the King, yet?" Bentrik asked him.

He turned. "No. Nobody we've questioned so far knows anything later than a month ago about him. He just disappeared." He was going to say something else, saw Bentrik's face, and changed his mind.

"He's dead," Bentrik said dully. "They tortured him and brainwashed him and used him as a ventriloquist's dummy on the screen as long as they could; when they couldn't let the people see him any more, they stuffed him into a converter."

They did find Zaspar Makann, hours later. Maybe he could have told them something, if he had been alive, but he and a few of his fanatical followers had barricaded themselves in the Throneroom and died trying to defend it. They found Makann on the Throne, the top of his head blown away, a pistol death-gripped in his hand, and the Great Crown lying on the floor, the velvet inner cap bullet-pierced and spattered with blood and brain-tissue. Prince Bentrik picked it up and looked at it disgustedly.

"We'll have to have something done about that," he said. "I really didn't think he'd do just this. I thought he wanted to abolish the Throne, not sit on it."

Except for one chandelier smashed and several corpses that had to be dragged out, the Ministerial Councilroom was intact. They set up headquarters there. Boake Valkanhayn and several other ship-captains joined them. There was fighting going on in several places inside the Palace, and the city was still in a turmoil. Somebody managed to get in touch with the captains of the *Damnthing*, the *Harpy* and the *Curse of Cagn* and bring them to the Palace. Trask attempted to reason with them, to no avail.

"Prince Trask, you're my friend, and you've always dealt fairly with me," Roger-fan-Morvill Esthersan said. "But you know just how far any Space Viking captain can control his crew. These men didn't come here to correct the political mistakes of Marduk. They came here for what they could haul away. I could get myself killed trying to stop them now . . ."

"I wouldn't even try," the captain of the *Curse of Cagn* put. "I came here for what I could make out of this planet, myself."

"You can try to stop them," the captain of the *Harpy*

237

said. "You'll find it even harder than what you're doing now."

Trask looked at some of the reports that had come in from elsewhere on the planet. Harkaman had landed on one of the big cities to the east, and the people had risen against Makann's local bosses and were helping wipe out the People's Watchmen with arms they had been furnished. Valkanhayn's exec. had landed on a large concentration-camp where close to ten thousand of Makann's political enemies had been penned; he had distributed all his available weapons and was calling for more. Gompertz of the *Grendelsbane* was at Drepplin; he reported just the reverse. The people there had risen in support of the Makann regime, and he wanted authorization to use nuclear weapons against them.

"Could you talk your people into going to some other city?" Trask asked. "We have a city for you; big industrial center. It ought to be fine looting. Drepplin."

"The people there are Mardukan subjects, too," Bentrik began. Then he shrugged. "It's not what we'd like to do, it's what we have to. By all means, gentlemen. Take your men to Drepplin, and nobody will object to anything you do."

"And when you have that place looted out, try Abaddon. You were aground there, Captain Esthersan. You know what all Dunnan left there."

A couple of Space Vikings—no, Royal Army of Tanith men—brought in the old woman, dirty, in rags, almost exhausted.

"She wants to talk to Prince Bentrik; won't talk to anybody else. Says she knows where the King is."

Bentrik rose quickly, brought her to a chair, poured a glass of wine for her.

"He's still alive, your Highness. The Crown Princess Melanie and I—I'm sorry, your Highness; Dowager Crown Princess—have been taking care of him, the best way we could. If you'll only come quickly . . ."

Mikhyl VIII, Planetary King of Marduk, lay on a pallet of filthy bedding on the floor of a narrow room behind a mass-energy converter which disposed of the rubbish and sewage and generated power for some of the fixed equipment on one of the middle floors of the east wing of the palace. There was a bucket of water, and on a rough wooden bench lay a cloth-wrapped bundle of food. A woman, haggard and disheveled, wearing a suit of greasy mechanic's coveralls and nothing else, squatted beside him. The Crown Princess Melanie, whom Trask remembered as the charming and gracious hostess of Cragdale. She tried to rise, and staggered.

"Prince Bentrik! And it's Prince Trask of Tanith!" she cried. "Just hurry; get him out of here and to where he can be taken care of. Please." Then she sat down again on the floor and fell over, unconscious.

They couldn't get the story. The Princess Melanie had collapsed completely. Her companion, another noblewoman of the court, could only ramble disconnectedly. And the King merely lay, bathed and fed in a clean bed, and looked up at them wonderingly, as though nothing he saw or heard conveyed any meaning to him. The doctors could do nothing.

"He has no mind, no more mind than a new-born baby. We can keep him alive, I don't know how long. That's our professional duty. But it's no kindness to his Majesty."

The little pockets of resistance in the Palace were wiped

out, through the next morning and afternoon. All but one, far underground, below the main power-plant. They tried sleep-gas; the defenders had blowers and sent it back at them. They tried blasting; there was a limit to what the fabric of the building would stand. And nobody knew how long it would take to starve them out.

On the third day, a man crawled out, pushing a white shirt tied to the barrel of a carbine ahead of him.

"Is Prince Lucas Trask of Tanith here?" he asked. "I won't speak to anybody else."

They brought Trask quickly. All that was visible of the other man was the carbine-barrel and the white shirt. When Trask called to him, he raised his head above the rubble behind which he was hiding.

"Prince Trask, we have Andray Dunnan here; he was leading us, but now we've disarmed him and are holding him. If we turn him over to you, will you let us go?"

"If you all come out unarmed, and bring Dunnan with you, I promise you, the rest of you will be let outside this building and allowed to go away unharmed."

"All right. We'll be coming out in a minute." The man raised his voice. "It's agreed!" he called. "Bring him out."

There were fewer than two score of them. Some wore the uniforms of high officers of the People's Watchmen or of People's Welfare Party functionaries; a few wore the heavily braided short jackets of Space Viking officers. Among them, they propelled a thin-faced man with a pointed beard, and Trask had to look twice at him before he recognized the face of Andray Dunnan. It looked more like the face of Duke Angus of Wardshaven as he last remembered it. Dunnan looked at him in incurious contempt.

"Your dotard king couldn't rule without Zaspar Makann, and Makann couldn't rule without me, and neither can you," he said. "Shoot this gang of turncoats, and I'll rule Marduk for you." He looked at Trask again. "Who are you?" he demanded. "I don't know you."

Trask slipped the pistol from his holster, thumbing off the safety.

"I am Lucas Trask. You've heard that name before," he said. "Stand away from behind him, you people."

"Oh, yes; the poor fool who thought he was going to marry Elaine Karvall. Well, you won't, Lord Trask of Traskon. She loves me, not you. She's waiting for me now, on Gram."

Trask shot him through the head. Dunnan's eyes widened in momentary incredulity; then his knees gave way, and he fell forward on his face. Trask thumbed on the safety and holstered the pistol, and looked at the body on the concrete in front of him.

It hadn't made the least difference. It had been like shooting a snake, or one of the nasty scorpion-things that infested the old buildings in Rivington. Just no more Andray Dunnan.

"Take that carrion and stuff it in a mass-energy converter," he said. "And I don't want anybody to mention the name of Andray Dunnan to me again."

He didn't look at them haul Dunnan's body away on a lifter-skid; he watched the fifty-odd leaders of the overthrown mis-government of Marduk shamble away to freedom, guarded by Paytrik Morland's riflemen. Now there was something to reproach himself for; he'd committed a separate and distinct crime against Marduk by letting each one of them live. Unless recognized and killed by somebody outside, every one of them would be at some villainy before next sunrise. Well, King Simon I could cope with that.

He started when he realized how he had thought of his friend. Well, why not? Mikhyl's mind was dead; his body would not survive it more than a year. Then a child Queen, and a long regency, and long regencies were dangerous. Better a strong King, in name as well as power. And the succession could be safeguarded by marrying Steven and Myrna. Myrna had accepted, at eight, that she must someday marry for reasons of state; why not her playmate Steven?

And Simon Bentrik would see the necessity. He was neither a fool nor a moral coward; he only needed to take some time to adjust to ideas. The rabble who had bought their lives with their leader's had gone, now. Slowly, he followed them, thinking.

Don't press the idea on Simon too hard; just expose him to it and let him adopt it. And there would be the treaty —Tanith, Marduk, Beowulf, Amaterasu; eventually, treaties with the other civilized planets. Nebulously, the idea of a League of Civilized Worlds began to take shape in his mind.

Be a good idea if he adopted the title of King of Tanith for himself. And cut loose from the Sword-Worlds; especially cut loose from Gram. Let Viktor of Xochitl have it. Or Garvan Spasso. Viktor wouldn't be the last Space Viking to take his ships back against the Sword-Worlds. Sooner or later, civilization in the Old Federation would drive them all home to loot the planets that had sent them out.

Well, if he was going to be a king, shouldn't he have a queen? Kings usually did. He climbed into a little hall-car and started up a long shaft. There was Valerie Alvarath. They'd enjoyed each other's society on the *Nemesis*. He wondered if she would want to make it permanent, even on a throne . . .

Elaine was with him. He felt her beside him, almost tangibly. Her voice was whispering to him; *She loves you, Lucas. She'll say yes. Be good to her, and she'll make you happy.* Then she was gone, and he knew that she would never return.

Goodbye, Elaine.

BEST-SELLING
Science Fiction
and
Fantasy

THE CHILDE CYCLE SERIES

By Gordon R. Dickson